THE COMPLETE ADVENTURES OF
ROMNEY PRINGLE

THE COMPLETE ADVENTURES OF
ROMNEY PRINGLE

R. AUSTIN FREEMAN &
JOHN J. PITCAIRN

COACHWHIP PUBLICATIONS

Landisville, Pennsylvania

The Complete Adventures of Romney Pringle, by R. Austin Freeman &
   John J. Pitcairn.
Copyright © 2011 Coachwhip Publications
No claim made on public domain material.

Stories published originally under the pseudonym Clifford Ashdown.
The Adventures first published 1902.
The Further Adventures first published 1903.

ISBN 1-61646-090-3
ISBN-13 978-1-61646-090-7

Cover Image: Bicycle © Dorota Caderek

CoachwhipBooks.com

CONTENTS

PREFACE

In the course of the present year there died suddenly at Sandwich, a gentleman who had only a short time previously taken up his residence in one of the curious old red-brick houses which, surrounded by large gardens, sleepily nestle in the shade of its venerable towers. He was reputed wealthy, his name given as Romney, being popularly supposed to denote ancestral, if not actual, connection with the town and district of that name on the South Coast. A man of highly-cultured tastes and of rare and varied information, he led a very retired life, divided between his books, the cataloguing of a valuable collection of antique gems, and cycle-rides into the surrounding country—for he was an ardent cyclist. A chance meeting on the Sandwich Flats, whereon he had lost his way one misty evening, was the commencement of a close friendship with the present writers, who, on Mr. Romney's demise soon after, were found to be designated his literary executors. A series of MS. stories, apparently intended for publication, furnished the sole explanation of this somewhat surprising provision. Whether, as might be imagined from their intimate record of the chief actor's career, they were derived from the notes of actual experience, or whether they were simply the result of imagination, they are here presented exactly as left by the author.

THE ASSYRIAN REJUVENATOR

As six o'clock struck, the procession of the un-dined began to stream beneath the electric arcade which graces the entrance to Cristiani's. The doors swung unceasingly; the mirrors no longer reflected a mere squadron of tables and erect serviettes; a hum of conversation now mingled with the clatter of knives and the popping of corks; and the brisk scurry of waiters' slippers replaced the stillness of the afternoon.

Although the restaurant had been crowded some time before he arrived, Mr. Romney Pringle had secured his favourite seat opposite the feminine print after Gainsborough, and in the intervals of feeding listened to a selection from Mascagni through a convenient electrophone, price sixpence in the slot. It was a warm night for the time of year, a muggy spell having succeeded a week of biting north-east wind, and as the evening wore on the atmosphere grew a trifle oppressive, more particularly to those who had dined well. Its effects were not very visible on Pringle, whose complexion (a small port-wine mark on his right cheek its only blemish) was of that fairness which imparts to its fortunate possessor the air of youth until long past forty—especially in a man who shaves clean, and habitually goes to bed before two in the morning.

As the smoke from Pringle's Havana wreathed upwards to an extractor, his eye fell, not for the first time, upon a diner at the next table. He was elderly, probably on the wrong side of sixty, but with his erect figure might easily have claimed a few years' grace, while the retired soldier spoke in his scrupulous neatness, and in the trim of a carefully tended moustache. He had finished his dinner some little time, but remained seated, studying a letter with an intentness more due to its subject than to its length, which Pringle could see was by no means excessive. At last with a gesture almost equally compounded of weariness and disgust, he rose and was helped into his overcoat by a waiter, who held the door for him in the obsequious manner of his kind.

The languid attention which Pringle at first bestowed on his neighbour had by this time given place to a deeper interest, and as the swing-doors closed behind the old gentleman, he scarcely repressed a start, when he saw lying beneath the vacant table the identical letter which had received such careful study. His first impulse was to run after the old gentleman and restore the paper, but by this time he had disappeared, and the waiter being also invisible, Pringle sat down and read:—

> "*The Assyrian Rejuvenator Co.,*
> 82 *Barbican, E. C., April* 5.

"Dear Sir,

"We regret to hear of the failure of the 'Rejuvenator' in your hands. This is possibly due to your not having followed the directions for its use sufficiently closely, but I must point out that we do not guarantee its infallible success. As it is an expensive preparation, we do not admit the justice of your contention that our charges are exorbitant. In any case we cannot entertain your request to return the whole or any part of the fees. Should you act upon your threat to take proceedings for the recovery of the same, we must hold your good self responsible for any publicity which may follow.

> "Yours faithfully,
> "Henry Jacobs,
> "*Secretary.*

> "Lieut.-Col. Sandstream,
> 272 *Piccadilly, W.*"

To Pringle this business-like communication hardly seemed to deserve so much consideration as Colonel Sandstream had given it, but having read and pondered it over afresh, he walked back to his chambers in Furnival's Inn. He lived at No. 33, on the left as you enter from Holborn, and those who, scaling the stone stairs, reached the second floor, might observe on the entrance to the front set of chambers, the legend, "Mr. Romney Pringle, Literary Agent." According to high authority, the reason of being of the literary agent is to act as a buffer between the ravening publisher and his prey. But although a very fine oak bureau with capacious pigeon-holes stood conspicuously in Pringle's sitting-room, it was tenanted by no rolls of MS. or type-written sheets. Indeed little or no business appeared to be transacted in the chambers. The buffer was at present idle, if it could be said to have ever worked! It was "resting," to use the theatrical expression.

Mr. Pringle was an early riser, and as nine o'clock chimed the next morning from the brass lantern-clock which ticked sedately on a mantel unencumbered by the usual litter of a bachelor's quarters, he had already spent some time in consideration of last night's incident, and a further study of the letter had only served to thoroughly arouse his curiosity, and decide him to investigate the affair of the mysterious "Rejuvenator." Unlocking a cupboard in the bottom of the bureau, he disclosed a regiment of bottles and jars, and sprinkling a few drops from one on to a hare's-foot, he succeeded, with a little friction, in entirely removing the port-wine mark from his cheek. Then from another phial he saturated a sponge and rubbed it into his eyebrows, which turned in the process from their original yellow to a jetty black. From a box of several, he selected a waxed moustache (that most facile article of disguise), and having attached it with a few drops of spirit-gum, covered his scalp with a black wig, which, as is commonly the case, remained an aggressive fraud in spite of the most assiduous adjustment. Satisfied with the completeness of his disguise, he sallied out in search of the offices of the "Assyrian Rejuvenator," affecting a military bearing which his slim but tall and straight-backed figure readily enabled him to assume.

"My name is Parkins—Major Parkins," said Pringle, as he opened the door of a mean-looking room on the second floor of No. 82 Barbican. He addressed an oleaginous-looking gentleman, whose curly locks and beard suggested the winged bulls of Nineveh, and who appeared to be the sole representative of the concern. The latter bowed politely, and handed him a chair.

"I have been asked," Pringle continued, "by a friend who saw your advertisement to call upon you for some further information."

Now the subject of rejuvenation being a delicate one, especially where ladies are concerned, the business of the company was mainly transacted through the post. So seldom indeed did a client desire a personal interview, that the Assyrian-looking gentleman jumped to the conclusion that his visitor was interested in quite another matter.

"Ah, yes! You refer to 'Pelosia,'" he said briskly. "Allow me to read you an extract from the prospectus."

And before Pringle could reply, he proceeded to read from a small leaflet with unctuous elocution:—

"PELOSIA.

The sovereign remedy of MUD has long been used with the greatest success in the celebrated baths of Schwalbach and Franzenbad. The proprietors of PELOSIA having noted the beneficial effect which many of the lower animals derive from the consumption of earth with their food, have been led to investigate the internal uses of mud. The success which has crowned the treatment of some of the longest-standing cases of dyspepsia (the disease so characteristic of this neurotic age), has induced them to admit the world at large to its benefits. To thoroughly safeguard the public, the proprietors have secured the sole right to the alluvial deposits of a stream remote from human habitation, and consequently above any suspicion of contamination. Careful analysis has shown that the deposit in this particular locality, consisting of finely divided mineral particles practically free from organic admixture, is calculated

to give the most gratifying results. The proprietors are prepared to quote special terms for public institutions."

"Many thanks," said Pringle, as the other momentarily paused
for breath; but I think you are under a slight misapprehension. I
called on you with reference to the 'Assyrian Rejuvenator.' Have I
mistaken the offices?"

"Pray excuse my absurd mistake! I am secretary of the 'Assyrian
Rejuvenator Company,' who are also the proprietors of 'Pelosia."
And he regarded Pringle in evident concern. It was not the first
time he had known a diffident person to assume an interest in the
senility of an absent friend, and he mentally decided that Pringle's
waxed moustache, its blue-blackness speaking loudly of hair-dye,
together with the unmistakable wig, were evidence of the decrepi-
tude for which his new customer presumably sought the Company's
assistance.

"Ours, my dear sir," he resumed, leaning back in his chair, and
placing the tips of his fingers in apposition; "ours is a world-
renowned specific for removing the ravages which time effects in
the human frame. It is a secret which has been handed down for
many generations in the family of the original proprietor. Its success is frequently remarkable, and its absolute failure is impossible. It is not a drug, it is not a cosmetic, yet it contains the prop-
erties of both. It is agreeable and soothing to use, and being best
administered during the hours of sleep, does not interfere with the
ordinary avocations of every-day life. The price is so moderate—
ten and sixpence, including the Government stamp—that it could
only prove remunerative with an enormous sale. If you—ah, on
behalf of your friend!—would care to purchase a bottle, I should
be most happy to explain its operation."

Mr. Pringle laid a half-sovereign and a sixpence on the table,
and the secretary, diving into a large packing-case which stood on
one side, extracted a parcel. This contained a card-board box
adorned with a representation of Blake's preposterous illustration
to "The Grave," in which a centenarian on crutches is hobbling into
a species of banker's strong-room with a rocky top, whereon is
seated a youth clothed in nothing but an ecstatic expression.

"This," said Mr. Jacobs impressively, "is the entire apparatus!" And he opened the box, displaying a moderate-sized phial, and a spirit-lamp with a little tin dish attached. "On retiring to rest, a teaspoonful of the contents of the bottle is poured into the receptacle above the lamp which is then lighted, and the preparation being vaporized, is inhaled by the patient. It is best to concentrate the thoughts on some object of beauty whilst the delicious aroma soothes the patient to sleep."

"But how does it act?" inquired the Major a trifle impatiently.

"In this way," replied the imperturbable secretary. "Remember that the appearance of age is largely due to wrinkles; that is to say, to the skin losing its elasticity and fulness—so true is it that beauty is only skin-deep." Here he laughed gaily. "The joints grow stiff from loss of their natural tone, the figure stoops, and the vital organs decline their functions from the same cause. In a word, old age is due to a loss of *elasticity*, and that is the very property which the 'Rejuvenator' imparts to the system, if inhaled for a few hours daily."

Mr. Pringle diplomatically succeeded in maintaining his gravity while the merits of the "Rejuvenator" were expounded, and it was not until he had bidden Mr. Jacobs a courteous farewell, and was safely outside the office, that he allowed the fastening of his moustache to be disturbed by an expansive grin.

About nine o'clock the same evening, the housekeeper of the Barbican offices was returning from market, her thoughts centred on the savoury piece of fried fish she was carrying home for supper.

"Mrs. Smith?" said a man's voice behind her, as she produced her latch-key.

"My name's 'Odges," she replied unguardedly, dropping the key in her agitation.

"You're the housekeeper, aren't you?" said the stranger, picking up the key and handing it to her politely.

"Lor', sir! You did give me a turn," she faltered.

"Very sorry, I'm sure. I only want to know where I can find Mr. Jacobs of the 'Assyrian Rejuvenator Company.'"

"Well, sir, he told me I wasn't to give his address to any one. Not that I know it either, sir, for I always send the letters to Mr. Weeks."

"I'll see you're not found fault with. I know he won't mind your telling me." A sovereign clinked against the latch-key in her palm.

For a second she hesitated, then her eye caught the glint of the gold, and she fell.

"All I know, sir, is that when Mr. Jacobs is away I send the letters—and a rare lot there are—to Mr. Newton Weeks at the Northumberland Avenue Hotel."

"Is he one of the firm?"

"I don't know, sir, but there's no one comes here but Mr. Jacobs."

"Thank you very much, and good-night," said the stranger, and he strode down Barbican, leaving Mrs. Hodges staring at the coin in her hand as if doubting whether, like fairy gold, it might not disappear even as she gazed.

The next day Mr. Jacobs received a letter at his hotel:—

> "*April* 7.
>
> "Sir,
>
> "My friend Col. Sandstream informs me he has communicated with the police, and has sworn an information against you in respect to the monies you have obtained from him, as he alleges, by false pretences. Although I am convinced that his statements are true, a fact which I can more readily grasp after my interview with you to-day, I give you this warning in order that you may make your escape before it is too late. Do not misunderstand my motives; I have not the slightest desire to save you from the punishment you so richly deserve. I am simply anxious to rescue my old friend from the ridiculous position he will occupy before the world should he prosecute you.
>
> "Your obedient servant,
"Joseph Parkins, Major.
>
> "Newton Weeks, Esq.,
>> *Northumberland Avenue Hotel.*"

Mr. Jacobs read this declaration of war with very mixed feelings.

So his visitor of yesterday was a friend of Colonel Sandstream's! Obviously come to get up evidence against him. Knowing old dog that Sandstream! But then how had they run him to earth? That looked as if the police had got their finger in the pie. Mrs. Hodges was discreet. She would never have given the address to any but the police. It was annoying though, after all his precautions; seemed as if the game was really up at last. Well, it was bound to come some day, and he had been in tighter places before. He could hardly complain; the "Rejuvenator" had been going very well lately. But suppose the whole thing was a plant—a dodge to intimidate him?

He read the letter through again. The writer had been careful to omit his address, but it seemed plausible enough on the face of it. Anyhow, whatever the Major's real motive might be, he couldn't afford to neglect the warning, and the one clear thing was that London was an unhealthy place for him just at present. He would pack up so as to be ready for all emergencies, and drive round to Barbican and reconnoitre. Then, if things looked fishy, he could go on to Cannon Street and catch the 11.5 Continental. He'd show them that Harry Jacobs wasn't the man to be bluffed out of his claim!

Mr. Jacobs stopped his cab some doors from the "Rejuvenator" office, and was in the act of alighting when he paused, spellbound at the apparition of Pringle. The latter was loitering outside No. 82, and as the cab drew up he ostentatiously consulted a large pocket-book, and glanced several times from its pages to the countenance of his victim as if comparing a description. Attired in a long over-coat, a bowler-hat, and wearing thick boots of a constabulary pattern, to the nervous imagination of Mr. Jacobs he afforded startling evidence of the police interest in the establishment; and this idea was confirmed when Pringle, as if satisfied with his scrutiny, drew a paper from the pocket-book and made a movement in his direction. Without waiting for further developments, Mr. Jacobs retreated into the cab and hoarsely whispered through the trap-door, "Cannon Street as hard as you can go!"

The cabman wrenched the horse's head round. He had been an interested spectator of the scene, and sympathized with the evident desire of his fare to escape what appeared to be the long arm of the law. At this moment a "crawling" hansom came up and was promptly hailed by Pringle.

"Follow that cab and don't lose it on any account!" he cried, as he stood on the step and pointed vigorously after the receding hansom,

While Mr. Jacobs careered down Barbican, his cabman looked back in time to observe this expressive pantomime, and with the instinct of a true sportsman, lashed his unfortunate brute into a hand-gallop. But the observant eye of a policeman checked this moderate exhibition of speed just as they were rounding the sharp corner into Aldersgate Street, and had not a lumbering railway-van intervened, Pringle would have caught him up, and brought the farce to an awkward finish. But the van saved the situation. The moment's respite was all that the chase needed, and in response to the promises of largesse, frantically roared by Mr. Jacobs through the trap-door, he was soon bounding and bumping over the wood-pavement with Pringle well in the rear.

Then ensued a mad stampede down Aldersgate Street.

In and out, between the crowded files of vans and 'buses, the two cabs wound a zig-zag course; the horses slipping and skating over the greasy surface, or ploughing up the mud as their bits skidded them within inches of a collision. In vain did policemen roar to them to stop—the order fell on heedless ears. In vain did officious boys wave intimidating arms, or make futile grabs at the harness of the apparent runaways. Did a cart dart unexpectedly from out a side street? the inevitable disaster failed to come off. Did an obstacle loom dead ahead of them? it melted into thin air as they approached. Triumphantly they piloted the narrowest of straits, and dashed unscathed into St. Martin's-le-Grand.

There was a block in Newgate Street and the cross traffic was stopped. Mr. Jacobs' hansom nipped through a temporary gap, grazing the pole of an omnibus, and being lustily anathematized in the process. But Pringle's cabman, attempting to follow, was imperiously waved back by a policeman.

"No go, I'm afraid, sir!" was the man's comment, as they crossed into St. Paul's Churchyard after a three minutes' wait. "I can't see him nowhere."

"Never mind," said Pringle cheerfully. "Go to Charing Cross telegraph office."

There he sent the following message:—

"To Mrs. Hodges, 82 Barbican. Called away to country. Mr. Weeks will take charge of office—Jacobs."

About two the same afternoon, Pringle, wearing the wig and moustache of Major Parkins, rang the housekeeper's bell at 82.

"I'm Mr. Weeks," he stated, as Mrs. Hodges emerged from the bowels of the earth. "Mr. Jacobs has had to leave town, and has asked me to take charge of the office."

"Oh, yes, sir! I've had a telegram from Mr. Jacobs to say so. You know the way up, I suppose."

"I think so. But Mr. Jacobs forgot to send me the office-key."

"I'd better lend you mine, then, sir, till you can hear from Mr. Jacobs." She fumbled in her voluminous pocket. "I hope nothing's the matter with him?"

"Oh, dear no! He found he needed a short holiday, that's all," Pringle re-assured her, and taking the key from the confiding woman, he climbed to the second floor.

Sitting down at the secretarial desk, he sent a quick glance round the office. A poor creature, that Jacobs, he reflected, for all his rascality, or he wouldn't have been scared so easily. And he drew a piece of wax from his pocket and took a careful impression of the key.

He had not been in possession of the "Rejuvenator" offices for very long before he discovered that Mr. Jacobs' desire to break out in a fresh place had proved abortive. It will be remembered that on the occasion of his interview with that gentleman, Mr. Jacobs assumed that Pringle's visit had reference to "Pelosia," whose virtues he extolled in a leaflet composed in his own very pronounced style. A large package in the office, Pringle found to contain many thousands of these effusions, which had apparently been laid aside for some considerable time. From the absence in the daily correspondence of any inquiries thereafter, it was clear that the public had failed to realize the advantages of the internal administration of mud, so that Mr. Jacobs had been forced to stick to the swindle that was already in existence. After all the latter was a paying concern—eminently so! Besides, the patent-medicine trade is rather overdone.

The price of the "Assyrian Rejuvenator" was such as to render the early cashing of remittances an easy matter. Ten-and-sixpence being a sum for which the average banker demurs to honour a cheque, the payments were usually made in postal-orders; and Pringle acquired a larger faith in Carlyle's opinion of the majority of his fellow-creatures as he cashed the previous day's takings at the General Post Office on his way up to Barbican each morning. The business was indeed a flourishing one, and his satisfaction was only alloyed by the probability of some legal interference, at the instance of Colonel Sandstream, with the further operations of the Company. But for the present Fortune smiled, and Pringle continued to energetically despatch parcels of the "Rejuvenator" in response to the daily shower of postal-orders. In this indeed he had little trouble, for he had found many gross of parcels duly packed and ready for posting. One day while engaged in the process which had grown quite a mechanical one by that time, he listened absently to a slow but determined step which ascended the stairs and paused on the landing outside. Above, on the third floor, was an importer of cigars made in Germany, and the visitor evidently delayed the further climb until he had regained his wind. Presently, after a preliminary pant or two, he got under way again, but proceeded only as far as the "Rejuvenator" door, to which he gave a peremptory thump, and opening it, walked in without further ceremony.

There was no need for him to announce himself. Pringle recognized him at the first glance, although he had never seen him since the eventful evening at Cristiani's restaurant.

"I'm Colonel Sandstream!" he growled, looking round him savagely.

"Delighted to see you, sir," said Pringle with assurance. "Pray be seated," he added politely.

"Who am I speaking to?"

"My name is Newton Weeks. I am—"

"I don't want to see *you!*" interrupted the Colonel testily. "I want to see the secretary of this concern. I've no time to waste either."

"I regret to say that Mr. Jacobs—"

"Ah, yes! That's the name. Where is he?" again interrupted the old gentleman.

"Mr. Jacobs is at present out of town."

"Well, I'm not going to run after him. When will he be here again?"

"It is quite impossible for me to tell. But I was just now going to say that as the managing director of the Company, I am also acting as secretary during Mr. Jacobs' absence."

"What do you say your name is?" catechized the other, still ignoring the chair which Pringle had offered him.

"Newton Weeks."

"Newton Weeks," repeated the Colonel, making a note of the name on the back of an envelope.

"Managing director," added Pringle suavely.

"Well, Mr. Weeks, if you represent the *Company*"—this with a contemptuous glance from the middle of the room at his surroundings— "I've called with reference to a letter you've had the impertinence to send me."

"What was the date of it?" inquired Pringle innocently.

"I don't remember!" snapped the Colonel.

"May I ask what was the subject of the correspondence?"

"Why, this confounded 'Rejuvenator' of yours, of course!"

"You see we have a very large amount of correspondence concerning the 'Rejuvenator,' and I'm afraid unless you have the letter with you—"

"I've lost it or mislaid it somewhere."

"That is unfortunate! Unless you can remember the contents I fear it will be quite impossible for *me* to do so."

"I remember them well enough! I'm not likely to forget them in a hurry. I asked you to return me the money your 'Rejuvenator,' as you call it, has cost me, because it's been quite useless, and in your reply you not only refused absolutely, but hinted that I dare not prosecute you."

As Pringle made no reply, he continued more savagely—

"Would you like to hear my candid opinion of you?"

"We are always pleased to hear the opinion of our clients."

Pringle's calmness only appeared to exasperate the Colonel the more.

"Well, sir, you shall have it. I consider that letter the most impudent attempt at blackmail that I have ever heard of!" He ground out the words from between his clenched teeth in a voice of concentrated passion.

"Blackmail!" echoed Pringle, allowing an expression of horror to occupy his countenance.

"Yes, sir! Blackmail!" asseverated the Colonel, nodding his head vigorously.

"Of course," said Pringle, with a deprecating gesture, "I am aware that some correspondence has passed between us, but I cannot attempt to remember every word of it. At the same time, although you are pleased to put such an unfortunate construction upon it, I am sure there is some misunderstanding in the matter. I must positively decline to admit that there has been any attempt on the part of the Company of such a nature as you allege."

"Oh! so you don't admit it, don't you? Perhaps you won't admit taking pounds and pounds of my money for your absurd concoction, which hasn't done me the least little bit of good in the world— nor ever will! And perhaps you won't admit refusing to return me my money? Eh? Perhaps you won't admit daring me to take proceedings because it would show up what an ass I've been! Don't talk to me, sir! Baugh!" Having poured this out in a *crescendo* of disgust, the old gentleman flung himself into the chair, forgetful that his dignity had hitherto prevented him from accepting it.

"I'm really very sorry that this unpleasantness has arisen," began Pringle, "but—"

"Pleasant or unpleasant, sir, I'm going to stop your little game! I mislaid your letter or I'd have called upon you before this. As you're the managing director I'm better pleased to see you than your precious secretary. Anyhow I've come to tell you that you're a set of swindlers! Of *swindlers*, sir!" And he, emphasized the word with a thump of his malacca that made the windows rattle.

"I can make every allowance for your feelings," said Pringle, drawing himself up with an air of pained dignity, "but I regret to see a holder of His Majesty's commission so deficient in self-control."

"Damn your impertinence, sir!" vociferated the veteran. "I'll let the money go, and I'll prosecute the pair of you, no matter what it costs me! Yes, you, and your rascally secretary too! I'll go and swear an information against you this very day!" He bounced out of the room, and explosively snorted downstairs.

Pringle followed in the rear, and reached the outer door in time to hear him exclaim, "Mansion House Police Court," to the driver of a motor-cab, in which he appropriately clanked and rumbled out of sight.

Returning up-stairs, Pringle busied himself in making a bon-fire of the last few days' correspondence. Then, collecting the last batch of postal-orders, he proceeded to cash them at the General Post Office, and walked back to Furnival's Inn. "After all, the farce couldn't have lasted much longer. Some one else was sure to kick, even if that old fire-eater hadn't turned up. It would be good to see his face though when he found the nest empty!" Arrived at Furni-val's Inn, Pringle rapidly divested himself of the wig and mous-tache, and assuming his official port-wine mark, became once more the unemployed literary agent.

It was now half-past one, and after lunching lightly at a near restaurant, he lighted a cigar and strolled leisurely eastward.

By the time he reached Barbican three o'clock was reverberat-ing from St. Paul's. He entered the private bar of a tavern nearly opposite, and calling for some whisky of a comparatively innocu-ous kind, sat down by a window which commanded a view of No. 82.

As time passed and the quarters continued to strike in rapid succession, Pringle felt constrained to order further refreshment; and he was lighting a third cigar before his patience was rewarded.

Happening to glance up at the second-floor window, he caught a glimpse of a strange man engaged in taking a momentary survey of the street below.

The march of events had been rapid. He had evidently resigned the secretaryship not a moment too soon!

Not long after the strange face had disappeared from the window, a four-wheeled cab stopped outside the tavern. It appeared to be waiting of set purpose, as no one alighted. After a few moments' pause, the cab-door was opened gently, and an individual wearing a pair of large blue spectacles, and carrying a Gladstone bag, got out and carefully scrutinized the offices of the "Rejuvenator." Mr. Jacobs, for it was he, did not intend to be caught napping this time.

At length, being satisfied with the normal appearance of the premises, he crossed the road, and to Pringle's intense amusement, disappeared into the house opposite. The spectator had not long to wait for the next act of the drama. The curtain fell for but a very brief interval.

About ten minutes after Mr. Jacobs' disappearance, the man who had looked out of the window emerged from the house and beckoned to the waiting cab. As it drew up at the door, a second individual came down the steps, fast holding Mr. Jacobs by the arm. The latter, in very crest-fallen guise, re-entered the vehicle, being closely followed by his captor, and the first man having taken his seat with them, the party adjourned to a destination as to which Pringle had no difficulty in hazarding a guess. Satisfying the barmaid he sallied into the street. The "Rejuvenator" offices seemed once more to be deserted, and the postman entered in the course of his afternoon round. Pringle walked a few yards up the street, and then, crossing as the postman re-appeared, turned back and entered the house boldly. Softly mounting the stairs, he knocked at the door. There was no response. He knocked again more loudly, and finally turned the handle. As he expected, it was locked securely, and satisfied that the coast was clear, he inserted his own replica of the key and entered. The books tumbled on the floor in confused heaps, the wide-open and empty drawers, and the over-turned packing-cases, showed how thoroughly the place had been ransacked in the search for compromising evidence. But Pringle took no further interest in these things. The letter-box was the sole object of his attentions. He tore open the batch of newly-delivered letters, and crammed the postal-orders into his pockets; then, secreting the correspondence behind a rifled packing-case, he went out and silently locked the door.

As he strolled down the street, on a last visit to the General Post Office, the two detectives passed him on their way back in quest of the "Managing Director."

THE FOREIGN OFFICE DESPATCH

"*Rien ne va plus*—the ball rolls!"

The silence was only broken by the rattle of the ivory ball over the diamond-shaped studs around the circumference of the disc. Every now and then there was a sharp click, as it struck a partition between two numbers and was viciously jerked on to the studs again.

Round and round the ball went. It was only for a minute, but to the men gathered by the green cloth it seemed a century. Suddenly the noise ceased. The disc continued to revolve, but the ball lay snugly resting in one of the little pens.

The *tailleur* placed his finger on the capstan and stopped the disc. "Twelve—*rouge—manque—pair*," he intoned monotonously. Then he raked the stakes off the spaces painted on the green cloth. The table had won for the eighth time in succession, with payment to hardly a single player. A kind of suppressed groan ran round the board, and the fleeced ones crowded to the bar at the end of the room for consolation.

The life at the marble caravanserais which largely now do duty for clubs was repellent to Mr. Pringle, and doubtless on Pope's principle that

"The proper study of mankind is MAN,"

when the ostensible calls of his mysterious literary agency did not take him in other directions, the "Chrysanthemum Club" had many attractions for him. As to the club itself, election was a process

24

scarcely more exacting than a mere scrutiny by the hall-porter; the
"Chrysanthemum" was not too exclusive, and although situated in
a fashionable street off Piccadilly, the subscription was almost a
nominal one.

As Pringle inhaled his cigarette and watched the last disastrous
success of the table, a young man got up from the board and flung
himself abruptly into a low chair opposite. Presently a waiter placed
on the marble table at his elbow a bottle of *Pommery*, to which he
applied himself assiduously. There was nothing in his appearance
to differentiate him from any of the thousands of well-dressed and
well-groomed men who frequent club-land, but somehow or other
as they sat opposite one another, his eye continually caught that
of Pringle, who at length rose and crossed the room. The Club was
not so large that a member need consider himself insulted did a
stranger address him without a previous introduction, and the
other displayed no emotion when Pringle sat down beside him and
entered into conversation.

"The table seems to be having all the luck to-night," he remarked.

"That's true," agreed the youth frankly. "I never heard of such luck."

"Been playing long?" inquired Pringle sympathetically.

"I'm not a member, you know. I was introduced as a visitor for
the first time to-night." Then growing confidential as the wine cir-
culated in his brain, he continued— "I cashed a cheque for eighty
pounds when I began to play, and I staked ten every time."

"So you lost it all?"

"Lost it all," the youth echoed gloomily.

"But why not go on? Professor Bond calculates that the chances
in favour of the Bank are only as thirty-seven to thirty five."

"I changed my last sovereign there," he tapped the bottle.
"Think I'd better go now." And he rose somewhat unsteadily. His
libations to Fortune had evidently commenced very early in the
evening.

"Try your luck again," persuaded Pringle. "Allow me the pleasure of helping you to get your revenge," said he, producing a handful of gold from his pocket.

"You're really very good, but—"

"Not at all! The luck's sure to run by this time," urged the tempter. Pringle was not entirely a stranger to generous impulses, and he felt some pity for the youth.

"Well, I'll take eight pounds, and thanks awfully, Mr.— Really I don't know your name; mine's Redmile."

"Mine is James," said Pringle. "Now go in and win!"

Once more Redmile took his seat at the green board and watched the play eagerly. The table was no longer winning, and the interest in the game had revived. After a few turns he ventured a sovereign on the *Pair* or even numbers. "Twenty-six" was called, and he was richer by as much more. Still cautious, he placed three sovereigns below the first column of figures. "Nineteen" was the winning number, and six more sovereigns were added to his three.

"I congratulate you!" whispered Pringle behind him. "Didn't I say the luck would change?"

"A good guess," laughed Redmile. "Only let me win enough to redeem that cheque, and I shall be contented."

"Try the twelves," Pringle suggested.

Redmile arranged five sovereigns on the space allotted to the first twelve numbers.

"Thirty-one!" the *tailleur* called. Pringle shrugged his shoulders as the money was raked into the bank.

Without looking round but breathing heavily Redmile placed a sovereign on "*rouge*," another on "*impair*," and after a second's hesitation dropped two more on "twenty-one." Even as he withdrew his hand the *tailleur* uttered his parrot-cry "*Rien ne va plus*," and, spinning the disc, reversed the ball against it.

"Twenty-one—*rouge*—*passe*—*impair*," he droned, as the ball rested.

Redmile had won seventy-two pounds at one stroke! He rose from the table and vigorously shook hands with Pringle.

"I've only got eighty-two pounds altogether, and I must get that cheque back from the manager," he said. "Do you mind coming round to my rooms? Only as far as Dover Street, and I'll give you a cheque for what you so kindly lent me."

"With pleasure," said Pringle, as Redmile, now flushed with success in addition to the wine, darted off to redeem his cheque.

"I've had as much as is good for me, or we'd have had another bottle to celebrate the occasion," he remarked as they strolled down Piccadilly together.

"Rather more," thought Pringle, adding politely, "I should not have noticed it."

"Perhaps not, but I must have a clear head to-morrow. I'm in the 'F. O.' you know, and we're very busy just now."

"Indeed!" exclaimed Pringle, much interested. "You must have had a harassing time lately—over this Congo affair, for instance?"

"Yes, harassing isn't the word to describe it. Come in!"

He drew out his latch-key, and after some ineffectual efforts, succeeded in opening the door. Then he insisted on writing the cheque in spite of all Pringle's protestations, and opening a box of cigars, put whisky and soda on the table. The fresh air had completed the work of the alcohol. He was evidently becoming very drunk, and laughed inanely when, missing the tumbler, he directed the cascade from a syphon over the table-cloth.

"We'll just have a night-cap before you go," he hiccoughed. "Yes, as you were saying, we've had a deuce of a time lately. I'm one of Lord Tranmere's secretaries, and the berth's not all beer and sk-skittles! Why, you mightn't think it, but I have to examine and minute every blessed despatch and telegram that passes between London and Paris every day, Sundays and all, and that means some work just now, I can tell you! Yesterday was no d-day of rest for me."

He unlocked a despatch-box and held up an official envelope for Pringle to see. The direction was printed in bold letters:—

On His Britannic Majesty's Service.
HIS EXCELLENCY THE RIGHT HONBLE.
THE VISCOUNT STRATHCLYDE, G.C.B.,
HIS BRITANNIC MAJESTY'S AMBASSADOR
EXTRAORDINARY AND PLENIPOTENTIARY,
ETC. ETC. ETC.
PARIS.

O
Foreign Office.

"This is the finish to the whole business," he said. "Rather short and rather sweet. I only finished dr-drafting it this evening. It will be franked by the Secretary of State in the morning, and I think by this time to-to-morrow, the F. O. officials will sleep sounder in both capitals."

"Will they indeed!" exclaimed Pringle. "I am delighted to find that diplomacy is not a lost art in England. But talking of that, I suppose you know the story of the King's Messenger and that affair of the Emperor of Austria's razors?"

Redmile had never heard it, and settled himself comfortably to listen. But as the combined result of his potations and the lateness of the hour, his head began to nod, and long before Pringle arrived at the climax of the story, a loud snore proclaimed that his audience was asleep.

After waiting a little while to make sure of his host's unconsciousness, Pringle cautiously reached towards the despatch-box which still lay open on the table, and possessed himself of an addressed envelope and several sheets of foolscap embossed with the Foreign Office stamp. He then turned his attention to the waste-paper basket, and after a search, as noiseless as possible, among its rustling contents, found a torn envelope bearing a nearly perfect Foreign Office seal in wax. Placing all the stationery carefully in his pocket, he gave vent to a loud sneeze.

Redmile woke up with a start, and Pringle as if finishing the story remarked calmly, "So that's how the affair ended."

"Dear me! I'm awfully sorry," apologized Redmile thickly. "I'm afraid I've been asleep. It must have been that whisky that did it!"

"More likely the prosiness of my story," Pringle suggested with a smile. "But anyhow, I must be moving."

"Come and look us up any time you're passing," said the other sleepily.

When he reached Furnival's Inn Pringle did not trouble to go to bed. He had a hard night's work before him, and the dawn found him still busily engaged.

Drawing up the blinds he admitted the morning light. The Venetian mirror which hung above the mantel had seldom reflected such a scene of confusion as the usually neat room presented. Pringle's hat crowned one of the two choice pieces of Delft which flanked the brass lantern-clock, while his over-coat sprawled limply across the reading-easel. On a table in one corner stood a glass vessel containing a clear blue solution. In this, well-coated with black-lead, was immersed the seal abstracted from the waste-paper basket, which with a plate of copper, also hanging in the solution, was connected with the wires of a detached electric-lamp; in the course of the night the potent electricity had covered the wax with a deposit of copper sufficiently thick to form a perfect reverse *intaglio* of the seal. A centre-table was littered with pieces of paper, scrawled over with what appeared to be the attempts of a beginner in the art of writing. A closer inspection would have revealed a series of more or less successful reproductions of Redmile's handwriting; his cheque for eight pounds being pinned to a drawing-board, and serving Pringle as a copy. With frequent reference to a Blue-book which lay open before him, Pringle penned a communication, in a couple of short paragraphs, which he carefully copied on to one of the sheets of foolscap. Then, folding it into the envelope, he sealed it with a neat impression from the copper electrotype.

One thing only remained to complete the official appearance of the package; that was the "frank." Turning to the dado of dwarf book-cases which ran round the room, Pringle took down an album containing the portraits and autographs of celebrities of the day, and looked up that of the Foreign Secretary. Lord Tranmere's signature was a bold and legible one, and with the skill of an expert copyist, he soon had a facsimile of it written in the lower left-hand corner of the envelope.

Eight o'clock was striking just as he had finished. He rose and stretched himself languidly, when his eye fell on the cheque. Unpinning it from the board, he attached a "y" to the written word "eight," and deftly inserted a cipher after the somewhat unsteady figure which sprawled in the corner, thus converting it into a cheque for eighty pounds!

His task was now done, and after swallowing a cup of chocolate brewed over a spirit-lamp, he made a hurried but careful toilet.

Endowed by nature with a fresh complexion which did much to conceal the ravages of a sleepless night, he presented his usual youthful appearance on leaving the Inn, and, having chartered a passing cab, was swallowed up in the sea of traffic already beginning to surge down Holborn.

Work, as a general rule, begins later at the Foreign Office than elsewhere, but although it was only a little past nine when Pringle dismissed his cab in Downing Street and entered the portico of Lord Palmerston's architectural freak, several cabs and a miniature brougham were already waiting in the quadrangle. He inquired at the door for Redmile, and was directed up the magnificent staircase to a waiting-room on the first-floor.

"I will not detain Mr. Redmile long if he is at all busy," he remarked to the messenger who took his name.

"Mr. Redmile is always busy, sir," was the man's impressive reply. You see as a member of the Foreign Office staff he was of course a diplomatist.

Pringle sat down and devoted himself to a study of *The Times*, and it was fully a quarter of an hour before the messenger returned and led him along a dismal and vault-like corridor to an apartment overlooking the Horse Guards' Parade.

The room was empty, but he had scarcely had time to seat himself when a side-door, through which he caught a glimpse of a vast and lofty room beyond, suddenly opened and Redmile entered with a packet in his hand.

"Good morning! er—Mr. James," he said rather stiffly, and remained standing.

"I must apologize for intruding upon you when you are so busy," Pringle commenced.

Redmile said nothing, but glanced at the paper he held, which Pringle at once recognized as the momentous despatch which the other in his vinous indiscretion had shown him the previous evening.

"I should not have troubled you so early," continued Pringle, "but on looking at your cheque when I got home, I found that instead of repaying me my small loan you had drawn it for a much larger sum." And he handed the altered cheque to Redmile, who started when he saw the amount. He stared at it a second or two before he spoke, and then it was in a much more cordial tone.

"Pray sit down, Mr. James. Excuse my not having offered you a chair. I am really greatly obliged to you. As a man of honour, which I see you are, may I ask you to do what I shall regard as an even greater service—that is, to forget that you saw me at that infernal club? I had only been there once before with Lord Netherfield"— he named a well-known man about town— "and I should not have gone there again had I not dined rather too freely with an old friend last night. I remember very little of what occurred, and I need not tell you how fatal the events of last night would be to my official position if they became known."

"You may rely on me implicitly, Mr. Redmile. I do not play myself, and indeed I only regard the 'Chrysanthemum' as an interesting place to pass an idle hour. One can study there emotions more realistic than any which are travestied on the stage."

The whole time he was speaking, Pringle's eyes never left the packet which Redmile had placed on the table. It was duly sealed and franked by the Secretary of State, the latter operation having evidently just been concluded when Redmile brought it into the room, and Pringle, mentally comparing it with the one reposing in his coat-pocket, decided that they bore a sufficient family likeness to render them practically indistinguishable. Suddenly starting up and turning to the window, he exclaimed, as he pointed to something outside, "Extraordinary!"

"What is the matter?" inquired Redmile, going up to the window and looking over the Park.

"Excuse me, but that man walking along there is the very image of Karazoff, the accomplice of Grenevitsky who assassinated the Czar of Russia in '81."

"Is he indeed!" said Redmile, gazing with much interest at an innocent-looking pedestrian who was approaching from the direction of the Mall.

"I never saw a more astounding likeness. You may remember that Grenevitsky shared the same fate as the Czar by the explosion of the bomb, but Karazoff, who was standing a little further back, was unhurt, and was at once arrested."

"Did you see the assassination, then?"

"No, but I was in St. Petersburg afterwards, and saw Karazoff and the other accomplices hanged. I shall never forget his face as long as I live—he went to his death with the air of a martyr. How it snowed too that day!"

"Marvellous fanaticism," murmured Redmile, as the Nihilist's double, who was in point of fact a Congregationalist minister, ascended the steps leading to Downing Street. He continued to stare out of the window until the imperative whirr of an electric bell made him turn with a start.

"I must really ask you to excuse me," he said. "I have a most important despatch to send off to Paris, and there isn't a moment to lose. I'll send you another cheque on as soon as I have some time to spare. Will you give me your address?"

"Don't let such a small matter as that trouble you. I will look in at your chambers again one evening, if I may."

"Pray do! Excuse me, but the King's messenger is waiting. I haven't a moment—good-morning—good-morning!"

Descending the grand staircase, Pringle hurried into Parliament Street, and hailing a cab drove back to his chambers. To resume the artificial port-wine mark was but the work of a moment, after which he strolled into the City.

Making the circuit of the Bank, he turned into Throgmorton Street, and entered a large doorway whose passage-walls were plastered with names from floor to ceiling. Opening a door on the ground-floor, "Is Mr. Hedsor in?" he inquired.

"Just gone over to the House," replied a smart clerk.

"Would you kindly let him know Mr. Pringle would like to speak to him."

It was a band-boxed gentleman in morning costume, wearing a tall hat of effulgent glossiness, who entered the office soon after.

"How do you do, Mr. Pringle? How's literature?" was his greeting.

"Very quiet just now."

"Same here!"

"Nothing doing?"

"Ab—so—*lute*—ly nothing!"

"Really?" And Pringle, with a smile, glanced round the office. A clerk was sitting ankle-deep in a pile of wrappers and envelopes, which gradually submerged his legs as he attacked a heap of letters and circulars; beside him another incessantly tapped correspondence out of a type-writer; whilst a third divided his attention between response to the calls of a telephone, and the sundering of a tape disgorged in endless snaky coils from the unresting little machine in one corner.

"Fact!" asseverated the broker, leading the way to a little den separated from the office by a glazed window-frame partition. "Truth is, Paris has got the hump, and ditch-water's sparkling compared to the present state of things."

"What about Consols to-day?"

"Consols?"

"I suppose you're open to do business?"

"Oh, of course it can be done. Depends what you want to do, though."

"Will you sell for me?"

"How much?" inquired the broker, producing a little book.

"What do you say to fifty thousand?"

The other looked dubiously at him, and sucked the top of his pencil. "There's always a large bear account open—I shall want some cover," he remarked after a pause.

"Will you take one per cent.?"

"Why, yes, I'll take that. From any one else I should ask two—indeed I don't like it much at any price. They're high enough, goodness knows, now, but who's to say they won't go higher?"

"What are they at?"

Mr. Hedsor went into the outer office and consulted the board on which the tapes were impaled. "A hundred and ten and an eighth," said he returning. "Lord! what a price!"

"Well, I think I'll trust my luck," Pringle remarked quietly.

"You need something better to trust to than luck in these hard times."

"Did you ever hear of a company called the 'Lobatsi Consolidated'?"

"Yes, you were lucky there, I own, for a mere bit of stagging."

"And wasn't there another called the 'Bokfontein Development'?"

"By Jove! I never thought you'd get out of that as well as you did."

"And the 'Topsipitsi Deep Level'?"

"Oh, hang it all! Your proper place is inside the House. I'd forgotten the 'Topsipitsi.' Come out and have a drink."

The world was rather less tranquil when Mr. Hedsor awoke the next morning. Indeed it was many years since the newspapers had offered the public such a sensational bill-of-fare as their posters promised. In the journals themselves, the news was displayed in startling headlines, *The Times* so far forgetting its dignity as to double-lead its leader on the momentous news.

Towards one a.m. the previous night there had come over the wires from the matter-of-fact Reuter the following piece of news, which dislocated the "make-up" of the papers, reducing the sub-editors to a condition of frenzy.

"*Paris*—In accordance, it is understood, with instructions from London, Lord Strathclyde leaves for Calais tomorrow, diplomatic relations having been abruptly broken off between the two countries."

Further particulars from "our own" correspondents confirmed the news, adding that crowds were parading the streets of Paris, singing patriotic songs, and smashing the windows of every shop which bore an English name. Troops were being held in readiness in case of emergencies with which the police would be unable to cope, as it was feared the opponents of the settled order of things would foment disturbances, which, in the electric condition of the public mind, might have serious results.

The news, although startling, was not altogether unexpected. For some time past the relations between France and England had been in the condition euphemistically described by diplomatists as "strained." Events in Africa had constituted a chronic source of friction, and the annexation of the Congo Free State by the French, who claimed rights of pre-emption, had brought matters to a crisis. Nevertheless, it seemed as if the resources of diplomacy would heal the breach, and the public, lulled to a sense of tranquility, were simply paralyzed by the morning's news, which burst on the nation like a thunder-clap.

Some of the papers accused the Government of precipitancy, alleging that England was quite unprepared for war with such a power as France; others preferred to look upon the war as having been inevitable, and only regretted that a more favourable opportunity had not been selected to commence hostilities: but they were unanimous in the opinion that we were about to enter upon a life-and-death struggle which it would be impossible to confine to the two Powers chiefly concerned.

In every place where men congregated there was the wildest commotion. At the London railway-stations, in the trains and omnibuses hasting to disgorge their daily suburban load, the tidings dwarfed every other topic. But naturally it was at the Stock Exchange that the greatest excitement prevailed, and "Gorgonzola Hall" was in a delirious ferment. There had been a feeling of uneasiness for some days past, and even the most intensely aureate of gilt-edged securities had shown jelly-like movements. But on this eventful morning the bears carried all before them, and an hour before the springing of the rattle which announces the commencement of business, prices had begun to crumble away like snow beneath the sun.

As the day wore on and the news spread, the crowd outside the Exchange became a surging mob, which was swollen every second by the cabs depositing perspiring clients in search of absent brokers. Those privileged to pass the janitors had literally to fight their way in. One of the glass panels in the Shorter's Court doorway was shivered early in the day, and its fellow had to be boarded over to protect it from a similar fate. Round in Capel Court half-a-dozen policemen had been posted as a breakwater, against which the uninitiated broke in impotent waves. And ever, as the glass-doors swung to and fro, a dull, drumming, persistent roar, like the whirring of distant factory-looms, reverberated down the passages, and mingled with the noise of the traffic on the clattering asphalt roadway.

About noon the tall slim figure of Pringle joined the crowd around the Capel Court entrance, and after an arduous struggle succeeded in getting within hailing distance of the blue-coated porter, who as a rule reposes majestically in the leather chair by the door. The present was no time for repose, however, and in response to a fervent appeal from Pringle, he condescended to transmit his inquiry for Mr. Hedsor through a speaking-tube to the arcana of the House. Pringle had a weary wait of over half-an-hour before the broker appeared, and even then, so dense was the pressure of the crowd, mostly passing inward, that after a few ineffectual struggles, Mr. Hedsor, whose stature was not of the bulkiest, was reduced to a desperate squirm at short intervals with the sole purpose of retaining his position quite apart from any idea of making progress. How long this captivity might have lasted, or whether it might not have terminated in the incontinent collapse of the broker is uncertain, had not the janitor at length caught sight of him, and clearing a passage through the mob, with an authoritative "By your leave," extracted him by the remnants of his coat-collar.

"Whatever do you want?" gasped the palpitating broker, as he pettishly endeavoured to adjust his tattered garments. "I'm frightfully busy." And mopping his brow, he edged towards a clear space at the side, left by the eddying crowd.

"I'm sorry to trouble you, but I came to ask your advice as to what I had better do," apologized Pringle, as he dusted him down.

"Advice!" repeated the broker. "Why, I tell you, you ought to be one of us! You've got the luck of old Nick himself! Who on earth would have thought this was going to happen? And I don't believe it would either, if you hadn't taken it into your head to do a bear."

"You see I have faith in my luck, as I told you yesterday. But what are Consols standing at now?"

"*Standing* do you call it? They're falling—*falling*, man!" The broker grinned sardonically, he was too breathless to laugh.

"Well, what have they fallen to?"

"Why, they were ninety-seven ten minutes ago, and the Lord only knows when they'll touch bottom! They were eighty-five in the Crimea, and this little show'll be worse than half-a-dozen Crimeas before it's done with."

"I suppose I ought to buy, then?"

"Oh, the innocence of the man! As if you didn't know the game to play! Lucky dog that you are." Mr. Hedsor sighed enviously, and began to work a little sum in his note-book. "Look here, I sold fifty thou' for you yesterday at a hundred and nine seven-eighths. If you buy them back now at ninety-seven—or suppose we say ninety-six or thereabouts, you'll make thirteen per cent. more or less. Now I can't come out here again. You must just go round to the office and wait, and I'll telephone through to you as soon as the job's done. You can amuse yourself by figuring out how much you've made in the last twenty-four hours. Oh, you lucky dog!"

"Delighted, I'm sure," smiled Pringle sweetly. "And in that case you can hold over my cheque till the settlement. And look here, I think this movement has been overdone, so, while closing the bear, just buy me a bull of another fifty thousand, and I shouldn't be surprised if that thirteen per cent. turns out more like twenty-six when we come to close the bull."

"Right you are, my boy! And, look here, next time you've got a good thing on, you might give me the tip, and let's get in on the ground-floor."

Pringle shook his head in deprecation as the broker, with a knowing wink, dived once more into the crowd, and was borne inwards with the stream.

Coasting along the outskirts of the turmoil, Pringle got safely down Throgmorton Street, only taking ten minutes over a journey which under ordinary circumstances he could have accomplished in as many seconds, and was about to enter the office, when a tremendous hubbub arose, distinctly audible above the all-pervading uproar. From the height of the three or four steps up to the door-way he commanded a view of the scene. Looking back, he saw a news-boy crying an evening paper, surrounded by a yelling mob, which struggled and fought madly for the sheets. Presently a small group detached itself from the rest, and frantically rushed towards the entrance to the Exchange in the wake of a hatless individual, who had seized a contents-bill, which he waved triumphantly above his head. As it floated like a banner in the van of the little army, Pringle with some difficulty spelt out:—

British Ambassador Hoaxed.
Forged Paris Despatch,
Scene in the House of Commons.

He turned abruptly and entered the office, and even as he shut the door behind him, the telephone gong whirred. He sprung to the receiver, and before the clerk could reach it, pressed the handle.

"Are you there?"

"Yes."

"Is it Mr. Barker?"

"No, Pringle."

"Oh, all serene! Fifty thou' at ninety-six and a half."

"Thank you. How much do you make it?"

"I said about thirteen per cent., didn't I? Roughly it's six thousand five hundred that you've made. I say, were you born with a silver spoon in your mouth? It's settling day next week, and I'll send you the full account then. Ta, ta!"

Out in Throgmorton Street, Pringle managed to secure a paper, and this was what he read:—

The Threatened War Averted.
Statement by the Foreign Under-Secretary.
Extraordinary Story.
Is It A Hoax?

When the House of Commons assembled to-day at noon there was an unusual attendance of members, and hardly a seat on the floor of the chamber was vacant, except on the Treasury Bench, whose sole tenant was the Foreign Under-Secretary. Immediately after prayers Mr. Grammaty rose and said:—

"Sir, I have to crave the indulgence of the House for the purpose of making a statement on behalf of the Government, in view of the very serious news published in the morning papers. The Government has never had any intention of breaking off diplomatic relations with France, and Lord Strathclyde, while doing so in all good faith, appears to have acted on misleading and unauthorized instructions. I can assure the House that the matter will form the subject of the most searching investigation, and in the meantime Lord Strathclyde has been requested to offer the amplest apologies to the French Government. I am happy to inform the House that the relations of this country with France have never been more friendly than they are at the present moment."

This statement was received with profound silence, only broken by the cheers which arose on all sides at the conclusion. Immediately Mr. Grammaty resumed his seat, the House rapidly emptied, and the lobby was thronged with members eagerly discussing the situation.

We understand that Lord Tranmere was in attendance at the Foreign Office at an unprecedented hour, and that a brisk exchange of telegrams between London and the Paris Embassy has been in progress all the morning.

It is stated that our relations with France have, within the last few days, assumed a most amicable complexion, and no one was more surprised at the morning's news than the officials at the Foreign Office. Although the utmost reticence is being observed by the department in question, we are in a position to state that the despatch in accordance with which Lord Strathclyde acted, was nothing less than a clever forgery, which was mysteriously substituted for a genuine one of quite a different complexion. How or by what means

the exchange was effected, and how the spurious document
was allowed to reach the Paris Embassy undetected, appears
to be an unsolved mystery pending the result of the investigation promised by the Government.

Pringle folded the paper, and glanced at the scene around him.
The individual so hotly denounced was not likely to stand in the
pillory—the Chrysanthemum Club's cellar had insured that!

He walked on past the entrance to the Exchange. The murmur
of the crowd which filled every approach was answered by a roar
from the Temple of Mammon, deeper, and more thunderous than
any that had hitherto escaped the swing-doors, now wedged wide
open by the surging mass.

The pendulum had swung back. The bulls were triumphantly
rushing prices up again.

THE CHICAGO HEIRESS

It was a warm morning towards the end of June, and London, that is to say the West End, was fast becoming an arid wilderness. But although almost everybody who was anybody, had long left town, there was one place which enjoyed a popularity unaffected by the flight of fashion or the seasons.

The weirdly zoological collection which frequents the reading-room of the British Museum was very much in evidence. The juvenile and cheerful lady who edited the magazine, the elderly and unhappy one who copied hymns, the retired tragedian in the cloak who spent the day in sleep, were all there. So, too, was the red-whiskered gentleman of uncertain age, who seldom rested, but perambulated the room in search of the book which some one had always taken from the lower shelves just when he wanted to consult it. He was still on patrol-duty; his shuffles across the hills and valleys of the linoleum being almost the only sounds which broke the stillness of the warm, leathery atmosphere.

Perhaps it was on account of the heat, at any rate the blue dome was free from echoes of the groans, grunts, and still more fearsome noises with which the staple reader is wont to accompany his literary studies.

The reading-room was a locality which appealed to Mr. Pringle with a two-fold concern. As a (supposititious) literary agent he was bound to be interested in the focal point of modern hack-writing; but it was rather as a student of human nature that he frequented the chamber which has succeeded to the heritage of Grub Street.

41

The room, then, was very full, and Pringle had made the circular tour twice over before he espied a seat which another reader was in the act of vacating. It was at the end of one of the long desks, and taking a volume of Froude's *England* from the nearest shelf he sat down. Next to him was a man whom he at first took to be asleep, but a closer inspection showed that he was merely leaning back regarding the dome with an abstracted air. His uncropped hair and beard, together with a large pair of spectacles, gave him the look of a student, which was heightened by the sombrero-looking wide-awake which reposed on the shelf in front of him. He was evidently in search of inspiration from the vault above, as several sheets of notepaper on the desk appeared to be copies of a half-written letter which he was unable to finish. Littered all about were books of ponderous size, many resplendent with gilding. Peerages and directories, from the reference library, mingled in confusion with more recondite works from the inmost recesses of the establishment. Burke jostled Debrett, and was in turn overlaid by Dod, while Burke's *County Families* and sundry genealogies and court-guides were smothered by Zeimssen's many-volumed *Medicine*. Here and there about the heap were scattered stained and dirty clippings of newspaper, carefully backed with postage-stamp edging at the well-worn creases.

The creator of all this chaos was by no means a fluent writer, for Pringle had curiously watched him for perhaps half-an-hour before he completed the letter to his satisfaction. He then made a fair copy, and folded it into an envelope, which he addressed with elaborate care. Rising, he chanced with his elbow to push one of the medical tomes, which fell to ground with a resounding thud. As he stooped to pick it up, Pringle leant across and read the address on the laborious composition:—

The Most Noble the Marquis of Lundy,
65 *Clarges Street, Mayfair, W.*

Sorting out his volumes, the unknown took some of them up to the central desk to redeem the vouchers, and Pringle made use of the opportunity to exchange blotting-pads. As it happened, the two were stained in a not very dissimilar manner, and he had just time to complete the manoeuvre before his neighbour returned. Pringle's intuition was remarkably prophetic, for tearing his tickets in half and flinging them under the desk, the letter-writer deliberately proceeded to remove the top sheet of the blotter with a paper-knife! The mere possibility of the substitution did not appear to even enter his mind, and carefully placing the sheet, together with his other papers, in a leathern pocket-book, he walked out of the room.

As soon as he was gone, Pringle groped under the desk for the torn fragments of the tickets. The signature on one of them was intact, and he read in long-looped characters the name "Julius Schillinghammer."

Schillinghammer—he was a German, then, reflected Pringle. No wonder he found English composition such a labour. He looked too respectable for a begging letter-writer; besides, it was evident he regarded the letter as an important one, or why had he been so careful to remove the blotting-paper? But Pringle had lived long enough to be surprised at nothing, and congratulating himself on his opportune exchange of the blotters, he hastily appropriated the incriminating top-sheet and followed the German out.

When Pringle reached the cloak-room, the way was blocked by an irascible old gentleman who had lost the tally for a small black bag, and was expressing grave doubts as to the logic of the attendant's refusal to return him his property. "Words" were passing freely, and Pringle lost several minutes in the endeavour to recover his own walking-stick. At length he got off, but, as he expected, there was no sign of the stranger in the entrance-hall. As he ran down the steps, however, he caught a glimpse of him passing out of the front-gate, and hurried across the gravel-path in time to see the German turn into Museum Street. Crossing Oxford Street, Mr. Schillinghammer kept straight on through Drury Lane and Wych Street, then, skirting St. Clement Danes, he turned into Essex Street, and suddenly disappeared about half-way down. Pringle, who had followed all the time at an unobtrusive pace, fixed

the spot by its vicinity to a street-lamp, and after what he judged a
discreet interval, walked past. The house into which Mr. Schillinghammer had disappeared proved to be one of the smaller ones in
the street, and, like the majority, was let in offices—or, to be exact, an office; for there was but a single brass-plate upon the door,
and it bore the inscription—*Essex Private Inquiry Agency. British and Continental.*

Pringle strolled on down the slope of Essex Street towards the
flight of steps leading to the Embankment. But he never reached
that thoroughfare, for, pausing a moment at the top of the flight to
take a perspective view of the "Inquiry Agency," he saw a figure
abruptly emerge from the office and walk with quick step towards
the Strand. Without a moment's hesitation Pringle turned back and
started in pursuit, for although garbed in the frock-coat and tall
hat of advanced civilization, there was no mistaking the identity
of Mr. Julius Schillinghammer!

At the top of the street the German paused, and appeared to be
in search of a conveyance, as he carefully scrutinized the procession of omnibuses. A vacant garden-seat at length invited him to
one bound westward, and Pringle, who had feigned absorption in
the literary contents of a shop-window which accurately reflected
the other's movements, ran after it, and took an inside seat as far
as possible from the door. Towards Piccadilly his watchfulness increased, and as they drew near the Green Park it was rewarded by
seeing Mr. Schillinghammer dismount and walk up Clarges Street.
He was evidently in a hurry, and by the time Pringle, who had followed, but on the other side of the street, was abreast of No. 65,
the German was engaged in conversation with a man-servant, to
whom he was handing a letter. Pringle walked on, and, turning the
corner into Bolton Row, looked back at the house; but the door
was already closed, and as he ventured a step back into Clarges
Street, he was just able to see Mr. Schillinghammer amble round
the corner into Piccadilly.

Returning to Furnival's Inn, Pringle commenced the work of
deciphering the hieroglyphics on the blotting-paper.

Mr. Schillinghammer appeared to have used a "J" pen—a course which had its disadvantages as well as its advantages. For if the individual words were bold and distinct, the thickness of the pen had only served the more thoroughly to run one word into another on the blotting-paper. After some thought, Pringle decided to hunt first for any semblance to the signature on the book-ticket, and, with the aid of a looking-glass to reverse the script, he was at length rewarded by the sight of a blurred *lius Schilling* in one corner. This was satisfactory in so far as it offered proof that the writer had signed the letter with his own name. But when Pringle endeavoured, amid the confused mass of blots and smudges, to decipher some additional words, or even letters, the task appeared well-nigh hopeless. But he was not the man to be daunted by obstacles, however insurmountable they might at first sight appear, and he patiently returned to the charge, using the book-ticket to verify and distinguish the German's handwriting from that of any previous user of the pad. Fortunately the upper sheet was almost unblemished, and at the cost of a racking headache, his eyes almost blinded by the use of a magnifying-lens, he made out a series of words from the boldest part of the writing—doubtless derived from the fair copy of Mr. Schillinghammer's literary effort.

When set out on paper this is how they appeared—

92 Lang, seeing, possession, brother, business, good, heard, you, obtained, concealed, history, repair, value, thousand, inform, require, family, notes, nothing, be, and the signature.

There were also numerous fragments of words with a fair quantity of scattered conjunctions and articles. These he copied on to a separate sheet of paper, and after a laborious study of their relative sequence on the pad, he constructed a skeleton of the letter, thus—

92 Lang—seeing—an—mis—Chic—repair—occurred—possession—y—history—be—value—y's—family—you—doc—

evi—cide—brothers—concealed—unde—inform—e—Engl—
business—y—many—thousand—require—good—obtain—
notes—nothing—heard—fully—Julius Schillinghammer.

Having completed this patchwork, Pringle lit a cigarette, and,
sitting down, took up a newspaper in the desperate endeavour to
give his brain a short respite. It was the *Park Lane Review* that
he had picked up, and although it required no great intellectual
effort for its perusal, his thoughts incessantly strayed to the skeleton letter.

Just as the faintest ray of light in a dark room is enough to
indicate the position of an outlet, so a single syllable was the means
of solving the riddle. Determined to concentrate his attention on
the paper, he re-read a paragraph which his eye had skimmed without assimilating it.

An event which I predicted some weeks ago, shows that
alliances with the British aristocracy are still popular with
our fair American cousins. It is now formally announced
that the Marquis of Lundy is to be shortly married to Miss
Petasöhn, the only child of the well-known Chicago million-
aire, and who aroused so much interest by her beauty and
graceful presence during the late season.

Flinging the paper aside, Pringle impulsively seized the skeleton letter. There it was, sure enough!—*Chic*—a fragmentary word
which had hitherto baffled him completely. It stood for Chicago,
of course! And, encouraged by the discovery, he sat down again,
and studied the paper with avidity.

For many years the Lundy estates have been greatly im-
poverished, partly by bad seasons, but mainly by the ex-
travagance and mismanagement of former owners; Thorpe
Regis, the palatial family residence in Norfolk, having been
long unoccupied. The present Marquis, as a younger son,
had at one time little chance of succeeding to the title, had

not the death of both his brothers opened the way for him. It is a curious fact that the late peer and his two sons all ended their lives by some misadventure; the eldest son being found dead in a wood as the result of a gun-accident when shooting; while the second, who bid fair to take a high position in the House of Commons, and had a brilliant future before him, took poison by mistake. The late Lord Lundy was drowned soon afterwards, having mistaken his way on a dark night. The present peer, better known as Lord William Pownall, has always been a favourite in society, and I understand he has been simply overwhelmed with congratulations on his approaching wedding, which will be one of the social events of the year.

Could Schillinghammer be a blackmailer, after all, Pringle pondered. There was *notes* plainly written, and also the significant term *thousand*. Were not the words almost enough to explain the whole letter? The German appeared to be asking for a thousand pounds in notes. That was a large sum to demand. It must be a valuable secret to have such a price put upon it. There was a hint at a family mystery to be read between the lines of the *Park Lane Review*. The riddle was certainly a very piquant one, and Pringle returned to his task with a renewed zest.

A little further search for disconnected words in the mazes of the blotting-paper, a little re-arrangement of the disjointed syllables, a happy guess or two, and he clothed the bare bones of the skeleton thus:—

> "92, *Langbourne Street*,
> "*Leicester Square.*

"My Lord,

"Seeing the announcement of your betrothal to Miss Petasöhn of Chicago, which I hope will repair your fortunes, it has occurred to me that I am in possession of facts concerning your family history which may be considered of value by the lady's family. When I tell you that I have documentary evidence of the suicide of your father and two brothers, facts which have been successfully concealed hitherto, you will understand my reasons for informing you that I wish to leave England and start a business in Germany. The sum of a thousand pounds is what I require, and should your lordship be good enough to assist me to obtain this sum in notes, I promise you nothing more shall be heard of the matter.

"Yours respectfully,

"Julius Schillinghammer."

This, then, or something very like it, must have been the letter which Mr. Schillinghammer had not thought fit to trust to the post, and Pringle contemplated his solution of the mystery with very pardonable pride.

Obviously the paragraphs in the *Park Lane Review* had struck the key-note of Mr. Schillinghammer's little plot, whilst the details might have been worked up from papers which had come under his notice, most probably in the offices of the "Inquiry Agency," of which he must be a member, if not the principal. As to the address, Pringle was already acquainted with it as a notorious place where letters were received, and he had little difficulty in recognizing it in the fragmentary address of the skeleton.

The next step was to make sure of the valuable information he had acquired. He had spent all the afternoon over his task. It had now gone six. Mr. Schillinghammer, it is true, had been denied the Marquis when he called, but it was probable that the latter, even if not dining at home, would be returning to dress shortly. He must be interviewed immediately.

Pringle had never much difficulty in removing the port-wine mark on his cheek with a little spirit, and a smart application of chemicals soon darkened his fair hair. Then, putting on a "bowler" and a light covert-coat, he turned his face westward.

"Can I see Lord Lundy?"

The footman was discreetly doubtful, but if Pringle would give his name he would make inquiries.

"Tell his lordship I have an important message from the German gentleman who called here this morning," Pringle added, and a few minutes later was following the servant up-stairs.

He was ushered into a room on the first-floor, half library, half smoking-room, with the solid mahogany door and elegantly-carved mantel of an eighteenth-century London mansion. A tall young man, with a closely-cropped beard, was sitting smoking in an easy-chair. He half rose as the door opened, and, without acknowledging Pringle's bow, waited until the servant had retired before speaking.

"I was not expecting you before to-morrow," he said curtly; "but since you are here, be good enough to state your business briefly, as my time is limited."

"I must first tell your lordship that I have no interest in any German you are expecting, beyond being desirous of arresting him."

"Arresting him!" exclaimed the Marquis.

"Yes; I am a member of the Criminal Investigation Department, and have charge of the case of some foreign anarchists who are wanted on the Continent."

"May I ask why you trouble to come here then?" inquired the peer, only a trifle less icily.

"One of those anarchists, Hödel by name, was traced to this street to-day in company with a man named Eppelstein, who was seen to call here."

"But what has that to do with me?"

"Only this. By a gross neglect of duty on the part of the officer who was observing them, Hödel was lost sight of, and in the hope that your lordship will assist the ends of justice, I have come to ask you for some information as to his companion who called here."

"Pray sit down. May I ask your name?" and Lord Lundy pushed a box of cigars across the table towards Pringle.

"My name is Fosterberry," said Pringle, as he took a chair, respectfully declining the cigars.

"Well, I should be very glad to help you if I could, but the man who called here this morning didn't give the name of Hödel."

"No; it was his companion, Eppelstein, who came here."

"That wasn't the name either. I didn't see the man, as I was out at the time, but he left a letter which I found waiting for me this afternoon, and he said he would call again at half-past ten to-morrow morning."

"What name did he leave behind?"

"Schillinghammer."

"Schillinghammer? An *alias* I was unacquainted with. May I ask what his object was in calling here?"

Lord Lundy coughed and fidgeted in his chair.

"Pray excuse me," apologized Pringle. It is, of course, no business of mine. I merely asked the question, as I presume your lordship is not acquainted with him."

"Acquainted with him! I never heard of the scoundrel before to-day!" exclaimed the peer, as he dealt the table beside him a resounding blow with his fist. Then, his indignation getting the better of his caution, he drew a letter from his pocket. "This is a letter he left for me. It seems as if the blackguard has got hold of some information which I have the best of reasons for wishing to keep private, and he offers not to make any use of it, but to leave the country if I will give him a thousand pounds."

"Indeed," mused Pringle. "This is news to me. I had no idea he did anything in that line. Not but what he is quite capable of it, but he must be getting in rather low water if he has begun to play such a risky game."

"All I can say is that he appears to be a professional blackmailer."

"May I ask your lordship if you intend to pay?"

"Well, I need hardly say I don't like it, but, so far as I can see, I must either allow him to bleed me like this, or I must submit to the loss of a very much larger sum; together with other inconveniences which cannot be estimated quite so easily."

As he spoke his eye wandered to the mantelpiece. There, in a silver frame, stood the photograph of a strikingly handsome girl. Across one corner had been scrawled in a bold, almost masculine hand—*à vous, Bernice Petasöhn.*

Pringle, who had followed the direction of his glance, took in these details before the marquis, recovering himself with a start, exclaimed almost pettishly— "Can't you arrest this Schilling-hammer, or whatever his name is, when he comes here again to-morrow?"

"It's rather unfortunate that he is not wanted. He is well known to both the London and Continental police as an associate of foreign anarchists, but Hödel is the man we are really anxious to arrest."

"You can't possibly arrest the other brute, then?"

"I'm afraid not. I have no doubt he is as great a scoundrel as Hödel, especially after what your lordship has just told me; but as the German police have not applied for his extradition, we have no grounds for interfering with him. Of course, my lord, if you are ready to proceed against him for attempting to blackmail you, the matter becomes a very simple one, and we shall be—"

"No, no, no! Publicity is the very thing of all others I want to avoid," exclaimed the peer hurriedly, adding, "and he knows it too."

"Then I'm afraid there's nothing for it but to pay."

Lord Lundy sighed and passed his hand wearily across his brow.

"You can't advise anything else?" he asked despondently.

"The case is really a very clear one," argued Pringle. "If, as you say, this man is able to do your lordship some substantial injury, which you are naturally anxious to avoid, and if at the same time you are unwilling to avail yourself of the protection of the law, what other course is open to you?"

The peer drummed an impatient tattoo on the table without speaking for a few minutes. "I thought," he remarked at length, "of giving him only half what he asks for now, and of sending the remainder to be paid to him personally by a German banker."

"A very excellent plan," agreed Pringle. "You will make certain at any rate that he is safely out of the country. Under the circumstances, I should advise you to give him cash. You see a cheque has obvious disadvantages if you wish to keep the affair private, and if you give him notes and he had any difficulty in passing them, as he might have, your object would be again defeated. I am sorry," he added, as he arose to go, "that I can be of no service to your lordship in the matter."

"Not at all," exclaimed the marquis, "your advice has been most valuable." And ringing the bell for the footman, he politely bowed Pringle out.

About half-past ten the next morning Lord Lundy was sitting in his study. A number of letters lay unopened on the desk, and he held a newspaper in front of him. But he did not read. His eyes were fixed upon the photograph on the mantelpiece. At length, as he continued to gaze, a tear slowly trickled down his cheek, and, as it pattered against the crisp sheet upon his knee, he started and, flinging the paper down, moved towards the desk. At this moment the distant rattle of an electric-bell ascended from the hall, and stopping short he turned away, and strode nervously up and down the room.

"Mr. Schillinghammer, my lord," the footman said, and ushered that gentleman in according to orders.

The marquis took up a position on the hearthrug, and Mr. Schillinghammer saluted him with a profound bow, which he supplemented by a sweep of the tall hat as the servant withdrew.

"I have de honour—" he began, but the peer cut him short.

"Have the goodness, sir," he exclaimed, "to dispense with any unnecessary formalities. I have read the letter which you left here yesterday. What is the information you have to sell?" He remained standing, as perforce did Mr. Schillinghammer.

"Some information which may be useful to Misder Petasöhn."

"Then why not take it to Mr. Petasöhn?"

"It is a madder of commerce. I coom to you. I have someding valuable to sell. You do not buy it. Very well, I go to Misder Petasöhn. I will tell him for noding. Berhaps he pay me after I tell him—berhaps not. But he will be gradeful. I have lived in America. I have been an *employé* of Misder Petasöhn in his great pig-business. I know the American fader. He is more particular than de English. I will tell Misder Petasöhn your fader killed himself, likewise your two broders. He will not led his daughter marry such a family-man. Dat is all. I coom to you first, den if you do not buy I go on to Misder Petasöhn and tell what I know. And den, my lord, and den, and den—you lose Miss Petasöhn, de great, great heiress!" Here he spread his arms expansively.

"How did you obtain this valuable information?" inquired Lord Lundy, with difficulty repressing his inclination to kick Mr. Schillinghammer downstairs.

"I am a brivate inquiry agent! It is my brofession to know everyding about everybody," and he smiled superciliously.

"But have you no documents or papers to give me if I consent to pay you? What proofs have you of your statement?"

The German produced his pocket-book, and extracted from it the bundle of papers and cuttings which Pringle had seen in his possession at the Museum.

"Here," said he, "you give me a tousand pounds and dey are yours."

He held the bundle towards Lord Lundy, who received it with an air of disgust which he took no pains to conceal, but sitting down at the desk, untied the piece of tape surrounding it, and fastidiously handling the uppermost paper, commenced to read. Tossing it contemptuously aside when he had done, he took up the next slip, and so on, till he had perused the whole budget.

"Are you aware of the value of this collection of papers?" he asked, turning suddenly towards Mr. Schillinghammer, and laying his hand upon the scattered heap as he spoke.

"I have told you what is de brice I ask," replied the inquiry agent doggedly.

"You are insolent, sir! These papers are worth at the very most about half-a-crown, and you have the effrontery to ask me to give you a thousand pounds for them!"

"It is my silence I will sell you—not de pabers. Dey may be worth only half-a-crown, but de newspabers are out of brint, and de oders cost much money to collect. I do not desire to sell de pabers. I will give dem to you if you buy my silence."

"You are most generous," remarked the peer dryly.

"You say, where are my broofs?" continued Mr. Schillinghammer, without noticing the sarcasm. "You have dem dere beside you in black and white. Every one nearly who ever knew has forgot de matter, and Misder Petasöhn will not believe me if I cannot show him dose pabers. Dere are de accounts of de inquests on your broders and your fader. All died by deir own hand. De Doctor say your broder could not fire by accident de gun. De valet of your older broder say he bought de poison for him to take. Dere is copy of de corresbondence with de Insurance Office which refused to pay your fader's life-policy because he killed himself. Dese have cost much money and time to get, but I tink Misder Petasöhn will understand dat."

"I wonder you are not afraid to let such valuable documents leave your possession for a moment."

"*Noplesse oplige,*" returned Mr. Schillinghammer, with another bow and wave of his hat, adding with a snigger, "Beside, dere is no fire in de grate."

Once again did Mr. Schillinghammer narrowly escape a rapid ejectment from the room; but Lord Lundy simply asked

"I consent to your terms, what will you do?"

"I will return to Germany. I desire to start a business in Hamburg."

"But what security have I that you will leave England?"

"De word of one gentleman to anoder!"

"I prefer to trust to something more tangible. I will send you the money as soon as I am sure you have actually reached Germany."

"But I cannot reach Germany widout de money!" Mr. Schillinghammer expostulated.

"I have not de tariff! I have also money owing for rent, and food, and bills! I am a poor, very poor man, but I will not rob my creditors. I am honest!"

"I will pay you five hundred pounds now, and will send the rest to Germany as soon as I know you have arrived."

"No, it will not do," said the German decisively. "Misder Petasöhn shall help me return to Germany." And he made towards the door.

"Stop!" exclaimed the Marquis, taking something from the writing-desk. "See, here are five hundred sovereigns." He dropped a canvas-bag upon the table with a thud.

At the very threshold Mr. Schillinghammer paused, and Lord Lundy hastened to pursue his advantage.

"If you will return to Germany at once, an order shall be sent to a Hamburg banker to pay you another five hundred."

Painful was Mr. Schillinghammer's situation! Impelled in one direction by his innate distrust of his fellow-beings, in another by the sight, or, to be more accurate, by the sound of the specie, he wavered and stood irresolutely fingering the door-handle. At length the irresistible argument of a cash transaction prevailed, as the Marquis had calculated, over every obstacle, and drawn to the table by the magnetic attraction of the gold, Mr. Schillinghammer, oblivious of the pressing claims of his creditors, exclaimed with reckless generosity, "I will be fair wid you. Here are de pabers, my lord. I will start for Hamburg to-night."

Seizing the bag, he stuffed it into his coat-pocket. At the door he turned, "I wish your lordship all health and happiness;" and with a final bow and wave of the hat towards the photograph, added, "and her ladyship also!"

Despite the weightiness of the specie, it was with an elastic step that the blackmailer left the house. The Street happened to be almost deserted, except for a four-wheeler which was waiting a few doors off. As Mr. Schillinghammer approached, he observed that a man was standing beside its open door; he was tall and clean-shaven, wore a bowler hat and a covert-coat, also he was shod in an uncompromisingly stout pair of boots: in short, it was Mr. Romney Pringle.

The German passed on unsuspectingly, but Pringle seized him by the arm. "Mr. Schillinghammer, I believe?" And before the latter had regained sufficient presence of mind to deny his identity, Pringle continued— "I am Inspector Fosterberry, of the Criminal Investigation Department, and I arrest you on a warrant for obtaining money by threats and false pretences from the Marquis of Lundy. I must ask you to come with me quietly."

He gently but firmly urged Mr. Schillinghammer into the cab, and still grasping his arm, sat down beside him and closed the door. The cabman, who had received his instructions, drove up Clarges

Street, and they had traversed Mayfair before Mr. Schillinghammer recovered from the astonishment which, for the moment, had rendered him speechless.

"Why do you arrest me?" he demanded, after several ineffectual efforts to speak.

"I have already told you. The warrant has been issued on the sworn information of the Marquis of Lundy."

"He is a liar! I am a respectable man."

"You will have every opportunity of explaining matters; in the meantime you must come with me."

"Where are we going? I will not go to de prison."

"I am taking you before the sitting magistrate at Marlborough Street police-court."

"I will not go! I warn you it is a serious madder. I am a German subject—I will write to de German ambassador! You will be severely punished!" And volubly protesting, he began to struggle violently, and endeavoured to reach the door-handle. But he was muscularly flabby and out of condition, and Pringle had little difficulty in overpowering him. They were crossing Bond Street, and Pringle had reasons of his own for wishing to avoid a scene just there.

"If you don't keep still I shall be compelled to handcuff you," warned Pringle. "What's this? A revolver! I must take it from you."

He had been feeling a hard lump in the breast of Mr. Schillinghammer's coat, and inserting his free hand, he drew out the bag of sovereigns and placed it in his own pocket. Mr. Schillinghammer's nerves, although severely tried, were not too shattered to quench all resentment at this high-handed proceeding had not the cab stopped at this moment.

"What's the matter?" asked Pringle, putting his head out.

"Ere we are, sir," said the cabman, pointing ahead with his whip. The cab had traversed Regent Street and Argyll Place and was now drawn up at the end of Great Marlborough Street.

Pringle stepped on to the pavement, and stared intently in the direction of the police-court a few yards further on, as if waiting for some one to appear. Meanwhile Mr. Schillinghammer, with an agility with which he could hardly have been credited, scrambled through the open window on the off-side of the cab. Alighting, he nearly fell into the arms of a constable who was crossing the road.

"Hulloa! What's the little game?" said the man.

But Mr. Schillinghammer, ignoring the question, dodged round the cab and raced frantically up Argyll Street.

The constable looked at Pringle, who was still regarding the police-court with undiminished interest, apparently quite unaware of Mr. Schillinghammer's movements.

"What did he want to get out of the window for?" said the gentleman in blue inquisitively.

"Window!" said Pringle, turning with a well-assumed start, and looking into the cab. "Do you mean the cab-window? By Jingo, so he has! Here, help me to stop him—he's my prisoner!"

The constable, with a condescending grin at Pringle's innocence, obligingly started in pursuit of Mr. Schillinghammer, who by this time was nearly in Oxford Street. Pringle slipped a half-sovereign into the cabman's hand, and followed at a pace scarcely commensurate with any great interest in the prospective capture. Half-way up Argyll Street he turned short off to the left, and entering Regent Street, hailed a cab.

As the policeman, having reached Oxford Street, stood hopelessly scanning the crowd for a glimpse of the blackmailer, Pringle drove by on his way to Furnival's Inn.

THE LIZARD'S SCALE

"You'll have to ground-bait very carefully," said the chatty old gentleman. "You won't do much with the roach unless you do. I found them quite off yesterday."

"Which is the best Broad for the fishing?" inquired Pringle as he reached across the table for the coffee.

"Pike! ah, poor sport just now," was the irrelevant reply. "No good before September."

Pringle repeated his question.

"Eh? Yes, I'm on my way back to Stanlowe after breakfast. Sorry I didn't hear you. I've gone rather deaf since I saw you last, and I can't find my conversation-tube this morning."

Since he first took his seat at the table, the deaf one had treated Pringle with a cordiality unusual, to say the least of it, between total strangers, and it began to dawn upon him that the old gentleman mistook him for some one else. Mr. Pringle, having turned his back on the shadowy literary agency which he professed in Furnival's Inn, had been bronzing his fair complexion for the last few days in the East Anglian sun. The fishing had proved disappointing, although the yachting had afforded some slender compensation, and the quietude of the little inn was not distasteful to a town-dweller.

"Have I had the pleasure of meeting you before?" roared Pringle, as politely as the elevation of his voice permitted.

"Windrush? I've not seen him for a week or so. He was asking if I had heard anything of you the last time I went over."

He was certainly very deaf, and a connected conversation seemed hopeless.

"Who is that? I'm afraid I don't know him," Pringle vociferated in a supreme effort at disillusion.

"Oh, he's at Axford House, under Fernhurst's care, you know. I forgot you were away North at the time."

Worse and worse, thought Pringle. And, abandoning any further attempt at explanation, he contented himself with smiling and bowing, as the other continued to discourse with the loudness characteristic of the deaf.

"Yes, it was a sad business!" the old gentleman continued, "but what we should have done without Percy, I don't know. Uncharitable people might say he's making a good thing out of it; but, after all, he's John's nearest relative, and he was certainly most devoted in the way he looked after his brother. Indeed, he acted most sensibly throughout, and was entirely guided by my advice in all that he did. I must say I never cared very much for him before, and between ourselves I had regarded him as a bit of an unscrupulous adventurer, but I've quite altered my opinion of him now." He rose and collected his fishing-tackle. "You should go over and see John at Axford. It's only the fourth station beyond Stanlowe. But you ought to know the way! Tell him I shall be over next week if you do." And cordially shaking hands, the chatty old gentleman mounted a dog-cart which had been brought round to the door, and drove off.

"Who is that deaf old gentleman?" inquired Pringle of the landlord's son as he entered the bar.

"What! Dr. Toddington? Didn't yew iver see him when yew was at Thorpe Stanlowe, sir? He's gone wonful deaf, sure."

Pringle gasped. Was the whole place inhabited by lunatics, he asked himself, or had he taken leave of his senses?

"Look here," he said desperately, "I never saw that old gentleman before, and I was never at Thorpe what-d'you-call-it in my life!"

"Ain't yew Mr. Coatbridge, then?"

"Certainly not!" Pringle repudiated.

"Sars o' mine! Noo I come te look at yew I see he hain't got that there mark on the cheek—beggin' yar pardon fur a-mentionin' it."

"But who is he?"

"He were a great friend o' Mr. Windrush."

"And who on earth is Mr. Windrush?"

"My oo'd master at Thorpe Stanlowe."

"Am I so like Mr. Coatbridge, then?"

"Like as tew peas, sir!"

Pringle remembered that on arriving at the inn he had never been asked for his name, also that he had been welcomed with effusion; facts which at the time he ascribed to the rustic simplicity of the place. "I suppose Dr.—Toddington do you say his name is?—he thought I was Mr. Coatbridge, too?"

"Yes, sir! I toold him it were yew when he come here yes'day, an' he said he'd stop th' night jes' to see yew, but yew'd garn to bed any."

After all, then, mused Pringle, the chatty old gentleman was not so eccentric as he had thought. There were possibilities too in having a double!

"Does the Doctor live far away?" he asked at length.

"Up Thorpe Stanlowe, agin' th' Hall, sir. Matter o' 'leven mile from hare. Th' rain's kep' awa' wholly, sir, an' ef yew care fur a sail I could come now fawther's downd."

As they hoisted the little anchor and the sail filled, Pringle stretched his long limbs in the stern, and grasped the tiller in indolent attention to the discursive stream which flowed from the lips of the crew.

"See him theer, sir!" exclaimed the youth presently; "doon't he shine?"

The sedges rustled, shook, and then parted, as a foot or so of delicate olive-green, with a splash of yellow at the near end, shot whiplike from the bank. For a moment its lustrous belly-scales flashed in the sun, and then the snake glided gracefully into the water with a frog writhing between its powerful little jaws.

"*Tropidonotos natrix,*" murmured Pringle with an expansive yawn.

"Iver see a fiery sarpent, sir?"

"Do you mean fireworks?"

"Noo, a rale livin' one."

"Can't say I ever did. Did you?"

"Noo. Mr. Windrush did, tho';" and hauling the sheet more aft, he sat down on the weather-gunwale, as the little craft heeled to the wind roaring in miniature hurricane across the lonely expanse of the Broad. "He were haunted by th' funniest kinds of kewerious impets an' things yew iver set eyes on. Ah! th' best master as iver breathed. I were under-gardener at Thorpe Stanlowe fur oover three yare. I were eighteen when I went theer, an' stayed till the place were broke up. Mr. Percy wanted me to stay—didn't want no truck with *him!* Soo's fawther were a-gettin' oo'd, an' couldn' manage th' place, I come hoome."

"Who was Mr. Percy?"

"The master's brother, leastways half-brother. Fawther married twice, they said. But he's th' master now. Ah, I'm a-wishin' it'd been him 'stids o' Mr. Windrush."

"Why, is Mr. Windrush dead?"

"Worser'n that," said the youth, shaking his head mysteriously. "Noo, things was all right afore Mr. Percy come te live 'long with th' master, but in 'bout six months Mr. Windrush went wrong in his head. Dr. Toddington said he mustn't be 'loone, soo Mr. Percy took te sleepin' in master's dressin'-room. I didn't see noo difference in him—seemed th' same kinder-spoken gen'l'man he'd always been. Howsiver, they called down 'nother doctor from Lun'on, an' I hard they took an' held a crowner's 'quest on him, for all the warl' as if he'd been dead! An' jury they said he must goo 'way to a mad'us, an' he's now at Axford. Doctor from Lon'on couldn't hev been much account anyways. I hard he thought Mr. Windrush drunk a won'ful lot, an' a soberer man niver breathed! Theer were one o' um lifted his little finger, but 't 'twasn't Mr. Windrush! Doon't I mind how oo'd Percy fell oover some rails in th' dark won night? Lork! His face were that swelled he couldn't see outer his eyes fur a week. Nex' day he took an' had th' rails a-painted with that theer whitey stuff that shines oof th' dark, an' th' key-hole

a-painted, soo's he couldn't miss a-seein' of it. Givin' hisself a nice
character, I calls it. Ah! them tew differed as Wroxham and Barton.
Oo'd Percy now'd niver take no notice o' yew 'cept he gonned yew
some order or other. A'most th' only time I remember he iver did
speak to me were once when Mr. Windrush were a-talkin' to me
'bout yottin', an' Percy were a-standin' by a-listenin', an' a-grinnin'
from are to are, an' he upped an' says I were only a fresh-water
sailor, an' didn't know nothin' 'bout it—quite maliceful-like! *Me*,
mind yew! Me as were born an' bred on th' Broads in the manner
o' speakin'! Some said he'd been to sea hisself, an' I hard tell as
he'd studied fur a doctor. Anyhow they said if Mr. Windrush hadn't
took pity on him he'd have had to go to th' Work'us. Ah, he knowed
a thing or two, did Percy."

"Yachting on the Broads for instance?" suggested Pringle slyly.

The youth snorted contemptuously. "Seems to me all he knowed
an' all he didn't know'd have made a big book! Howsiver, he were
a riddy kind o' chap. He were fur everlastin' 'sperimentin' with
animals. Coachman's gals kep' guinea-pigs, an' they used to bring
'um to Percy when they got over-run. I hard 'um say he'd git 'um to
bring all manner o' live animals; snakes like that theer, an' lizards, an' sech-like. Won day I found a pig jes' a-dyin' back o' the
tule-shed, an' when I gonned it a tech, it shruck horrud! Seem'd 's
if that's been shaved an' painted all over with sticky stuff. Won o'
oo'd Percy's 'speriments, I thot. A'most th' only frien' he had were
th' mad'us doctor fr' Axford wheer master is now. Dr. Fernhurst
an' he were thick as thieves. Now th' house 'tis hired-let, an' Percy
he lives up o' Lon'on. He's 'pointed to look tew th' money fur Mr.
Windrush, an' lork! they've hot on th' right man fur that job!"—
Here the youth digressed into a chronicle of Stanlowe small-beer,
and Pringle, who had been an attentive listener up to this point,
fell into a reverie which lasted for the rest of the voyage.

The morning sail had given Pringle an appetite for lunch, and
after a hearty meal he walked briskly to the little station and took
the train to Axford. He had no difficulty in finding Dr. Fernhurst's
asylum. It was a three-story Manor-house built in the prim but
substantial style of Queen Anne's days, and as Pringle crossed the

pleasaunce surrounding it, he noted, with the grateful eye of a con- noisseur, the elaborate fan-light and the handsome pilasters which flanked the doorway supporting a pediment of chaste design. Pull- ing the wrought-iron bell-handle, he inquired for Mr. Windrush, and was ushered into a waiting-room. Here in a few moments he was joined by a smart young man looking like a superior valet, who introduced himself as the chief attendant of the Asylum.

"Dr. Fernhurst is out at present," he said, "but Mr. Windrush will be glad to see you if you will step this way. I believe, sir, that you are an old friend of his?"

"Not so very," replied Pringle ingenuously.

Ascending the stairs, they entered a room on the first-floor, with a cheerful outlook over a formal garden bordered with yew- trees fantastically trimmed into the shape of mushrooms, peacocks, chickens, and, in one instance, of a cup and saucer. "Mr. Windrush, here is your friend Mr. Coatbridge to see you," announced the at- tendant, immediately retiring and closing the door behind him. A tall, dejected-looking man, with a student's stoop and hair prema- turely grey, rose hesitatingly, with an exclamation of surprise, from the chair in which he had been reading.

"Why, you're never Coatbridge!" he cried.

"Hush! Please don't speak so loudly—I have something for your private ear alone." Pringle sprang to the door and opening it, looked out for a moment. "Excuse me for this slight deception," he con- tinued, as he resumed his seat: "I took the liberty of assuming the name of one whom I know to be your friend in order to have freer access to you."

The lunatic subsided irresolutely into his chair and began to nervously finger the leaves of the book he held. He did not attempt to read, although he kept his eyes downcast, but threw an occa- sional furtive glance at Pringle as he spoke.

"My real name is Pringle," said that gentleman. "I live in Lon- don, and have accidentally acquired some information which leads me to think that the facts connected with your case appear to re- quire investigation." Windrush started and opened his lips as if to speak, but he repressed the impulse and continued to listen intently.

"How I got to know of it is of no immediate consequence. I have been lucky enough to find you alone, and, as we may be interrupted at any moment, we mustn't waste precious time. What I want you to understand at present is that I have come to see you with a view of extricating you from this very unpleasant position."

Still Windrush made no reply, but assuming a less constrained attitude he regarded Pringle more openly and with a shade less suspicion.

"I am inclined to think," continued Pringle, "that your old medical attendant, Dr. Toddington, has been the victim of a very suspicious train of circumstances."

"But surely," exclaimed Windrush, at length breaking silence, "you did not get your information from him? He is the last person in the world to throw any fresh light upon the case! Why, the old simpleton firmly believes I am insane, and has been the chief means of putting me here!"

"No, no! It was from quite a different source."

"I must confess," said Windrush after a pause, during which he appeared to be reflecting deeply; "I must confess that I am very curious as to the means by which you, a total stranger, have got to know so much about my private affairs."

"I will tell you with the greatest pleasure, only, as I said before, time is precious, and I must ask you not to waste it by interrupting me. I will be as brief as I can." And in a few words, Pringle informed him of his accidental interview with the Doctor and the innkeeper's son. "Now," he said in conclusion, "may I ask you to regard me as a friend, and to speak to me unreservedly?"

"I really don't know how you are going to help me, Mr. Pringle, but I can only say that I shall be eternally grateful to any one who will rescue me from this miserable position. It is quite true that I see things at night, but I swear to you positively they are realities, and not delusions! Why, only last night I saw a fiery object of some sort while I was in bed. It was about six or eight inches long and appeared to run along the floor. I feel that if these things continue to trouble me much longer, my brain will indeed give way under the strain." He covered his face with his hands and sobbed passionately. "You must excuse me," said he, regaining his composure after a pause, during which Pringle had affected to be examining the garden, "but if you knew all that I have gone through during the last few months, you would wonder that I am as sensible as I am. I often wonder at it myself," he added with a melancholy smile.

"Do I understand you to say that these fiery apparitions only occur at nights?" inquired Pringle.

"They have never appeared at any other time. As a rule I see them on first retiring. I cannot even have the poor consolation of believing they are merely a nightmare horror."

"I should very much like to look at the room where all these things take place. Is your bedroom anywhere near?"

"Only through here."

Windrush led the way into an adjoining apartment where a man sat reading. "This is my attendant," he said, as the man rose on their entry and bowed.

"Would you mind asking him to inquire if Dr. Fernhurst is anywhere about the place? I should like to see him," said Pringle.

As the man departed on his errand, Pringle continued in a low voice, "I only want to get rid of him."

Windrush nodded with a look of intelligence, and opened a door on the further side of the room, The bedroom was plainly but substantially furnished, and overlooked the garden at a point where the clipped yews were replaced by a more pleasing vegetation, the mingled scent of jasmine and day-lily floating in through the open window.

"Where does that lead to?" asked Pringle, pointing to a door opposite the one by which they had entered.

"To Dr. Fernhurst's room. The door is usually locked, but either he or Bonting, the chief attendant, always sleeps there in case I should want their services during the night. Then Jenkinson, my own attendant, always sleeps in the ante-room. I am well looked after you see!" Again the melancholy smile.

Pringle went down on his hands and knees and commenced to make a rigid examination of the floor. The room was carpeted with a chocolate-coloured linoleum scattered over with a rug or two, and apparently presented nothing likely to repay such an elaborate investigation. After a prolonged tour of the room, including a temporary disappearance under the bedstead, Pringle rose to his feet and placed something carefully between the leaves of a book of cigarette-papers, just as the attendant was heard returning from a fruitless search.

"Dr. Fernhurst is nowhere about, sir, and is not expected back till late," the man announced.

"Never mind," said Pringle cheerily. "And now, Windrush, I must be going. I'm delighted to find you so comfortably housed and so well looked after. Keep up your spirits, I shall hope to see you again soon." He grasped Windrush's hand with an eloquent pressure which was gratefully returned.

Walking slowly back to the station, Pringle took the train to Thorpe Stanlowe, and inquired for Drgoo. Toddington. He had had to wait some time for the train at Axford, and the evening was drawing in as he approached the house. The doctor was reading, or rather dozing, in his study when the servant announced "Mr. Pringle." Seizing the conversation-tube which lay beside him, he adjusted it too late to grasp the name of his visitor, but rose to welcome the tall figure of Pringle as he entered, suave and well-groomed as ever.

"Pardon my intrusion at so late an hour," Pringle apologized in his most insinuating tones; "but will you allow me to consult an Encyclopaedia?"

The doctor courteously referred Pringle to a revolving bookcase and watched him curiously, as with the volume open at a plate of *Lacertilia*, he sat glancing from it every now and again to something in his hand, which he examined through a Coddington magnifier.

"I feel," said Pringle at length as he returned the volume to its place, "that I owe you an apology for making use of you in this very unceremonious fashion, especially when I tell you that I come here under false pretences."

"False pretences! I hardly follow you, Mr. Coatbridge," said the doctor stiffly.

"To make a long story short, I am not Mr. Coatbridge, although I am told I resemble him greatly. My real name is Pringle—here is my card, and I am a literary agent in London." He did not think it necessary to add the information that his agency was a sinecure!

The doctor rose abruptly, dropping the conversation-tube in his agitation. Pringle sprang forward to recover it, but was majestically motioned away by the old gentleman, and the two stood facing one another.

"I don't know, sir," began the doctor very slowly and deliberately, "on what ethical grounds you can justify your extraordinary conduct; under a false name, and assuming a false interest in an unfortunate man, you have succeeded in involving me in a very serious breach of professional etiquette."

"Excuse me," said Pringle, seizing the free end of the tube as the doctor paused in his somewhat pompous admonition; "I never assumed any name! I was not responsible for the innkeeper's mistake. I tried to explain to you this morning that I knew nothing of what you were talking about, but could not make you understand, and I have come now partly to explain matters, and partly to tell you that I have just left Mr. Windrush."

"Mr. Windrush! What your motives may be, sir, I cannot imagine, but if I may judge them from your mode of procedure they are of a nature that will scarcely bear investigation."

"I am painfully aware," said Pringle, "that my conduct must appear liable to misconstruction, but all I ask is that you bear with me for a moment. A mere accident has led me to think that Mr. Windrush has been the victim of a conspiracy to declare him insane, and this appears to me to be the work of the chief person to benefit by its success—Percy Windrush!"

"May I ask where you acquired this information, which appears to seriously affect my professional character?"

"After you left this morning, I went for a sail on the Broad. The landlord's son said he had been in Mr. Windrush's service, and in the course of conversation he made statements—"

"And do you mean to tell me, sir, that you are relying on the chatter of an ignorant bumpkin like that!"

"He only suggested a line of thought, and the more I speculated upon it, the stronger grew my suspicions."

"I really am not prepared to go into the matter with you," returned the doctor icily; "but what I should like to know is how you gained access to Mr. Windrush? I may tell you that as legal difficulties arose in connection with the management of the estate, there was an 'inquisition' or inquiry before a Master in Lunacy with a jury, and by them Mr. Windrush was declared insane, and irresponsible. He then became the ward of the Lord Chancellor, and any interference with him is likely to be severely dealt with!"

"To confirm my theory of the case," said Pringle, "it was absolutely necessary that I should have an interview with him. As I appear to be so like his friend Coatbridge, it occurred to me that I would, just for that single occasion, assume his name. I was thus admitted to see him, and, as a result, I have now no doubt whatever that Percy was in the habit of introducing snakes and other animals which he had coated with luminous paint and so on, into John's bed-room. That explains his solicitude for his brother, shown by his sleeping in the next room, and the boy said that John only became queer after Percy's arrival."

"But how do you account for the visions still appearing?" inquired the doctor cautiously.

"Of course they do!" cried Pringle. "And they'll continue to appear so long as he remains under Dr. Fernhurst's care."

"What! Do you say that Dr. Fernhurst is concerned in the plot as well?

"I know it! When I got to Axford this morning he was out—very luckily, as it happened! I gained Windrush's confidence after a little explanation; especially when he saw that I didn't ridicule his having seen some fiery animal last night, and then I got him to take me to the theatre of the apparitions. I managed to get rid of the attendant, and so had a good look round. As I anticipated, the room communicates with the doctor's own room, and under the bed I found this trace of the fiery object he saw." Pringle laid on the table his book of cigarette-papers, and carefully placing in his palm a morsel of what appeared to be one of the leaves, handed

Toddington the magnifier, and motioned him to inspect the object through it.

"This," said Pringle, "appears to be a flake of cuticle such as lizards are periodically casting, and the lines on it correspond to those found on the head of the common green lizard. Now the Encyclopaedia, which I just consulted in case my memory was misleading me, gives this marking as a means of differentiating the species; therefore I know it was a *common green lizard* which Windrush saw in his room last night!"

"But I thought you said he told you it was fiery?"

"Turn down the light, please, while I reverse the scale. Thanks! Now look over here." Without the lamp the room was quite dark, and, as the doctor looked, a faint shimmering glow from the direction of Pringle's hand gradually dawned on his gaze.

"Will that satisfy you?" asked Pringle exultingly.

"Wonderful!" exclaimed the other in admiration, "you must really allow me to apologize for anything I may have said to hurt your feelings. But you will understand, if you put yourself in my place, how particularly unpleasant it was to find I had been discussing the private affairs of a patient and a friend with a stranger."

"I quite understand," said Pringle cordially. "But the question now is, how we can help Windrush?"

"I am afraid the others are too strong for us. Percy Windrush is his brother's *committee*, the person appointed to manage his affairs, and the other member of the *committee* with whom the charge of his person rests is Dr. Fernhurst. They have got it all their own way, I fear. As you say, he is never likely to recover as long as he remains in their hands. It would be no use calling the attention of the Lord Chancellor to your discoveries, and to help him to escape would be a criminal offence."

"That's no good at all," decided Pringle. "Percy is playing a very deep game, and this Fernhurst must be as thorough-paced a scoundrel as he, and no doubt gets well paid for his share of the work. No; the only thing to do is to take the bull by the horns, and frighten the pair of them out of the country! Then the 'hallucinations' will disappear, and Windrush can be officially declared of sound mind."

"I don't much like the idea," Toddington objected.

"There's nothing else to be done. Where's your evidence? Moral proof is not legal proof. Suppose you took proceedings and failed, as you would, for want of evidence, you'd be confronted with any amount of actions for libel and what not. No, no! You let me have all the documents in the case and any letters of Fernhurst's you have, and I'll see if I can't work on their terrors."

And when Pringle departed, his pockets bulged with a miscellaneous collection of documents.

A day or two after, as Mr. Percy Windrush was sitting in his chambers, he was informed that a messenger from Dr. Fernhurst was waiting to see him.

"What does he want?" he asked.

"He wouldn't tell me, sir," replied the servant. "He says his message is for you only, and very important."

"Bring him up then," and Percy began to bite his nails. As managing his brother's estate he had let Thorpe Stanlowe, himself retiring to chambers in Piccadilly, where he lived as much a Sybarite as his somewhat gross ideals permitted.

"What's the matter?" he snapped, as the messenger, a spruce young man with side-whiskers, entered the room.

"Dr. Fernhurst told me to give you this letter, sir, and await your reply," he said with a respectful bow.

Percy opened the letter in some trepidation, and read:—

"*Axford, July* 25.

"Dear Percy,

"I send this by my chief attendant (Bonting), as I must have an answer this afternoon. Jenkinson, the attendant I selected for John, as not being too 'cute, came home drunk last night, and when I reprimanded him, got very cheeky before some of the others, so I sacked him on the spot. This morning he asked to see me privately concerning John, and then told me he knew all about IT! He said he didn't mind leaving, as he wanted to join his brother at the new goldfields of Adansi; but, unless I would give him £500 down he would split to the L.C.'s visitor. I can't think how he got to know, but he said enough to show he *does* know, so there seems no help for it. Fortunately he agrees to go by the mail which leaves in a couple of days, and I hear most people leave their bodies at Adansi—even if their spirits return! Bonting will see him safely off. Please give Bonting the cash in *small* notes. A cheque will only lead to delay and possible complications.

"Yours in haste,

"Arthur Fernhurst."

Having read this letter, Windrush scanned it closely, as if hoping to read into it another meaning than that which appeared on the surface.

"The doctor was rather in a hurry when he wrote this?" he remarked at length.

"I didn't see him write it, sir, but I know that he was rather upset this morning."

Windrush hastily scribbled a note, and enclosing a cheque in it, rang the bell. "James," to the servant, "take this round to the Bank, and bring me back the answer as soon as possible."

"What had upset the doctor then?" he continued.

"Why, sir, I'm sorry to say that Mr. Windrush's attendant got drunk, and was very insolent to the doctor yesterday, so he dismissed him. But as he wants to go out to Africa, the doctor has very kindly helped him to a passage."

"Ah, very kind of the doctor, to be sure!" remarked Percy dryly. "I don't remember your face; have you been long with Dr. Fernhurst?"

"Not a great while, sir."

Percy again took up his pen. He was not a very ready correspondent, and sucked the holder for a minute or so between each sentence, so that it was only as the servant returned from the Bank that he finished his letter. Taking the packet, he enclosed it with the letter in a stout envelope, and handed it to Dr. Fernhurst's messenger.

"Be as quick as you can back," he said. "The doctor wants this as soon as possible, but be careful; its contents are valuable."

Pringle, for it was he, retired with a sense of having satisfactorily played the first hand in his game of bluff. He congratulated himself that his powers of penmanship had not deteriorated. True, Percy had detected a change in what purported to be Fernhurst's writing, but then that was explained by his presumed agitation at the time. Ah, they would both, in sober truth, be agitated before they were much older! Lucky he had secured some stamped paper when he was at the Asylum! Matters wouldn't have been quite so simple if old Toddington had refused to part with the correspondence. And as he passed eastward on an omnibus, Pringle opened Percy's letter, and having carefully pocketed the bank-notes, read with much satisfaction—

> "Dear Fernhurst,
> "I enclose fifty tenners as you ask, but you must distinctly understand this sort of thing can't go on. If you had only been careful, the brute could never have blackmailed me like this. I shall have to knock it off your next few cheques, as my balance will be nearly gone. Look out whom you choose to mind John, in future. Better come and see me as soon as you have got rid of Jenkinson and matters have *shaken down a bit.*
> "Yours,
> "Percy."

Arrived at his chambers at Furnival's Inn, Mr. Pringle's first care was to dispense with his whiskers and resume his official port-wine mark. Then he devoted the rest of the day to the concoction of two letters which would fire the train he had just laid.

This was the first:—

> "Axford.
> "Dear Windrush,
> "I packed Jenkinson off with his five hundred pounds the day but one after Bonting saw you. When he had gone I

took a look round his room, and found some torn-up paper which I had the curiosity to piece together. The skunk seems to have been playing a double game. So far as I could make out he has told old Toddington, and there was something about payment for making a statutory declaration for a warrant for conspiracy! Whatever this means, I think it better to take a holiday at your expense. Join me at Grand Hotel, Paris.

"In haste, yours,

"Arthur Fernhurst."

And this the second:

"Dear Fernhurst,

"Communicate with me through *Standard*, col. 2. I leave for the Continent at once, and should advise you to ditto. Just discovered that old Toddington has got wind of everything, and employed a detective who saw John the other day when you were out. T. intends to apply for warrant for conspiracy You can join me in Paris in a few days, when we can see how matters are going.

"Yours,

"Percy."

"The flowers are beautiful," commented Pringle. "It was certainly very kind of Mr. Windrush to send them all this way. Is this your first visit to London?"

"Farst time, sir; an' beggin' yar pardon, it bates me how people live here. Fared 's ef I couldn't brathe in them streets."

"So you're back in Mr. Windrush's service?" said Pringle, as he finished his note of thanks.

"O–o, I were rale glad to get back agin to th' oo'd place! I could ha' jumped outer my skin when master asked me to come back's head-gardener. I felt that horrud shut in th' bar all day, an' fawther were a-gettin' tired o' doin' nothin' and thought he'd like te work for a yare or tew more."

"But I thought the place was let."

"They went oof end o' las month! Master wouldn't 'new th' lease, as he were a-livin' 'long o' Dr. Toddington till they went."

"Then things are just as they were before?"

"Same ivery way, sir—'ceptin' won!" The youth grinned knowingly.

"What's that?"

"Mr. Percy! Thorpe Stanlowe 'll see him noo more. I hard he'd gone abroad fur fear they'd put him in Norwich Castle fur makin' tew free with th' money while master were 'way. Guilty conscience most-like!"

"Very probably!" agreed Pringle. "Then I shan't find you at the inn if I come down for any more yachting."

"Oo, fawther 'll be glad to see yew an' len' yew th' cutter. Thank yew kindly, sir—my best respec's te yew, sir!"

THE PASTE DIAMONDS

Mr. Romney Pringle was hunting through a portfolio of engravings in the afternoon.

One of the old prints which lightened the warm distemper of the sitting-room walls had just been summarily displaced. The cord breaking, it had reached the floor a complete wreck, a flower-bowl overturned in the descent having poured its cascade across the broken glass to the utter ruin of the print beneath. A substitute was required, and finding a worthy successor in a "Diogenes" of Salvator Rosa, engraved in laborious but beautiful line, Pringle was about to replace the portfolio when there came a knock at the outer door. Rising, he admitted a tall, slightly-stooping, grey-haired gentleman of spare habit, who seized his unresisting hand and shook it warmly.

"Why, surely you haven't forgotten me!" exclaimed the stranger, desisting as he observed a stony expression to gather over the face of his host. Pringle started, while his features relaxed into the winning smile which so ably seconded the magnetism of his address.

"What! Can it be Mr. Windrush?"

"Why, of course it is! But how stupid of me!—I ought to have remembered that you've only met me once before, and at that time I looked rather different from what I am now."

"Not so very different," was Pringle's tactful reply. "You certainly bore up manfully under a strain which would have crushed most people."

"Ah, that miserable Asylum! I shall never forget it, nor the way I was made to appear insane. And above all, I shall never forget the noble manner in which you worked for my release after you discovered the villainy of my brother and his accomplice."

"You have already thanked me beyond my deserts. Pray let us talk of something else. How kind of you to come and visit me!"

"Well, you've never come and seen me all this time, so I came to see if you were still alive!"

"You see my time is so much occupied with my work as a literary agent that my visits to any friends are necessarily angelic," and Pringle, with calm mendacity, waved his hands towards the empty bureau.

"Well, I've come now to ask your advice, and, if you can suggest it, your help."

"If you think my advice worth having, I shall be only too pleased to give it to you, but I'm afraid you rather over-rate my powers."

"Ah, I see you've all the modesty of true genius. But I won't waste time with compliments. Well now, a cousin of mine lives near me; her husband is head of one of the oldest families in our county, and I have always been on very affectionate terms with her. Well, I'm sorry to say she has lately got in with a rather fast set, and being in pressing need of about a thousand pounds, she took a very fine diamond star, which is a sort of family heirloom, to some West-end jewellers who do that sort of thing, and got an advance, and as she didn't want her husband to know anything about it, she got these people to make her a facsimile in paste. About a week or two ago, she found the central stone had dropped out. The jewellers said they couldn't replace it under a week, and she was at her wit's end, for they were entertaining a party of friends, and her husband would have wondered if she had never worn the diamonds all the time. Well, the jewellers suggested letting her have the real star, on hire for fifty pounds, until the sham stone was replaced, but they insisted on her giving them a cheque for the thousand they had lent her with interest, they agreeing to hold it over and return it to her when she returned the real diamonds. So she wore the star once or twice for the look of the thing, and then put it away. After the party broke up yesterday, she found to her horror the jewel-case was empty. She says it had been opened at the hinges."

"Ah, yes! By driving out the pins."

"That's it. Well, she was in despair. The jewellers would present the cheque if she didn't return the star; as she hadn't got more than a hundred or two at the bank, it would be dishonoured; and then her husband would learn the whole affair in the most disagreeable manner possible. Yesterday, she drove over to my place, and told me all, so I offered to lend her the money, and I came to town this morning and got her cheque back together with the paste. But we want to recover the real stones, and as she dreads having anything to do with the police—as you may suppose—I have come to ask your advice."

"Were there any traces of a burglary?"

"So far as I understand her, none. But it is possible that an expert might have found them."

"It seems to me," observed Pringle, "that the theft of an article so easily traceable, and so difficult to dispose of, could only be the work of a very stupid amateur, or of a very clever thief. Since the affair was managed so neatly, we are forced back on the latter alternative. Now an experienced jewel-thief would soon dispose of the stones, so it's doubtful if you'll ever see them again in the same form."

"Would you like to see the facsimile?"

"Of all things! Have you got it here?"

For reply Windrush drew a black leather case from his pocket, and opening it, displayed on a bed of blue velvet, what appeared to be a diamond star of such dazzling lustre as to deceive any eye but that of an expert.

"Very nice indeed," commented Pringle. "Evidently the work of a first-class artist. Would you have any objection to leaving it with me?"

"How long will you want to keep it?"

"It's rather how long can your cousin spare it?"

"Well, her husband is going for two or three weeks' yachting, so she can safely spare it for that time."

"That will do nicely," said Pringle, adding as the other rose to go, "Are you returning to Norfolk to-day?"

"No. I was afraid I mightn't catch you in, so I took a bed at the Great Eastern. Besides, it's gone six now, so I should have had to stop over-night in any case."

"If you are willing I should like to accompany you so far. By the bye, I was going to speak to you on rather a painful subject. Your brother Percy—have you heard anything of him lately?"

"As you say, it *is* a painful subject! In return for nothing but kindness from me, to not only make me appear insane, but to nearly drive me so in reality! You know, Mr. Pringle, no one better, what I suffered. I don't think I'm a vindictive man, but I feel that I cannot, at all events at present, hold any communication with him. My cousin saw him recently. Indeed, I understand he was staying with them last week, for although people know we are not on speaking terms, I think I have managed to keep the real reason a secret."

"No, there is nothing to be gained by washing your dirty linen in public."

"Do you think," Windrush said, as they stood an hour later in the vestibule of the hotel, "do you think it would help you to run down and take a look at the place? I am sure my cousin would be pleased to see you, and I need hardly say how delighted I shall be to put you up."

"Not just at present, thank you," declined Pringle, "I should like to do so eventually, and whilst I think of it I'll just go and get a time-table. Good-bye for the present. You mustn't be disappointed if you don't hear anything of me for a week or so."

Descending the sloping approach, Pringle entered the station. It was nearing half-past seven, and there was much bustle antecedent to the starting of the eight o'clock boat express. Having purchased his time-table, Pringle was about to return, when a hubbub arose by the booking-office, and he lingered a moment to listen.

"I tell yer, the cab stopped at my pitch! The eight-continental, ain't it, sir?"

"The gent 'anded the bag to me, didn't yer, sir? An' yer sez second class fur 'Arridge."

Two porters, very much in the attitude of the mothers in the judgment of Solomon as usually depicted, had seized the opposite ends of a Gladstone bag, whilst the owner, a burly, somewhat bloated individual, stood grasping a hold-all, in detached amusement at the scene. The contest merged into an East-End picturesqueness of abuse, when one of the men, espying an elderly lady possessed of a large quantity of luggage as yet unappropriated, abruptly raised the siege, and dropping the bag, went in pursuit of this more desirable client.

The appearance of the traveller was commonplace enough, but, as he moved off under the wing of the victorious porter, Pringle felt certain he had seen him before, and not so very long ago either. Staring absently after the man, he turned over in his mind all the likely and most of the unlikely places where they could have met, till a spasm of reminiscence showed him a luxuriously-furnished set of chambers. It was 256 Piccadilly of course, and equally of course the traveller was Percy Windrush! Harwich by the eight o'clock boat express! Pringle found himself wondering where on earth Percy could be going to. His objective could only be Rotterdam, but that was not a pleasure resort, while the slenderness of his luggage was incompatible with a more extended continental tour. He felt a sense of irritation against Percy for worrying him with such a problem. He turned impatiently to go, but suddenly stopped as a chance remark of John Windrush blazed vividly in his recollection— "My cousin saw him recently . . . he was staying with them last week."

Pringle sat down to reflect. This was the situation, it seemed. Percy's failure to keep his brother in an asylum, and their consequent rupture had deprived him of an easy means of livelihood. He was, no doubt, hard put to it for money, and unlikely to stop at anything to obtain it. He would know the way about his cousin's house, he could choose his opportunity, while his relationship would shield him from any suspicion. What more likely than that he had taken the diamonds, and if so, was now on his way to dispose of them? Pringle looked up the time-table. The boat was due at Rotterdam the next morning. At the very outside, to follow Percy to the Continent and back would not take more than three days, and he decided that the clue was worth following up. A bell clanged furiously. There was no time to lose, and the question of luggage had to be considered! Just by the booking-office stood one of those convenient toilet-establishments where hair-cutting and shaving are combined with the provision of travellers' requisites. Entering, he made a hurried investment, and emerged the richer by a bag packed with toilet and sleeping necessaries. Then, booking a through-passage to Rotterdam, he took his seat in the train a few seconds before it started. On arriving at Parkestone Quay he just obtained a glimpse of Percy Windrush hurrying, the first of all, on board the packet, where he promptly disappeared below, and as the night had set in dark and stormy, Pringle followed his example and was soon fast asleep.

The North Sea was in anything but a propitious mood when he awoke. The "Hook of Holland" route was not then in existence, and the crossing which, as a general rule, averaged twelve hours, now bid fair to lengthen into sixteen. It was a prolonged agony to the majority of the passengers, to whom the arrival and passing of the breakfast-hour had proved an event of no interest. Few but Pringle had dared to brave the wet and draughty horrors of the upper-deck, and it was only as the steamer entered the Maas, and Rotterdam with its wilderness of trees and masts appeared in sight, that a limp and draggled procession emerged from the saloon. As the deck filled, Pringle ceased his promenade and drew towards the rearmost rank. Nosing her way through the maze of shipping, the steamer slowly passed to her berth beside the Hull and Dunkirk packets, and was neatly moored alongside the tree-planted Boompjes where the shadows were already beginning to lengthen. The formalities of the Customs had been completed in the stream, and the crowd rapidly thinned and dispersed as the passengers streamed up the gangways on to grateful *terra firma*.

Percy was almost the last to appear, having remained below throughout; Pringle remembered that he was said to be a seasoned sailor, so he could hardly have stopped there on account of the prevalent malady. Recalling the historical precedent of Nelson only to dismiss it as inapplicable, he felt sure that Percy's reason for enduring such undoubted personal inconvenience could only have arisen from a desire to escape observation, and was more than ever determined not to lose sight of him. Pringle had little fear of being recognized himself. Although he had had no opportunity of removing his official port-wine mark as the putative literary agent, Percy would scarcely recognize, even if he remembered, the whiskered asylum-attendant in the slim, clean-shaven figure in the lounge-suit who followed him.

Resisting the siren importunities of the hotel touts, Pringle briskly strode across the elm-planted quay. He found Percy had already crossed the Scheepmaker's Haven by one of the innumerable swing-bridges of the city, and was upon another which spanned the Wijn Haven. Pringle followed, and Percy took the direction of the central railway-station. Beyond the Bourse he turned to the left towards the fish-market, and crossing the Zoete Bridge, passed by the Boijmann Gallery, and struck up Zand Straat. Block succeeded block along the street, and Pringle began to wonder when the promenade would end, when suddenly Percy dived down a turning on the right labelled Spoorweg Straat, which led towards the Delfsche Canal, and ascended the steps of a modest-looking house displaying the legend "Hotel Rotterdamsche."

As Pringle withdrew for a space into Zand Straat, he noted that his pursuit had landed him in anything but a select quarter of the town. The region of the best hotels and public buildings had been long left behind, and although there were plenty of large houses visible, their aspect was distinctly second-rate. Having waited sufficiently long to avoid any appearance of espionage, Pringle turned back into Spoorweg Straat, and entering the hotel, inquired for accommodation in his native tongue—the real *lingua franca* of the civilized world. For reply the clerk, whose knowledge of English appeared limited, handed him a dirty-looking visitors'-book. Pringle took up a pen, and glancing at the name last written, read in characters whose faintness indicated recent blotting, "Philip Winter." Percy had retained his own initials, although for some occult reason he had changed his name. Pringle was studying the signature, when the clerk laid a grimy, impatient finger on the first vacant line, and thus recalled to his surroundings, Pringle boldly signed "John M'Hugh," as a name well in keeping with the commercial atmosphere in which he found himself.

"Will you de straat or de vest overlook?" inquired the clerk; adding as a possible inducement, "Best for gentlemen de vest."

Realizing that he was asked to choose between an outlook to the street or the canal, Pringle selected the gentlemanly alternative, and hastened to reply, "The water—vest, vest!"

Following a porter with his bag, he was ushered up to a room on the first floor, at the end of a long and rather dark passage. The window opened on a broad balcony which ran the width of the house, and afforded a picturesque glimpse of the canal. Rather was it a basin, terminating one of the capillary offshoots of the main stream. It was bordered as usual with fine trees, whose branches seemed to form part and parcel of the spars of the craft which thronged the water, except towards the middle, where a fair-way, covered with the ubiquitous green scum, resembled a flat meadow. Pringle stepped to the window, which stood ajar, and leaned over the rail of the balcony. Gazing abstractedly at the shipping, the polished wood-work glistening in the sun which flashed again from innumerable points of bright metal, the calm unbroken by any sight or sound of task, he allowed the restful influence of the scene to steal lazily over him. But the sudden closing of a door near by, and a few words spoken in English broke the spell, and once again focused his thoughts on Percy Windrush.

"So here you are at last! I thought you'd have been here before me." The voice sounded through the next window, which must have been open, although its wooden sun-blind stood half across the balcony and effectually concealed it.

"Ma tear Mishdare Winder! It is a long, long way to come. I am poor man, and de hotel egspenche is great."

"Yes, I know all about that. I know you're the richest poor man in Amsterdam. Have you taken a room here?"

"Noomber eighteen—joost obbosite."

"Well, never mind the number so long as you are here. Have you brought any money with you?"

"A liddle."

"That's all right then. Is it cash as I told you?"

"Yes, goot bank English notes."

"You old villain! Every one of them 'known and stopped,' I suppose, that you've bought at eighty per cent. discount, and expect me to take at face-value." And the speaker gave an audible snort of disgust.

"We are all Hebrew and gendlemen in de stone trade," was the dignified response.

"So I've heard," Windrush observed acidly. "Well, suppose we come to business. I didn't invite you here to exchange compliments."

There was a pause in the conversation, and Pringle stepped gingerly towards the sun-blind. He did not advance too closely, but contented himself with an occasional glance between the hinges, which afforded him a very fair view of the room. Windrush was partially undressing, so as to remove a wash-leather packet which hung next his skin by a cord round the neck. Ripping it open with a pocket-knife, he removed several layers of tissue-paper, and finally a mass of cotton wool surrounding a diamond-star. As he held it up towards his companion, Pringle involuntarily grasped his own pocket to satisfy himself of the safety of the *facsimile*, so accurately did the two match in every particular. As for the Jew, from his gloating gaze, and the fondling gesture with which he handled it, the sight was one to rouse his utmost cupidity.

At length, as the other made no movement, but continued to stare, Percy broke the silence.

"Now then, Israels, what do you say?"

"Dey are very fair stones."

"Fair! 'Fair,' do you call them? You don't see such stones as they are every day, nor yet every year!"

"Dey are goot. I do not call dem de best."

"Look here, my Amsterdammer! It's not what you call them, but what I know they are. D'ye see?"

"What do you know they are?"

"I know they're worth every penny of three thousand pounds!"

Israels dropped the star on the table as if it had burnt him.

"Dree dousand!" he echoed, with an expression of amazement as his huckstering instincts asserted themselves.

"That's what I said."

"*Dree 'underd* you mean for surely!"

"I said three thousand and I meant it, and well you know it!"

"You are joking, Misdare Winder, to ask dat."

"You old fool! I didn't say I asked three thousand for them, did I?" growled Percy.

"Den what do you ask?" inquired Israels feebly.

"Fifteen hundred," said Percy with decision.

"To rob me you 'ave called me 'ere!" shrilly cried the Jew.

"Not much!" retorted Percy contemptuously. "Do you think if I wanted to do that I should have chosen this place?"

The Jew made no reply, but glanced uneasily through the window at the canal beyond.

"Look here, now," continued Percy. "I don't want any more humbug. You take 'em, or, by crumbs! I'll get some one who will."

"It cannot be done," said the Jew simply.

"Fifteen hundred's the figure," repeated Percy, as he leaned forward and clutched the star.

"I 'ave not so much," protested the Jew.

"All right, I'll find some one else who has," said Percy deliberately, and he commenced to wrap the jewel up again.

"Say one dousand," pleaded Israels.

Percy rose and pointed to the door.

"See," continued the Jew coaxingly, "I give you twelve 'underd."

"Fifteen," replied Percy firmly.

"Say twelve!" and Israels produced a wallet and flourished a handful of crisp paper in Percy's face.

"No! I tell you for the last time—Fifteen! And little enough too!" Percy clenched his ultimatum with a resounding slap on the table.

Loudly protesting that he was a ruined man, Israels reluctantly counted out the notes in front of the inexorable Percy, who affected to be engaged in examining the diamonds, which he held in full view of the other. When the notes lay, a rustling heap, upon the table, Percy pushed the star across to the Jew, who pounced upon it, and after another admiring glance, bundled it into a handbag which he jealously locked.

Percy, with a condescending air, counted the notes over again, whistling carelessly the while, then turning to Israels—

"Well, old stick-in-the-mud!" he said graciously, "I'll stand you a dinner. Yes, by Jingo! at the Weimar! There's nothing eatable to be got here. And then we'll go to the Diergaarden—it's slow, but it's the only thing to do in this cursed place."

"You are doo kind, Misdare Winder," sniggered the diamond-merchant, as he retired with the precious handbag.

The clock was nearing five when Pringle descended to the frowsy dining-room and reserved a seat for the *table d'hôte*. Then lighting a cigarette, he strolled out, and was soon absorbed in an inspection of the shop-windows of Zand Straat. He had not left the hotel very far behind, when Percy Windrush passed him with a jaunty swagger, which kept Israels, delighted with the prospect of a meal at another man's expense, at a perpetual trot. Still interested in the merchandise displayed in the shops, Pringle contrived to keep the pair in sight until they were safely housed in the Weimar, about the only passable restaurant in all Rotterdam; then boarding a tramcar, he returned northwards, and arriving at the hotel towards six, was assured by the evidence of most of his senses of the actuality of the *table d'hôte*.

Practically the whole hotel was dining, and the upper floors were quite deserted when he ascended to his room. The vault-like passage with the closing day was darker than ever, and the doorways of all the rooms were sunk in obscurity. Not a sound was to be heard except the distant murmur arising from the ground-floor, and after waiting a few minutes he tried the door of No. 18. As he expected, it was locked, and returning to his own room he took out the key and examined it. The simplicity of the wards augured little complication in any of the locks, and taking a bunch of skeleton keys from his vest-pocket, he selected the most likely-looking one. Once more he attacked No. 18, and after a little manipulation, the skeleton-key shot the bolt, and he entered. Carefully closing the door behind him, and re-locking it, he looked about for the hand-bag. It was nowhere to be seen! Israels had certainly not taken it out with him. Could he have given it into the custody of the land-lord? But the Jew's suspicious nature had negatived such an obvious precaution, and a very short search disclosed it under the far corner of the bed. As in most bags, especially when of continental make, the lock presented little difficulty to an expert, and a few minutes' work enabled Pringle to open it, and, having swathed the paste star in the solicitous wrappings of the genuine one, to pocket the latter leaving the paste in its stead. Then he locked the bag and returned it to its hiding-place.

He listened. All was quiet. Unlocking the door, he carefully closed and locked it again, then walked down-stairs without encountering a soul.

Dinner over, he endeavoured to amuse himself with a stroll through the town, but the intolerable dulness of the place drove him back to bed by ten o'clock, and notwithstanding the warmth of the night he soon dropped off to sleep. It seemed to him that he had slept for hours when he awoke with a start as the bed vibrated to a violent concussion. As he sat up his first thought was of the jewel-case. It was safe under the pillow where he had placed it on retiring. The moon had clouded, but there was sufficient light entering by the window for him to see that nothing was amiss in the room. The great clock of St. Lawrence struck one. Another concussion: then a confused bumping and jarring sounded somewhere near. He sprang out of bed, and opening the window looked on to the balcony. The sun-blinds were now hooked back, and he was just in time to see the windows of the next room start and burst open, as the flimsy fastenings gave way under the impact of a heavy weight.

Creeping to the window, Pringle looked in, and dimly discerned the creator of the disturbance in Percy Windrush, who, after a futile attempt to remove his boots, had reeled against the window, and now lay, fully dressed, snoring in a drunken stupor on the floor. Pringle waited and listened. But these vagaries had failed to rouse attention elsewhere, and the nasal solo was undisturbed.

Percy had rolled inward as he fell, and Pringle easily effected an entrance. He had only had a single opportunity of closely inspecting Percy before, and that was when the fortunes of the latter were at their zenith; times had changed since then! The younger Windrush was by no means an attractive object as he lay. His features, no doubt pleasing enough at one time, were bloated and drink-sodden, his limbs were flabby, and his waist, a region difficult to define, perilously approached the sixties. His linen was dirty, his clothes of loud cut, and with his swaggering air, proclaimed him the dissipated blackguard he was. Such then was the man against whom he had already pitted his wits and come off victoriously. Like most clever rogues, Percy had the wit to conceive an ingenious scheme, but at the psychological moment, his luck or his courage (which in such cases may be held to be synonymous) had deserted him.

The quarter struck from St. Lawrence. It was dangerous to remain long. Percy's slumbers were not so comatose that he could not be roused, and even as the clock struck, he turned over and muttered the refrain of some ditty—an item probably from the evening's entertainment.

A thought exploded in Pringle's mind. What a brilliant opportunity! It was now or not at all! He hurriedly glanced around. Percy's "hold-all" lay, collapsed and empty, in a corner where it had been tossed after unpacking. On a table near it stood the small Gladstone. Pringle gently pressed the lock and peeped in. A travelling-flask (empty), a change of linen (Percy had some claims to conventional decency), a panacea against headaches, a pipe, a golf-cap, pyjamas, a Baedeker, a pair of slippers—and that was all!

Strange that they were nowhere visible. But the bag would hardly have been unlocked in that case. Could Percy have gone one better than the Jew, and have handed them to the landlord for safe keeping? One more look round. Pringle tried the drawers in the rickety dressing-table. They were empty of all but dust and fluff; of course no one but a lunatic would have put them there—or a drunkard! Stay, what about his pockets? A wallet would be too large to be concealed very easily. He stepped towards the sleeper. The breath roared stertorously through his nostrils; his lips had ceased to move; and the uncomfortable position in which he lay, with one arm doubled under him, showed his complete and happy oblivion to externals. Pringle tenderly felt the ponderous carcass. The light was dim, and touch was about the only sense available. The coat gaped widely; there was something bulky inside. He cautiously withdrew a bundle from the breast-pocket. The sensation on pressing it, even more than a glance in the faint light, revealed it a letter-case stuffed to bursting with the bank-notes Mr. Israels had paid over that afternoon. A cloud slipped off the moon, and he counted them feverishly. One hundred and four tens, and twenty-three twenties. To seize them, and return the empty wallet to its owner's pocket was the work of a moment more. For the second time, and still unknown to Percy, had Pringle bested him; he might be forgiven the contemptuous smile with which he regarded his prostrate adversary. The snores still reverberated through the darkness, as he strode over the mountainous body, and out on to the balcony. How to close the windows was the difficulty, but after a little persuasion he succeeded in inducing the crazy bolt to tentatively engage the slot, and so conceal his retreat.

Pringle had slept long and soundly, and the morning had nearly "risen on mid-noon" when his slumbers were rudely disturbed by a torrent of abuse.

"You are a tief! A robber!! A rogue-villain!!!" The voice shrilled in *crescendo* as fresh terms of reproach in the English language crowded on the memory of the speaker.

As Pringle awoke, his head still dizzy with the profound and dreamless stupor which had crowned the stirring events of last night, he was in some doubt as to the origin of the uproar; but as memory returned he realized that it must be due to his own achievements. It was from the next chamber that the sounds of discord arose, and setting his door ajar, the better to hear, he commenced a leisurely toilet to the accompaniment of an acrimonious duet.

"What d'you want to wake me up for with your infernal row?" growled a deep bass, in farcical contrast to the falsetto of its interlocutor.

"*Gij hebt mij bezwendeld! Hets altemaal fopperij!! Ik zal gij voor den vrederegter doen verschijnen!!!*" ("You have swindled me! These are rubbish!! I will have you brought before the justice of the peace!!!") The words culminated in a scream, and were followed by a noise as if the speaker were executing a kind of double-shuffle round the room in his agitation.

"What are you talking about, you old fool? What is it you want?"

"*Der ster diamant!*"

"Talk English, will you? Damn you!"

"De stones!—you haf swintled me! Where are de real ones?"

"Here, get out of the room! You're drunk!"

"Drunk! *Gij hebt mij bezwendeld!*"

"You're mad then!" roared the bass with a hail of expletives.

"You are a pig-dog!" returned the falsetto, and to judge from an intermittent bouncing on the floor, he resumed his saltatory exercise.

"Let me see the (adjective) thing." A pause. "Well, what's all the fuss about?"

"Dey are paste! Give back my money."

"Paste be damned!"

"My money! I will call de police!"

"Here, take your money! I'll sell 'em to a man who knows good stuff when he sees it. Why, where the—" Another pause. Then suddenly the bass thundered, "You infernal Jew, you've robbed me!"

"You 'ave robbed *me!* My money or de police!"

"You dirty little swab, you know you've got it!"

"I 'ave it *not!*"

"Where are the notes then? Didn't you make me drunk last night at the Weimar? You thought you'd get the stones for nothing, eh? But I've got 'em, and by Jingo I'll stick to them!"

"Dey are paste."

"They're good enough for me. You can keep the notes you stole last night."

"It is you are a tief!"

"You stinking old hound, I'll wring your infernal neck!"

"*Policie—Moord! Moord! Policie!*" was gasped jerkily as from a body in a state of violent succussion.

Pringle walked calmly down-stairs and settled his bill.

"I rather think two gentlemen are fighting a duel up-stairs," he remarked in an apprehensive tone.

As he sallied out on his way to the quay, a series of loud shrieks, followed by the crashing of glass and other sounds of destruction, summoned the scandalized proprietor and a posse of waiters to the scene of strife.

THE KAILYARD NOVEL

The postman with resounding knock insinuated half-a-dozen packages into the slit in the outer door. He breathed hard, for it was a climb to the second floor, and then with heavy foot clattered down the stone stairs into Furnival's Inn. As the cataract descended between the two doors Mr. Pringle dropped his newspaper and stretched to his full length with a yawn; then, rolling out of his chair, he opened the inner door and gathered up the harvest of the mail. It was mostly composed of circulars; these he carelessly flung upon the table, and turned to the single letter among them. It was addressed with clerkly precision, *Romney Pringle, Esq., Literary Agent*, 33 *Furnival's Inn, London, E. C.*

Such a mode of address was quite a novelty in Pringle's experience. Was his inexistent literary agency about to be vivified? and wondering, he opened the envelope.

> "*Chapel Street, Wurzleford,*
> *August 25th.*

"Dear Sir,

"Having recent occasion to visit a solicitor in the same block in connection with the affairs of a deceased friend, I made a note of your address, and shortly propose to avail myself of your kind offices in publishing a novel on the temperance question. I intend to call it *Drouthy Neebors*, as I have adopted the Scotch dialect which appears to be so very

popular and, I apprehend, remunerative. Having no practical acquaintance with the same, I think of making a study
of it on the spot during my approaching month's holiday—
most likely in the Island of Skye, where I presume the language may be a fair guide to that so much in favour. I shall
start as soon as I can find a substitute and, if not unduly
troubling you, should be greatly obliged by your inserting
the enclosed advertisement for me in the *Undenominational Banner.* Your kindly doing so may lead to an earlier
insertion than I could obtain for it through the local agent
and so save me a week's delay. Thanking you in anticipa-
tion, believe me to be your very grateful and obliged

"Adolphus Honeyby (Pastor)."

Although "Literary Agent" stared conspicuously from his door,
Pringle's title had never hitherto induced an author, of however
aspiring a type, to disturb the privacy of his chambers, and it was
with an amused sense of the perfection of his disguise that he lighted
a cigarette and sat down to think over Mr. Honeyby's proposal.

Wurzleford—Wurzleford? There seemed to be a familiar sound
about the name. Surely he had read of it somewhere. He turned to
the Society journal that he had been reading when the postman
knocked.

Since leaving Sandringham the Maharajah of Satpura
has been paying a round of farewell visits prior to his return to India in October. His Highness is well known as the
owner of the famous Harabadi diamond, which is said to
flash red and violet with every movement of its wearer, and
his jewels were the sensation of the various state functions
which he attended in native costume last season.

* * * * * *

I understand that the Maharajah is expected about the
end of next week at Eastlingbury, the magnificent Sussex

seat of Lord Wurzleford, and, as a man of wide and liberal
culture, his Highness will doubtless be much interested in
this ancestral home of one of our oldest noble families.

Mr. Honeyby ought to have no difficulty in getting a *locum ten-ens*, thought Pringle, as he laid down the paper. He wondered how
it would be to—? It was risky, but worth trying! Why let a good
thing go a-begging? He had a good mind to take the berth himself!
Wurzleford seemed an attractive little place. Well, its attractive-
ness would certainly not be lessened for him when the Maharajah
arrived! At the very least it might prove an agreeable holiday, and
in any case would lead to a new and probably amusing experience
of human nature. Smiling at the ludicrous audacity of the idea,
Pringle strolled up to the mantelpiece and interrogated himself in
the Venetian mirror. Minus the delible port-wine mark, a pair of
pince-nez, blackened hair, and a small strip of easily applied whisker would be sufficient disguise. He thoughtfully lighted another
cigarette.

But the necessity of testimonials occurred to him. Why not say
he had sent the originals with an application he was making for a
permanent appointment, and merely show Honeyby the type-written copies? He seemed an innocent old ass, and Pringle would trust
to audacity to carry him through. He could write to Wurzleford
from any Bloomsbury address, and follow the letter before Honeyby
had time to reply. He had little doubt that he could clench matters
when it came to a personal interview; especially as Honeyby seemed
very anxious to be off. There remained the knotty point of doctrine. Well, the Farringdon Street barrows, the grave of theologi-
cal literature, could furnish any number of volumes of sermons,
and it would be strange if they could not supply in addition a very
efficient battery of controversial shot and shell. In the meantime
he could get up the foundation of his "Undenominational" opin-
ions from the Encyclopaedia. And taking a volume of the *Britan-nica*, he was soon absorbed in its perusal.

Mr. Honeyby's advertisement duly appeared in the *Banner*, and
was answered by a telegram announcing the application of the

"Rev. Charles Courtley," who followed close on the heels of his message. Although surprised at the wonderfully rapid effect of the advertisement, the pastor was disinclined to quarrel with his good luck, and was too eager to be released to waste much time over preliminary inquiries. Indeed, he could think of little but the collection of material for his novel, and fretted to commence it. "Mr. Courtley's" manner and appearance, to say nothing of his very flattering testimonials, were all that could be desired; his acquaintance with controversial doctrine was profound, and the pastor, innocently wondering how such brilliance had failed to attain a more eminent place in the denomination, had eagerly ratified his engagement.

"Well, I must say, Mr. Courtley, you seem to know so well what will be expected of you, that I really don't think I need wait over tonight," remarked Mr. Honeyby towards the end of the interview.

"I presume there will be no objection to my riding the bicycle I have brought with me?" asked Pringle, in his new character.

"Not at all—by no means! I've often thought of taking to one myself. Some of the church-members live at such a distance, you see. Besides, there is nothing derogatory in it. Lord Wurzleford, for instance, is always riding about, and so are some of the party he has down for the shooting. There is some Indian prince or other with them, I believe."

"The Maharajah of Satpura?" Pringle suggested.

"Yes, I think that is the name; do you know him?" asked Mr. Honeyby, impressed by the other's air of refinement.

"No—I only saw it mentioned in the *Park Lane Review*," said Pringle simply.

So Mr. Honeyby departed for London, *en route* for the north, by an even earlier train than he had hoped for.

About an hour afterwards Pringle was resting by the wayside, rather winded by cycling up one of the early undulations of the Downs which may be seen rising nearly everywhere on the Wurzleford horizon. He had followed the public road, here unfenced for some miles, through Eastlingbury Park, and now lay idle on the springy turf. The harebells stirred with a dry rustle in the imperceptible breeze, and all around him rose the music of the clumsy little iron-bells, clanking rhythmically to every movement of the wethers as they crisply mowed the herbage closer than any power of scythe. As Pringle drank in the beauty of the prospect, a cyclist made his appearance in the act of coasting down the hill beyond. Suddenly he swerved from side to side; his course grew more erratic, the zigzags wider: it was clear that he had lost control of the machine. As he shot with increasing momentum down the slope, a white figure mounted the crest behind, and pursued him with wild-waving arms, and shouts which were faintly carried onward by the wind.

In the valley beyond the two hills flowed the Wurzle, and the road, taking a sharp turn, crossed it by a little bridge with brick parapets; without careful steering, a cyclist with any way on, would surely strike one or other side of the bridge, with the prospect of a ducking, if not of a worse catastrophe. Quickly grasping the situation, Pringle mounted his machine, sprinted down to the bridge and over it, flinging himself off in time to seize the runaway by his handlebar. He was a portly, dark-complexioned gentleman in a Norfolk suit, and he clung desperately to Pringle as together they rolled into a ditch. By this time the white figure, a native servant, had overtaken his master, whom he helped to rise with a profusion of salaams, and then gathered up the shattered fragments of the bicycle.

"I must apologize for dragging you off your machine," said Pringle, when he too had picked himself up. "But I think you were in for a bad accident."

"No apology is necessary for saving my life, sir," protested the stout gentleman in excellent English. "My tire was punctured on the hill, so the brake refused to act. But may I ask your name?"

As Pringle handed him a card inscribed, "Rev. Charles Courtley," the other continued, "I am the Maharajah of Satpura, and I hope to have the pleasure of thanking you more fully on a less exciting occasion." He bowed politely, with a smile disclosing a lustrous set of white teeth, and leaning on the servant's arm, moved towards a group of cyclists who were cautiously descending the scene of his disaster.

In the jog-trot routine of the sleepy little place, where one day was very much like another, and in the study of the queer people among whom Pringle found himself a sort of deity, the days rapidly passed. To some of the church-members his bicycle had appeared rather a startling innovation, but his tact had smoothed over all difficulties, while the feminine Undenominationalists would have forgiven much to such an engaging personality, for Pringle well knew how to ingratiate himself with the more influential half of humanity. It was believed that his eloquence had, in itself, been the means of recalling several seceders to the fold, and it was even whispered that on several occasions gold coins graced the collection-plates—an event unprecedented in the history of the connection!

September had been an exceptionally hot month, but one day was particularly oppressive. Sunset had brought the slightest relief, and at Eastlingbury that evening the heat was emphatically tropical. The wide-open windows availed nothing to cool the room. The very candles drooped crescent-wise, and singed their shades. Although the clouds were scudding high aloft, and cast transient shadows upon the lawn, no leaf stirred within the park. The hour was late, and the ladies had long withdrawn, but the men still sat listening. It was a story of the jungle—of a fight between a leopard and a sambur-deer, and every one's pulse had quickened, and every one had wished the story longer.

"You are evidently an intrepid explorer, Mr. Courtley," commented the Earl, as his guest finished.

"And a keen observer," added the Maharajah. "I never heard a more realistic description of a fight. I have not had Mr. Courtley's good fortune to see such a thing in the jungle, although I frequently have wild-beast fights—*satmaris*, we call them—for the amusement of my good people of Satpura."

The Maharajah had found a little difficulty in inducing Lord Wurzleford to extend his hospitality to "Mr. Courtley." To begin with, the latter was an Undenominationalist, and only a substitute one at that! Then, too, the Maharajah had made his acquaintance in such a very unconventional manner. All the same, to please his Highness—

Pringle had thus a good deal of lee-way to make up in the course of the evening, and it says much for his success, that the ladies were unanimous in regretting the necessity for leaving the dinner-table. Indeed, from the very first moment of his arrival, he had steadily advanced in favour. He had not only talked brilliantly himself, but had been the cause of brilliancy in others—or, at least, of what passes for brilliancy in smart circles. His stories appeared to be drawn from an inexhaustible fund. He had literally been everywhere and seen everything. As to the Maharajah, who had of late grown unutterably bored by the smart inanities of the house-party, the poor man hailed him with unutterable relief. Towards the end of dinner, a youth had remarked confidentially to the lady beside him, that "that dissentin' fellow seemed a real good sort." He voiced the general opinion.

While Pringle, with the aid of a finger-bowl and some dessert-knives, was demonstrating the problem of the Nile *Barrage* to an interested audience, an earnest consultation was proceeding at the head of the table. The Maharajah, Lord Wurzleford, and the butler, were in solemn conclave, and presently the first was seen to rise abruptly and retire in unconcealed agitation. So obviously did the host share this emotion, that the conversation flagged and died out; and amid an awkward pause, numerous inquiring glances, which good breeding could not entirely repress, were directed towards the head of the table, where the butler, with a pallid face, still exchanged an occasional word with his master.

With a view to breaking the oppressive silence, Pringle was about to resume his demonstration, when Lord Wurzleford anticipated him.

"Before we leave the table," said the peer in a constrained voice, "I want to tell you that a most unpleasant thing has happened under this roof. The apartments of the Maharajah of Satpura have been entered, and a quantity of jewellery is missing. I understand that some one was heard moving about the room only half-an-hour ago, and a strange man was met crossing the park towards Bleakdown not long after. I am sending into Eastlingbury for the police, and in the meantime the servants are scouring the park. Pray let the matter be kept secret from the ladies as long as possible."

Consternation was visible on every face, and amid a loud buzz of comment, the table was promptly deserted.

"Will you excuse me?" said Pringle as he approached Lord Wurzleford, whose self-possession appeared to have temporarily deserted him. "I know the Bleakdown road well, and have cycled over it several times. I rode out here on my machine, and perhaps I might be able to overtake the burglar. Every moment is of importance, and the police may be some time before they arrive."

"I am greatly obliged to you for the suggestion!" exclaimed the peer, adding with a dismal attempt at jocularity, "Perhaps you may succeed in doing his Highness a further service with your cycle."

Between four and five miles from Eastlingbury the high road leaves the park, and crosses the Great Southern Canal. The bridge is of comparatively low span, and a sloping way leads down from the road to the towing-path. As the gradient rose towards the bridge, Pringle slowed up, and steering on to the path, dismounted on the grass, and leant the machine against the hedge. He had caught sight of a man's figure, some eighty yards ahead, standing motionless on the hither side of the bridge; he appeared to be listening for sounds of pursuit. In the silence a distant clock was striking eleven, and the figure presently turned aside and disappeared. When Pringle reached the bridge, the grinding of feet upon the loose gravel echoed from beneath the arch, and stealing down the slope to the towing-path, he peered round the corner of the abutment.

The clouds had all disappeared by now, and the moon flashing from the water made twilight under the bridge. On his knees by the water's edge a man was busily securing a bundle with a cord. To and fro he wound it in criss-cross fashion, and then threaded through the network what looked like an ebony ruler, which he drew from his pocket. A piece of cord dangled from the bundle, and holding it in one hand, he felt with the other along the board which edged the towing-path at this point. Presently he found something to which he tied the cord, and then lowered bundle and all into the canal.

For some time past a sound of footsteps approaching on the road above had been plainly audible to Pringle, although it was lost on the other, absorbed as he was in his task; now, as he rose from his cramped position, and was in the act of stretching himself, he paused and listened. At this moment Pringle slightly changed his position, and loosened a stone which plunged into the water. The man looked up, and catching sight of him, retreated with a muttered curse to the far side of the arch. For a second he scowled at the intruder, and then turned and began to run down the towing-path in the shadow of the bank.

"There he goes— See! On the towing-path!" shouted Pringle, as he scrambled up to the road and confronted two members of the county constabulary who were discussing the portent of the deserted bicycle. Seeing further concealment was useless, the fugitive now took to his heels in earnest, and ran hot-foot beside the canal with the two policemen and Pringle in pursuit.

But Pringle soon dropped behind; and when their footsteps were lost in the distance, he made his way back to the road, and hoisting the machine on his shoulder, carried it down the slope and rested it under the bridge. Groping along the wooden edging, his hand soon encountered the cord, and hauling on it with both hands, for the weight was not inconsiderable, he landed the bundle on the bank. What had appeared to be a ruler now proved to be a very neat jemmy folding in two. Admiring it with the interest of an expert, he dropped it into the water, and then ripped up the towel which formed the covering of the bundle. Although he anticipated the contents, he was scarcely prepared for the gorgeous spectacle which saluted him, and as he ran his hands through the confused heap of gold and jewels, they glittered like a milky way of stars even in the subdued pallor of the moonlight.

The striking of the half-hour warned him that time pressed, and taking a spanner from his cycle-wallet, he unshipped the handle-bar, and deftly packed it and the head-tube with the treasure. Some of the bulkier, and perhaps also less valuable articles had to be left; so rolling them up again in the towel, he sent them to join the folding-jemmy. Screwing the nuts home, he carried the cycle up to the road again, and pedalled briskly along the down-grade to Eastlingbury.

"Hi! Stop there!"

He had forgotten to light his lamp, and as a bull's-eye glared upon him, and a burly policeman seized his handle-bar, Pringle mentally began to assess the possible cost of this outrage upon the county bye-laws. But a semi-excited footman ran up, and turning another lamp upon him, at once saluted him respectfully.

"It's all right, Mr. Parker," said the footman. "This gentleman's a friend of his lordship's."

The policeman released the machine, and saluted Pringle in his turn.

"Sorry you were stopped, sir," apologized the footman, "but our orders is to watch all the roads for the burglar."

"Haven't they caught him yet?"

"No, sir! 'E doubled back into the park, and they lost 'im. One of the grooms, who was sent out on 'orseback, met the policemen who said they'd seen you, but didn't know where you'd got to after they lost the burglar. They were afraid 'e'd get back on to the road and make off on your bicycle, as you'd left it there, and they told the groom to ride back and tell us all to look out for a man on a bicycle."

"So you thought I was the burglar! But how did he get into the house?"

"Why, sir, the Indian king's 'ead man went up about ten to get the king's room ready. When 'e tried the door, 'e found 'e couldn't open it. Then 'e called some of the other Indians up, and when they couldn't open it either, and they found the door wasn't locked at all, they said it was bewitched."

Here the policeman guffawed, and then stared fixedly at the moon, as if wondering whether that was the source of the hilarity. The footman glanced reprovingly at him, and continued—

"They came down into the servants' 'all, and the one who speaks English best told us about it. So I said, 'Let's get in through the window.' So we went round to the tennis-lawn, underneath the king's rooms. The windows were all open, just as they'd been left before dinner, because of the 'eat. There's an old ivy-tree grows there, sir, with big branches all along the wall, thick enough for a man to stand on. So Mr. Strong, the butler, climbed up, and us after 'im. We couldn't see much amiss at first, but the king's 'ead man fell on 'is knees, and turned 'is eyes up, and thumped 'imself on the chest, and said 'e was a dead man! And when we said why? 'e said all the king's jewels were gone. And sure enough, some cases that 'eld diamond and ruby brooches, and necklaces, and things, were all burst open and cleaned out, and a lot of others for rings and small things were lying about empty. And we found the burglar 'd screwed wedges against the doors, and that was why they couldn't be opened. So we took them up and opened the doors, and Mr. Strong went down and reported it to 'is lordship, and 'e broke it to the king. But the 'ead man says the king took on about it terribly, and 'e's afraid the king 'll take 'im and 'ave a wild elephant trample on 'is 'ead to execute 'im, when 'e gets back to India!"

Here the footman paused for breath, and the constable seized the opportunity to assert himself.

"So you'll know the man again, if you should see him, sir," he chimed in.

"That I shall," Pringle asseverated.

"A pleasant-spoken gentleman as ever was!" observed the footman as Pringle rode away, and the policeman grunted emphatic assent.

Walking down North Street, the principal thoroughfare in the village, next morning, Pringle was accosted by a stranger. He was small but wiry in figure, dressed very neatly, and had the cut of a gentleman's servant out of livery.

"Are you Mr. Courtley, sir?" respectfully touching his hat.

"Yes. Can I be of any service to you?"

"I should like to have a quiet talk with you, sir, if I may call upon you."

"Shall we say six this evening, then?"

"If you please, sir."

Opining that here was a possible recruit for the connection gained by his eloquence, Pringle went on his way. He had just received a letter from Mr. Honeyby announcing his return, and was not dissatisfied at the prospect of the evening seeing the end of his masquerade. Not that it had grown irksome, but having exhausted the predatory resources of Wurzleford, he began to sigh for the London pavement. The pastor wrote that having completed his philological studies in the Island of Skye, he had decided to return South at once. But the chief reason for thus curtailing his stay was the extreme monotony of the climate, in which, according to local opinion, snow is the only variant to the eternal rain. Besides, he feared that the prevalent atmosphere of herring-curing had seriously impaired his digestion! On the whole, therefore, he thought it best to return, and might be expected home about twelve hours after his letter. He trusted, however, that Mr. Pringle would remain his guest; at all events until the end of the month.

Mr. Honeyby's study was an apartment on the ground-floor with an outlook, over a water-butt, to the garden. It partook somewhat of the nature of a stronghold, the door being a specially stout one, and the windows having the protection—so unusual in a country town of iron bars. These precautions were due to Mr. Honeyby's nervous apprehensions of burglary after "collection-days," when specie had to repose there for the night. It was none the less a cheerful room, and Pringle spent most of his indoor-time there. He was occupied in sorting some papers in readiness for the pastor's return, when, punctually as the clock struck six, the housekeeper knocked at his door.

"There's a young man come, sir, who says you're expecting him," she announced.

"Oh, ah! Show him in," said Pringle.

His chance acquaintance of the morning entered, and depositing his hat beneath a chair, touched his forehead and sat down. But no sooner had the door closed upon the woman than his manner underwent a complete change.

"I see you don't remember me," he said, leaning forward, and regarding Pringle steadily.

"No, I must confess you have rather the advantage of me," said Pringle distantly.

"And yet we *have* met before. Not so long ago either!"

"I have not the slightest recollection of ever having seen you before this morning," Pringle asserted tartly. He was nettled at the man's persistence, and felt inclined to resent the rather familiar manner in which he spoke.

"I must assist your memory then. The first time I had the pleasure of seeing you was last night."

"I should be glad to know where."

"Certainly!" Then very slowly and distinctly, "It was under a bridge on the Grand Southern Canal."

Pringle, in spite of his habitual composure, was unable to repress a slight start.

"I see you have not forgotten the circumstance. The time, I think, was about eleven p.m., wasn't it? Well, never mind that; the moon enabled me to get a better look at you than you got of me."

Pringle took refuge in a diplomatic silence, and the other walked across the room, and selecting the most comfortable chair, coolly produced a cigarette-case. Pringle observed, almost subconsciously, that it was a very neat gold one, with a monogram in one corner worked in diamonds.

"Will you smoke?" asked the man. "No? Well, you'll excuse me." And he leisurely kindled a cigarette, taking very detailed stock of Pringle while doing so.

"Now it's just as well we understood one another," he continued, as he settled himself in the chair. "My name is of no consequence, though I'm known to my associates as 'The Toff'; poor souls, they have such a profound respect for education! Now those who know me will tell you I'm not a man whom it pays to trifle with. Who you are, I don't know exactly, and I don't know that I very much care—it's rather an amusing thing, by the way, that no one else seems to be any the wiser! But what I do know"—here he sat straight up, and extended a menacing fist in Pringle's direction—

"and what it'll be a healthy thing for you to understand, is, that I'm not going to leave here to-night without that stuff!"

"My good man, what on earth are you talking about?" indulgently asked Pringle, who by this time had recovered his imperturbability.

"Now don't waste time; you don't look altogether a fool!" "The Toff" drew a revolver from his pocket, and carelessly counted the chambers which were all loaded. "One, two, three, four, five, six! I've got six reasons for what I've said. Let's see now—First, you saw me hiding the stuff; second, no one else did; third, it's not there now; fourth, the Maharajah hasn't got it; fifth, there's no news of its having been found by any one else; sixth, and last, therefore you've got it!" He checked the several heads of his reasoning, one by one, on the chambers of the revolver as one might tell them on the fingers.

"Very logically reasoned!" remarked Pringle calmly. "But may I inquire how it is you are so positive in all these statements?"

"I'm not the man to let the grass grow under my feet," said "The Toff" vain-gloriously. "I've been making inquiries all the morning, and right up to now! I hear the poor old Maharajah has gone to Scotland Yard for help. But it strikes me the affair will remain a mystery 'for ever and always,' as the people say hereabouts. And, as I said just now, you seem to be rather a mystery to most people. I spotted you right enough last night, but I wanted to find out all I could about you from your amiable flock before I tackled you in person. Well, I think I have very good grounds for believing you to be an impostor. That's no concern of mine, of course, but I presume you have your own reasons for coming down here. Now, a word to your principal, and a hint or two judiciously dropped in a few quarters round the place, will soon make it too hot for you, and so your little game, whatever it may be, will be spoiled."

"But supposing I am unable to help you?"

"I can't suppose any such thing! I am going to stick to you like tar, my reverend sir, and if you think of doing a bolt"—he glanced at the revolver, and then put it in his pocket— "take my advice and only *think* of it!"

"Is that all you have to say?" asked Pringle.

"Not quite. Look here now! I've been planning this job for the last four months and more, and I'm not going to take all the risk, and let you or any one else collar all the profit. By George, you've mistaken your man if you think that! I am willing to even go the length of recognizing you as a partner, and giving you ten per cent. for your trouble in taking charge of the stuff, and bringing it to a place of safety and so on, but now you've got to shell out!"

"Very well," said Pringle, rising. "Let me first get the house-keeper out of the way."

"No larks now!" growled "The Toff"; adding peremptorily, "I give you a couple of minutes only,—and leave the door open!"

Without replying, Pringle walked to the door, and slipping through, closed and double-locked it behind him before "The Toff" had time to even rise from his chair.

"You white-livered cur! You—you infernal sneak!" vociferated the latter as Pringle crossed the hall.

Being summer-time, the fire-irons were absent from the study. There was no other lethal weapon wherewith to operate. Escape by the window was negatived by the bars.

For the time then "The Toff" was a negligible quantity. Pringle ran down the kitchen-stairs. At the bottom was a gas-bracket, and stretching out his hand he turned on the gas as he passed. Out in the little kitchen there was much clattering of pots and dishes. The housekeeper was engaged in urgent culinary operations against Mr. Honeyby's return.

"Mrs. Johnson!" he bawled, as a furious knocking sounded from the study.

"Whatever's the matter, sir?" cried the startled woman.

"Escape of gas! We've been looking for it up-stairs! Don't you smell it out here? You must turn it off at the main!" He rattled off the alarming intelligence in well-simulated excitement.

"Gas it is!" she exclaimed nervously, as the familiar odour greeted her nostrils.

Now the meter, as is customary, resided in the coal-cellar, and as the faithful creature opened the door and stumbled forwards,

she suddenly found herself stretched upon the floor, while all became darkness. It almost seemed as if she had received a push from
behind, and her head whirling with the unexpected shock, she painfully arose from her rocky bed, and slowly groped towards the door.
But for all her pulling and tugging it held fast and never gave an
inch. Desisting, as the truth dawned upon her that in some mysterious way she had become a prisoner, she bleated plaintively for
help, and began to hammer at the door with a lump of coal.

Up the stairs again. Pringle glanced at the hall-door, then shot
the bolts top and bottom, and put the chain up. "The Toff" seemed
to be using some of the furniture as a battering-ram. Thunderous
blows and the sharp splintering of wood showed that, despite his
lack of tools, he was (however clumsily) engaged in the active work
of his profession, and the door shivered and rattled ominously
beneath the onslaught.

Pringle raced up-stairs, and in breathless haste tore off his
clerical garb. Bang, bang, crash! He wished the door were iron.
How "The Toff" roused the echoes as he savagely laboured for freedom! And whenever he paused, a feeble diapason ascended from
the basement. The study-door would soon give at this rate. Luckily
the house stood at the end of the town, or the whole neighbourhood
would have been roused by this time. He hunted for his cycling
suit. Where could that wretched old woman have stowed it? Curse
her officiousness! He almost thought of rushing down and releas-
ing her that she might disclose its whereabouts. Every second was
priceless. At last! Where had that button-hook hidden itself now?
How stiff the box-cloth seemed—he had never noticed it before.
Now the coat. Collar and tie? Yes, indeed, he had nearly forgotten
he still wore the clerical tie. No matter, a muffler would hide it all.
Cap—that was all! Gloves he could do without for once.

Bang, crash, crack!

With a last look round he turned to leave the room, and faced
the window. A little way down the road a figure was approaching.
Something about it looked familiar, he thought; seemed to be coming
from the direction of the railway-station, too. He stared harder.
So it was! There was no doubt about it! Swathed in a Scotch maud,

his hand grasping a portmanteau, the Rev. Adolphus Honeyby advanced blithely in the autumn twilight.

Down the stairs Pringle bounded, three at a time. "The Toff" could hear, but not see him as yet. The study-door was already tottering; one hinge had gone. Even as he landed with a thud at the foot of the stairs, "The Toff's" hand and arm appeared at the back of the door.

"I'd have blown the lock off if it wasn't for giving the show away," "The Toff" snarled through his clenched teeth, as loudly as his panting respiration would permit. "I'll soon be through now, and then we'll square accounts!" What he said was a trifle more full-flavoured, but this will suffice.

Crash! bang!! crack!!! from the study-door.

Rat-a-tat-a-tat! was the sudden response from the hall-door. It was Mr. Honeyby knocking! And, startled at the noise, "The Toff" took a momentary respite from his task.

Down to the basement once more. Mrs. Johnson's pummelling sounded louder away from the more virile efforts of the others. Fiercely "The Toff" resumed his labours. What an uproar! Mr. Honeyby's curiosity could not stand much more of that. He would be round at the back presently. The bicycle stood by the garden-door. Pringle shook it slightly, and something rattled; the precious contents of the head and handle-bar were safe enough. He opened the door, and wheeled the machine down the back-garden, and out into the little lane behind.

Loud and louder banged the knocker. But as a triumphant crash and clatter of wood-work resounded from the house, Pringle rode into the fast-gathering darkness.

THE SUBMARINE BOAT

Tric-trac! tric-trac! went the black and white discs as the players moved them over the backgammon board in expressive justification of the French term for the game. Tric-trac! They are indeed a nation of poets, reflected Mr. Pringle. Was not Teuf-teuf! for the motor-car a veritable inspiration? And as he smoked, the not unmusical clatter of the enormous wooden discs filled the atmosphere.

In these days of cookery not entirely based upon air-tights—to use the expressive Americanism for tinned meats—it is no longer necessary for the man who wishes to dine, as distinguished from the mere feeding animal, to furtively seek some restaurant in remote Soho, jealously guarding its secret from his fellows. But Mr. Pringle, in his favourite study of human nature, was an occasional visitor to the "Poissonière" in Gerrard Street, and, the better to pursue his researches, had always denied familiarity with the foreign tongues he heard around him. The restaurant was distinctly close—indeed, some might have called it stuffy—and Pringle, though near a ventilator, thoughtfully provided by the management, was fast being lulled into drowsiness, when a man who had taken his seat with a companion at the next table leaned across the intervening gulf and addressed him.

"*Nous ne vous derangeons pas, monsieur?*"

Pringle, with a smile of fatuous uncomprehending, bowed, but said never a word.

"*Cochon d'Anglais, n'entendez vous pas?*"

"I'm afraid I do not understand," returned Pringle, shaking his head hopelessly, but still smiling.

"*Canaille! Faue-il que je vous tire le nez?*" persisted the Frenchman, as, apparently still sceptical of Pringle's assurance, he added threats to abuse.

"I have known the English gentleman a long time, and without a doubt he does not understand French," testified the waiter who had now come forward for orders. Satisfied by this corroboration of Pringle's innocence, the Frenchman bowed and smiled sweetly to him, and, ordering a bottle of *Clos de Vougeot*, commenced an earnest conversation with his neighbour.

By the time this little incident had closed, Pringle's drowsiness had given place to an intense feeling of curiosity. For what purpose could the Frenchman have been so insistent in disbelieving his expressed ignorance of the language? Why, too, had he striven to make Pringle betray himself by resenting the insults showered upon him? In a Parisian restaurant, as he knew, far more trivial affronts had ended in meetings in the Bois de Boulogne. Besides, *cochon* was an actionable term of opprobrium in France.

The Frenchman and his companion had seated themselves at the only vacant table, also it was in a corner; Pringle, at the next, was the single person within ear-shot, and the Frenchman's extraordinary behaviour could only be due to a consuming thirst for privacy. Settling himself in an easy position, Pringle closed his eyes, and while appearing to resume his slumber, strained every nerve to discern the slightest word that passed at the next table. Dressed in the choicest mode of Piccadilly, the Frenchman bore himself with all the intolerable self-consciousness of the Boulevardier; but there was no trace of good-natured levity in the dark aquiline features, and the evil glint of the eyes recalled visions of an operatic Mephistopheles. His guest was unmistakably an Englishman of the bank-clerk type, who contributed his share of the conversation in halting Anglo-French, punctuated by nervous laughter as, with agonising pains, he dredged his memory for elusive colloquialisms.

Freely translated, this was what Pringle heard:

"So your people have really decided to take up the submarine, after all?"

"Yes; I am working out the details of some drawings in small-scale."

"But are they from headquarters?"

"Certainly! Duly initialed and passed by the chief constructor."

"And you are making—"

"Full working-drawings."

"There will be no code or other secret about them?"

"What I am doing can be understood by any naval architect."

"Ah, an English one?"

"The measurements, of course, are English, but they are easily convertible."

"You could do that?"

"Too dangerous! Suppose a copy in metric scale were found in my possession! Besides, any draughtsman could reduce them in an hour or two."

"And when can you let me have it?"

"In about two weeks."

"Impossible! I shall not be here."

"Unless something happens to let me get on with it quickly, I don't see how I can do it even then. I am never sufficiently free from interruption to take tracings; there are far too many eyes upon me. The only chance I have is to spoil the thing as soon as I have the salient points worked out on it, and after I have pretended to destroy it, smuggle it home; then I shall have to work out the details from them in the evening. It is simply impossible for me to attempt to take a finished drawing out of the yard, and, as it is, I don't quite see my way to getting the spoilt one out—they look so sharply after spoilt drawings."

"Two weeks you say, then?"

"Yes; and I shall have to sit up most nights copying the day's work from my notes to do it."

"Listen! In a week I must attend at the Ministry of Marine in Paris, but our military attaché is my friend. I can trust him; he shall come down to you."

"What, at Chatham? Do you wish to ruin me?" A smile from the Frenchman. "No; it must be in London, where no one knows me."

"Admirable! My friend will be better able to meet you."

"Very well, as soon as I am ready I will telegraph to you."

"Might not the address of the embassy be remarked by the telegraph officials? Your English post-office is charmingly unsuspicious, but we must not risk anything."

"Ah, perhaps so. Well, I will come up to London and telegraph to you from here. But your representative—will he be prepared for it?"

"I will warn him to expect it in fourteen days." He made an entry in his pocketbook. "How will you sign the message?"

"Gustave Zede," suggested the Englishman, sniggering for the first and only time.

"Too suggestive. Sign yourself 'Pauline,' and simply add the time."

"'Pauline,' then. Where shall the rendezvous be?"

"The most public place we can find."

"Public?"

"Certainly. Some place where everyone will be too much occupied with his own affairs to notice you. What say you to your Nelson's column? There you can wait in a way we shall agree upon."

"It would be a difficult thing for me to wear a disguise."

"All disguises are clumsy unless one is an expert. Listen! You shall be gazing at the statue with one hand in your breast—so."

"Yes; and I might hold a 'Baedeker' in my other hand."

"Admirable, my friend! You have the true spirit of an artist," sneered the Frenchman.

"Your representative will advance and say to me, 'Pauline,' and the exchange can be made without another word."

"Exchange?"

"I presume your Government is prepared to pay me handsomely for the very heavy risks I am running in this matter," said the Englishman stiffly.

"Pardon, my friend! How imbecile of me! I am authorized to offer you ten thousand francs."

A pause, during which the Englishman made a calculation on the back of an envelope.

"That is four hundred pounds," he remarked, tearing the envelope into carefully minute fragments. "Far too little for such a risk."

"Permit me to remind you, my friend, that you came in search of me, or rather of those I represent. You have something to sell? Good! But it is customary for the merchant to display his wares first."

"I pledge myself to give you copies of the working-drawings made for the use of the artificers themselves. I have already met you oftener than is prudent. As I say, you offer too little."

"Should the drawings prove useless to us, we should, of course, return them to your Admiralty, explaining how they came into our possession." There was an unpleasant smile beneath the Frenchman's waxed moustache as he spoke. "What sum do you ask?"

"Five hundred pounds in small notes—say, five pounds each."

"That is—what do you say? Ah, twelve thousand five hundred francs! Impossible! My limit is twelve thousand."

To this the Englishman at length gave an ungracious consent, and after some adroit compliments, beneath which the other sought to bury his implied threat, the pair rose from the table. Either by accident or design, the Frenchman stumbled over the feet of Pringle, who, with his long legs stretching out from under the table, his head bowed and his lips parted, appeared in a profound slumber. Opening his eyes slowly, he feigned a lifelike yawn, stretched his arms, and gazed lazily around, to the entire satisfaction of the Frenchman, who, in the act of parting with his companion, was watching him from the door.

Calling for some coffee, Pringle lighted a cigarette, and reflected with a glow of indignant patriotism upon the sordid transaction he had become privy to. It is seldom that public servants are in this country found ready to betray their trust—with all honour be it recorded of them! But there ever exists the possibility of some under-paid official succumbing to the temptation at the command of the less scrupulous representatives of foreign powers, whose actions in this respect are always ignored officially by their

superiors. To Pringle's somewhat cynical imagination, the sordid
huckstering of a dockyard draughtsman with a French naval attaché
appealed as corroboration of Walpole's famous principle, and as
he walked homeward to Furnival's Inn, the seat of his fictitious
literary agency, he determined, if possible, to turn his discovery to
the mutual advantage of his country and himself—especially the
latter.

During the next few days Pringle elaborated a plan of taking
up a residence at Chatham, only to reject it as he had done many
previous ones. Indeed, so many difficulties presented themselves
to every single course of action, that the tenth day after found him
strolling down Bond Street in the morning without having taken
any further step in the matter. With his characteristic fastidious
neatness in personal matters, he was bound for the Piccadilly
establishment of the chief and, for West-Enders, the only firm of
hatters in London.

"Breton Stret, do you knoh?" said a voice suddenly. And Pringle,
turning, found himself accosted by a swarthy foreigner.

"Bruton Street, *n'est-ce pas?*" Pringle suggested.

"*Mais oui,* Brruten Stret, *monsieur!*" was the reply in faint echo
of the English syllables.

"*Le voila! a droite,*" was Pringle's glib direction. Politely raising his hat in response to the other's salute, he was about to resume his walk when he noticed that the Frenchman had been joined
by a companion, who appeared to have been making similar inquiries. The latter started and uttered a slight exclamation on
meeting Pringle's eye. The recognition was mutual—it was the
French attaché! As he hurried down Bond Street, Pringle realised
with acutest annoyance that his deception at the restaurant had
been unavailing, while he must now abandon all hope of a counter-
plot for the honour of his country, to say nothing of his own profit.
The port-wine mark on his right cheek was far too conspicuous for
the attaché not to recognize him by it, and he regretted his neglect
to remove it as soon as he had decided to follow up the affair. Forgetful of all beside, he walked on into Piccadilly, and it was not
until he found himself more than half-way back to his chambers

that he remembered the purpose for which he had set out; but matters of greater moment now claimed his attention, and he endeavoured by the brisk exercise to work off some of the chagrin with which he was consumed. Only as he reached the Inn and turned into the gateway did it occur to him that he had been culpably careless in thus going straight homeward. What if he had been followed? Never in his life had he shown such disregard for ordinary precautions. Glancing back, he just caught a glimpse of a figure which seemed to whip behind the corner of the gateway. He retraced his steps and looked out into Holborn.

There, in the very act of retreat, and still but a few feet from the gate, was the attaché himself. Cursing the persistence of his own folly, Pringle dived through the arch again, and determined that the Frenchman should discover no more that day, he turned nimbly to the left and ran up his own stairway before the pursuer could have time to re-enter the Inn.

The most galling reflection was his absolute impotence in the matter. Through lack of the most elementary foresight he had been fairly run to earth, and could see no way of ridding himself of this unwelcome attention. To transfer his domicile, to tear himself up by the roots as it were, was out of the question; and as he glanced around him, from the soft carpets and luxurious chairs to the warm, distempered walls with their old prints above the dado of dwarf bookcases, he felt that the pang of severance from the refined associations of his chambers would be too acute. Besides, he would inevitably be tracked elsewhere. He would gain nothing by the transfer. One thing at least was absolutely certain—the trouble which the Frenchman was taking to watch him showed the importance he attached to Pringle's discovery. But this again only increased his disgust with the ill-luck which had met him at the very outset. After all, he had done nothing illegal, however contrary it might be to the code of ethics, so that if it pleased them the entire French legation might continue to watch him till the Day of Judgment, and, consoling himself with this reflection, he philosophically dismissed the matter from his mind.

It was nearing six when he again left the Inn for Pagani's, the Great Portland Street restaurant which he much affected; instead of proceeding due west, he crossed Holborn, intending to bear round by way of the Strand and Regent Street, and so get up an appetite.

In Staple Inn he paused a moment in the further archway. The little square, always reposeful amid the stress and turmoil of its environment, seemed doubly so this evening, its eighteenth-century calm so welcome after the raucous thoroughfare. An approaching footfall echoed noisily, and as Pringle moved from the shadow of the narrow wall the newcomer hesitated and stopped, and then made the circuit of the square, scanning the doorways as if in search of a name. The action was not unnatural, and twenty-four hours earlier Pringle would have thought nothing of it, but after the events of the morning he endowed it with a personal interest, and, walking on, he ascended the steps into Southampton Buildings and stopped by a hoarding.

As he looked back he was rewarded by the sight of a man stealthily emerging from the archway and making his way up the steps, only to halt as he suddenly came abreast of Pringle. Although his face was unfamiliar, Pringle could only conclude that the man was following him, and all doubt was removed when, having walked along the street and turning about at the entrance to Chancery Lane, he saw the spy had resumed the chase and was now but a few yards back.

Pringle, as a philosopher, felt more inclined to laughter than resentment at this ludicrous espionage. In a spirit of mischief, he pursued his way to the Strand at a tortoise-like crawl, halting as if doubtful of his way at every corner, and staring into every shop whose lights still invited customers. Once or twice he even doubled back, and passing quite close to the man, had several opportunities of examining him. He was quite unobtrusive, even respectable-looking; there was nothing of the foreigner about him, and Pringle shrewdly conjectured that the attaché, wearied of sentry-go, had turned it over to some English servant on whom he could rely.

Thus shepherded, Pringle arrived at the restaurant, from which he only emerged after a stay maliciously prolonged over each item of the menu, followed by the smoking of no fewer than three cigars of a brand specially lauded by the proprietor.

With a measure of humanity diluting his malice, he was about to offer the infallibly exhausted sentinel some refreshment when he came out, but as the man was invisible, Pringle started for home, taking much the same route as before, and calmly debating whether or no the cigars he had just sampled would be a wise investment; not until he had reached Southampton Buildings and the sight of the hoarding recalled the spy's discomfiture, did he think of looking back to see if he were still followed. All but the main thoroughfares were by this time deserted, and although he shot a keen glance up and down Chancery Lane, now clear of all but the most casual traffic, not a soul was anywhere near him.

By a curious psychological process Pringle felt inclined to resent the man's absence. He had begun to regard him almost in the light of a body-guard, the private escort of some eminent politician. Besides, the whole incident was pregnant with possibilities appealing to his keenly intellectual sense of humour, and as he passed the hoarding, he peered into its shadow with the half-admitted hope that his attendant might be lurking in the depths.

Later on he recalled how, as he glanced upwards, a man's figure passed like a shadow from a ladder to an upper platform of the scaffold. The vision, fleeting and unsubstantial, had gone almost before his retina had received it, but the momentary halt was to prove his salvation.

Even as he turned to walk on, a cataract of planks, amid scaffold-poles and a chaos of loose bricks, crashed on the spot he was about to traverse; a stray beam, more erratic in its descent, caught his hat, and, telescoping it, glanced off his shoulder, bearing him to the ground, where he lay dazed by the sudden uproar and half-choked by the could of dust.

Rapid and disconcerting as was the event, he remembered afterwards a slim and spectral shape approaching through the gloom. In a dreamy kind of way he connected it with that other shadow-figure he had seen high up on the scaffold, and as it bent over him he recognized the now familiar features of the spy. But other figures replaced the first, and, when helped to his feet, he made futile search for it amid the circle of faces gathered round him. He judged it an hallucination. By the time he had undergone a tentative dust-down he was sufficiently collected to acknowledge the sympathetic congratulations of the crowd and to decline the homeward escort of a constable.

In the privacy of his chambers, his ideas began to clarify. Events arranged themselves in logical sequence, and the spectres assumed more tangible form.

A single question dwarfed all others. He asked himself, "Was the cataclysm such an accident as it appeared?" And as he surveyed the battered ruins of his hat, he began to realise how nearly had he been the victim of a murderous vendetta!

When he arose the next morning, he scarcely needed the dilapidated hat to remind him of the events of yesterday. Normally a sound and dreamless sleeper, his rest had been a series of short snatches of slumber interposed between longer spells of rumination. While he marvelled at the intensity of malice which he could no longer doubt pursued him—a vindictiveness more natural to a mediaeval Italian state than to this present-day metropolis—he bitterly regretted the fatal curiosity which had brought him to such an extremity.

By no means deficient in the grosser forms of physical courage, his sense that in the game which was being played, his adversaries as unscrupulous as they were crafty, held all the cards, and, above all, that their espionage effectually prevented him filling the gaps in the plot which he had as yet only half-discovered, was especially galling to his active and somewhat neurotic temperament.

Until yesterday he had almost decided to drop the affair of the Restaurant "Poissonière," but now, after what he firmly believed to be a deliberate attempt to assassinate him, he realised the desperate situation of a duellist with his back to a wall—having scarce room to parry, he felt the prick of his antagonist's rapier deliberately goading him to an incautious thrust. Was he regarded as the possessor of a dangerous secret? Then it behooved him to strike, and that without delay.

Now that he was about to attack, a disguise was essential; and reflecting how lamentably he had failed through the absence of one hitherto, he removed the port-wine mark from his right cheek with his customary spirit-lotion, and blackened his fair hair with a few smart applications of a preparation from his bureau. It was with a determination to shun any obscure streets or alleys, and especially all buildings in course of erection, that he started out after his usual light breakfast.

At first he was doubtful whether he was being followed or not, but after a few experimental turns and doublings he was unable to single out any regular attendant of his walk; either his disguise had proved effectual or his enemies imagined that the attempt of last night had been less innocent in its results.

Somewhat soothed by this discovery, Pringle had gravitated towards the Strand and was nearing Charing Cross, when he observed a man cross from the station to the opposite corner carrying a brown-paper roll. With his thoughts running in the one direction, Pringle in a flash recognised the dockyard draughtsman. Could he be even now on his way to keep the appointment at Nelson's Column? Had he been warned of Pringle's discovery, and so expedited his treacherous task? And thus reflecting, Pringle determined at all hazards to follow him.

The draughtsman made straight for the telegraph office. It was now the busiest time of the morning, most of the little desks were occupied by more or less glib message-writers, and the draughtsman had found a single vacancy at the far end when Pringle followed him in and reached over his shoulder to withdraw a form from the rack in front of him.

Grabbing three or four, Pringle neatly spilled them upon the desk, and with an abject apology hastily gathered them up together with the form the draughtsman was employed upon. More apologies, and Pringle seizing a suddenly vacant desk, effected to compose a telegram of his own. The draughtsman's message had been short, and (to Pringle) exceptionally sweet, consisting as it did of three words— "Four-thirty, Pauline." The address Pringle had not attempted to read—he knew that already.

The moment the other left Pringle took up a sheaf of forms, and, as if they had been the sole reason for his visit, hurried out of the office and took a hansom back to Furnival's Inn.

Here his first care was to fold some newspapers into a brown-paper parcel resembling the one carried by the draughtsman as nearly as he remembered it, and having cut a number of squares of stiff tissue paper, he stuffed an envelope with them and pondered over a cigarette the most difficult stage of his campaign. Twice had the draughtsman seen him.

Once at the restaurant, in his official guise as the sham literary agent, with smooth face, fair hair, and the fugitive port-wine mark staining his right cheek; again that morning, with blackened hair and unblemished face. True, he might have forgotten the stranger at the restaurant; on the other hand, he might not—and Pringle was then (as always) steadfastly averse to leaving anything to chance. Besides, in view of this sudden journey to London, it was very likely that he had received warning of Pringle's discovery. Lastly, it was more than probable that the spy was still on duty, even though he had failed to recognize Pringle that morning.

The matter was clinched by a single glance at the Venetian mirror above the mantel, which reflected a feature he had overlooked— his now blackened hair. Nothing remained for him but to assume a disguise which should impose on both the spy and the draughtsman, and after some thought he decided to make up as a Frenchman of the South, and to pose as a servant of the French embassy.

Reminiscent of the immortal Tartarin, his ready bureau furnished him with a stiff black moustache and some specially stout horsehair to typify the stubbly beard of that hero. When, at almost a quarter to four, he descended into the Inn with the parcel in his hand, a Baedeker and the envelope of tissues in his pocket, a cab was just setting down, and impulsively he chartered it as far as Exeter Hall. Concealed in the cab, he imagined he would the more readily escape observation, and by the time he alighted, flattered himself that any pursuit had been baffled.

As he discharged the cab, however, he noticed a hansom draw up a few paces in the rear, whilst a man got out and began to saunter westward behind him. His suspicions alert, although the man was certainly a stranger, Pringle at once put him to the test by entering Romano's and ordering a small whiskey.

After a decent delay, he emerged, and his pulse quickened when he saw a couple of doors off the same man staring into a shop window! Pringle walked a few yards back, and then crossed to the opposite side of the street, but although he dodged at infinite peril through a string of omnibuses, he was unable to shake off his satellite, who, with unswerving persistence, occupied the most limited horizon whenever he looked back.

For almost the first time in his life, Pringle began to despair. The complacent regard of his own precautions had proved but a fool's paradise. Despite his elaborate disguise, he must have been plainly recognisable to his enemies, and he began to ask himself whether it was not useless to struggle further.

As he paced slowly on, an indefinable depression stole over him. He thought of the heavy price so nearly exacted for his interposition. Resentment surged over him at the memory, and his hand clenched on the parcel. The contact furnished the very stimulus he required. The instrument of settling such a score was in his hands, and rejecting his timorous doubts, he strode on, determined to make one bold and final stroke for vengeance.

The shadows had lengthened appreciably, and the quarter chiming from near St. Martin's warned him that there was no time to lose—the spy must be got rid of at any cost. Already could he see the estuary of the Strand, with the Square widening beyond; on his right loomed the tunnel of the Lowther Arcade, with its vista of juvenile delights.

The sight was an inspiration. Darting in, he turned off sharp to the left into an artist's repository, with a double entrance to the Strand and the Arcade, and, softly closing the door, peeped through the palettes and frames which hung upon the glass. Hardly had they ceased swinging to his movement when he had the satisfaction of seeing the spy, the scent already cold, rush furiously up the Arcade, his course marked by falling toys and the cries of the outraged stall keepers.

Turning, Pringle made the purchase of a sketching-block, the first thing handy, and then passed through the door which gave on the Strand. At the post-office he stopped to survey the scene. A single policeman stood by the eastward base of the column, and the people scattered round seemed but ordinary wayfarers, but just across the maze of traffic was a spectacle of intense interest to him.

At the quadrant of the Grand Hotel, patrolling aimlessly in front of the shops, at which he seemed too perturbed to stare for more than a few seconds at a time, the draughtsman kept palpitating vigil until the clock should strike the half-hour of his treason. True to the Frenchman's advice, he sought safety in a crowd, avoiding the desert of the square until the last moment.

It wanted two minutes to the half-hour when Pringle opened his Baedeker, and thrusting one hand into his breast, examined the statue and coil of rope erected to the glory of our greatest hero. "Pauline!" said a voice, with the musical inflection unattainable by any but a Frenchman. Beside him stood a slight neatly dressed young man, with close-cropped hair, and a moustache and imperial, who cast a significant look at the parcel.

Pringle immediately held it towards him, and the dark gentleman producing an envelope from his breast-pocket, the exchange was effected in silence. With bows and a raising of hats they parted, while Big Ben boomed on his eight bells.

The attaché's representative had disappeared some minutes beyond the westernmost lion before the draughtsman appeared from the opposite direction, his uncertain steps intermitted by frequent halts and nervous backward glances. With his back to the National Gallery he produced a Baedeker and commenced to stare up at the monument, withdrawing his eyes every now and then to cast a shamefaced look to right and left.

In his agitation the draughtsman had omitted the hand-in-the breast attitude, and even as Pringle advanced to his side and murmured "Pauline," his legs (almost stronger than his will) seemed to be urging him to a flight from the field of dishonor.

With tremulous eagerness he thrust a brown-paper parcel into Pringle's hands, and, snatching the envelope of tissue slips, rushed across the road and disappeared in the bar of the Grand Hotel.

Pringle turned to go, but was confronted by a revolver, and as his eye traversed the barrel and met that of its owner, he recognised the Frenchman to whom he had just sold the bundle of newspapers. Dodging the weapon, he tried to spring into the open, but a restraining grip on each elbow held him in the angle of the plinth, and turning ever so little Pringle found himself in custody of the man whom he had last seen in full cry up the Lowther Arcade.

No constable was anywhere near, and even casual passengers walked unheeding by the nook, so quiet was the progress of this little drama. Lowering his revolver, the dark gentleman picked up the parcel which had fallen from Pringle in the struggle. He opened it with delicacy, partially withdrew some sheets of tracing-paper, which he intently examined, and then placed the whole in an inner pocket, and giving a sign to the spy to loose his grasp, he spoke for the first time.

"May I suggest, sir," he said in excellent English with the slightest foreign accent, "may I suggest that in the future you do not meddle with what cannot possibly concern you? These documents have been bought and sold, and although you have been good enough to act as intermediary in the transaction, I can assure you we were under no necessity of calling on you for your help."

Here his tone hardened, and, speaking with less calmness, the accent became more noticeable; "I discovered your impertinence in selling me a parcel of worthless papers very shortly after I left you. Had you succeeded in the attempt you appear to have planned so carefully, it is possible you might have lived long enough to regret it—perhaps not! I wish you good-day, sir." He bowed, as did his companion, and Pringle, walking on, turned up by the corner of the Union Club.

Dent's clock marked twenty minutes to five, and Pringle reflected how much had been compressed into the last quarter of an hour. True, he had not prevented the sale of his country's secrets; on the other hand—he pressed the packet which held the envelope of notes. Hailing a cab, he was about to step in, when, looking back, at the nook between the lions he saw a confused movement about the spot.

The two men he had just left were struggling with a third, who, brandishing a handful of something white, was endeavouring, with varying success, to plant his fist on divers areas of their persons. He was the draughtsman.

A small crowd, which momentarily increased, surrounded them, and as Pringle climbed into the hansom two policemen were seen to penetrate the ring and impartially lay hands upon the three combatants.

THE KIMBERLY FUGITIVE

"Westerly and southwesterly breezes, close, thunder locally."

Twenty times that day had Mr. Pringle consulted the forecast, and then had tapped the barometer without inducing the pointer to travel beyond "change."

Indeed, as evening drew near with no sign of the promised storm, the prospect was quite sufficient to abate the philosophic calm which was his usual mask to the outer world. A morning drizzle had been so greedily licked by the scorching pavement, or lost in the sand and grit, that, inches deep, covered the roadway, that the plane trees on the Embankment, with a mottling where the rain had splashed their dusty leaves, were the sole evidence of a shower too fleeting to be remembered.

The drought was of many weeks' standing. The country lay roasting beneath a brazen sky, great fissures starred the earth, while a mat of peculiarly penetrating dust impartially floured the roads and hedges. London, with all its drawbacks, was more tolerable; at the least there was some shade to be found there, and Pringle had not yet been tempted from his chambers in Furnival's Inn.

When sunset came, and the daily traffic slackened, Pringle shouldered his cycle and carried it down the stone stairs from the second floor. His profession of the phantom literary agency, so gravely announced upon his door allowed him to dress with a disregard of convention, and it was in a bluish flannel suit and straw hat that he pedalled along Holborn in the comparative coolness.

By the bumpy slope of St. Andrew's Hill and the equally rough pavement of New Bridge Street, he reached Blackfriars, and turned to the right along the Embankment; it ran in his mind to go as far West as possible, inhaling whatever ozone the breeze might carry, returning later with the wind behind him.

The seats, crowded with limp humanity, the silent children too tired even to play, the general listlessness and absence of stir, all witnessed to the consuming heat. The roadway was almost deserted, but just by the Temple Pringle was conscious of the disagreeable sensation so full of meaning to a cyclist, of something striking his back wheel. From behind there came an exclamation, an oath from between close ground teeth, and as he sprinted on and dismounted these were punctuated by a loud crash.

Pringle knew the meaning of it all without turning. The shock had been too gentle and withal noiseless to be caused by anything but another cycle, ridden most likely by some ground-gazing scorcher, and knowing that with even the best of riders a collision with another machine in front means disaster, he was quite prepared for what he saw.

A few yards back a dilapidated-looking cyclist was examining his mount. His dark hair and moustache had acquired the same grey tint as his clothing, so generously had he been coated with dust in what must have been a long ride; but the machine appeared to have suffered more from the fall than its rider, who dolefully handled a pedal which declined to revolve.

"Can I be of any help?" inquired Pringle with his usual suavity. "I hope there's nothing serious the matter."

"Pedal pin's bent, and I've hurt my ankle," returned the cyclist. He spoke shortly, as if inclined to blame Pringle for the accident due to his own folly.

"Is it a sprain?" asked Pringle sympathetically. "Do you think you can ride with it?"

"Nothing much, I think." He walked round the machine with a slight limp, and added surlily, "But I can't ride a thing like that." He indicated the pedal with a pettish finger as he raised the machine from the ground.

"Oh, I think a few minutes' work will put that right," observed Pringle encouragingly.

"No! Really?" He brightened visibly as if Pringle had rid him of a certain incubus.

"I don't think we shall find a repairer open now—besides I don't know of one just about here. If you will allow me, I'll see what I can do to put it right. As you say, you can't ride it like that."

The stranger was obviously not a practical cyclist, and Pringle, leaning his own machine against the curb, had produced a spanner and was on his hands and knees beside the damaged cycle before the other had well got his pouch unstrapped. Pringle had put down his concern for the machine to the natural affection of an owner, but, with some of the dust and mud brushed off, it stood revealed as a hired crock, with cheap Belgian fittings. The dull enamel, the roughly machined lugs, the general lack of finish, showed the second-rate machine; and it was no drop-forging which yielded to the persuasion of a very moderately powerful wrench, the soft steel straightening under the leverage almost as readily as it had bent.

Meanwhile, the owner vented an unamiable mood in dispersing the inevitable boys crowding like vultures round the fallen cycle; and when Pringle, his labour ended, struck his shoulder beneath the handle-bar and was peppered with a shower of dust and pellets from the mud-guards, he had lost some of his former incivility, and, producing a handkerchief, insisted on dusting his benefactor with quite a gracious air.

"I see you've ridden far," remarked Pringle as he finished.

"Yes; from—er—er—Colchester," was the hesitating reply.

"Suppose we move on a bit from this crowd?" Pringle suggested. "I think we are both going westwards."

"I was on the look out for a quiet hotel somewhere near here," said the cyclist as they rode side by side.

"I think the 'Embankment' in Arundel Street would suit you; it's moderate and quiet—round here to the right. By the bye, it's some time since I was on the Colchester Road, but I remember what an awful hill there is at Hatfield Peverel. I don't know which is the worst—to come up or go down."

"Hatfield—Hatfield Peverel?" repeated the other musingly.

"Just this side of Witham, you know. Why, surely you must have noticed that hill!"

"Oh, yes. Witham—yes, a very nasty hill!"

"No, not Witham. You come to the hill at Hatfield Peverel."

"Yes, yes—I know." And then, as if anxious to change the subject, "Are we anywhere near the hotel?"

"Just the other side of that red-brick building. I see you've managed to pick up a little real estate on your way." The stranger started and glanced suspiciously at Pringle, who explained, "The mud, I mean."

"Oh! the mud. Ha! ha! ha!" There was more of hysteria than hilarity in the laugh and the man suddenly grew voluble. "Yes, I came through a lot of mud. Fact is, I was caught in the thunderstorm."

"Indeed! That's good news. Whereabouts was it?"

"Near Tonbridge."

"Tonbridge?"

"Tut! What am I talking about? I mean Colchester. But this is the place, isn't it? Good-night—good-night!" He dragged the machine into the hotel, leaving Pringle to silently debate whether his boorishness was due to his confusion, or his confusion to his boorishness.

With his foot on the step, Pringle was just remounting when a muffled rumble sounded overhead. The stars were hidden by a huge inksplash, and a pallid, ghostly light flickered in the south; then, with measured pat, huge blobs of rain began to fall, while a blast, as from all the furnaces across the stream, blew up from the Embankment. It was the long-deferred storm, and Pringle told himself his ride must be abandoned; he had wasted too much time over this ingrate.

Resigned to another night of stuffy insomnia, he turned and pedalled up towards the Strand. Beside him ran a newsboy, shouting

his alliterative bill: "Storm in the south! Rain in rivers." Cram-
ming a pink sheet into his pocket Pringle hurried on, and reached
Furnival's Inn as a blinding glare lit up the gateway, and the clouds
exploded with a crackling volley.

Fagged and dusty, his head throbbing to the reverberation of
the thunder, Pringle collapsed on his sofa and languidly unfolded
the paper; but, at the first glance he sat up again with a start, for
in the place of honour beneath the alliterative headlines he read:—

> The *Central News* reports that a violent thunder storm,
> which did some damage to the hop-fields, burst over the
> Tonbridge district early this afternoon. For a time many of
> the roads were impassable, the drains and ditches being
> choked by the sudden rush of stormwater. So far as is known
> no loss of life occurred. Further storms may be expected in
> the home counties and will be anxiously awaited by agri-
> culturists.

"Tonbridge!" thought Pringle. "Was there no storm in Essex?"
He scanned the rest of the paper with an eagerness which dismissed
his fatigue. The cyclist had positively named Colchester as the scene
of the storm. Strange that the paper said nothing about it—and
there was ample time for the news to have reached London, too.

He flicked a crumb of dry mud out of his turned-up trousers,
and recalled what an avalanche had poured from the stranger's
machine. That was no passing shower it had sped through. Stay—
why, of course! The man actually did say Tonbridge, and then made
haste to correct himself. And how clumsily he made his escape
afterwards! Supposing he had travelled up through Tonbridge, he
would probably cross Blackfriars Bridge, and thus his presence on
the Embankment would be explained. But why had he told a lie
about it? What could he possibly have to conceal?

Pringle absently turned the rest of the mud out of his trousers
and threw up the window. With wide-spread fingers he cast the
handful abroad, when a sudden inspiration bid him pause, and
tightly clasping the remnants of dust, he took a sheet of paper and

carefully scraped his palm over it. The *Britannica* stood ever ready to his hand, and taking a volume from its shelf he studied it intently for a while, murmuring, as he replaced it, "Essex, Thanet sands and London clay."

Across the room stood his oak bureau—the bureau which indifferently supplied an actor's make-up or a chemist's laboratory, and opening it, he drew out a test-tube and a bottle of hydrochloric acid. Shaking the dust into the tube he poured the acid in and watched the turbid solution as it slowly clarified after a brisk effervescence; then with a steady hand he added a few drops of sulphuric acid and his impassive features relaxed in a grim smile as the resulting opalescence deepened to opacity, and this in turn condensed into a woolly cloud.

The delicate test established the presence of chalk and the entire absence of clay. Thus, for all his clumsy lying, science, which cannot be deceived, declared that the cyclist had ridden into London over chalky roads—that is to say, not from Essex, but from the south.

The storm had passed. Clear moonlight succeeded the lambent spasms of the lightning, and a cool breeze sang past the upper windows of the Inn. Physical weariness would not be denied, and with the novel prospect of an unbroken night's rest before him, Pringle abandoned any present attempt to learn the motive of the stranger's deception.

The sun was shining brightly between the green blind-slats when he awoke. Tired out, he had slept long past his usual hour. Lighting the spirit-lamp to prepare his simple breakfast he glanced over the paper he found beneath his outer door. As he was accustomed to explain, he read the *Chronicle* not from any sympathy with its opinions, but as being the most really informing journal published in London.

The water boiled and boiled in the little kettle, the flame sputtered and died as the spirit burned out; but Pringle, intent on the newspaper, took no heed of his meal. There was barely a third of a column; but as he read and re-read the paragraphs the personality of the cyclist was ever before him, and remembering the chemical analysis, his suspicions all crowded back again—suspicions which he had laid aside with the headache of last night.

A TALE OF THE DIAMOND FIELDS

About a month ago, according to the South African papers just to hand, some sensation was caused in Kimberly by the disappearance of an outside broker named Thomas, who for some time past had been under the surveillance of the Diamond Fields police for suspected infractions of the Illicit Diamond Buying Act, colloquially known as I. D. B. Under this local Act arrest is lawful on much slighter evidence than would justify such a course elsewhere, but the police had little to work upon until some purloined stones were actually traced to Thomas just after he disappeared; the ordinary law was thereupon invoked by the police, and a warrant was granted for his apprehension.

The fugitive had a good start, and although traced to Cape Town, he never lost the advantage he had gained, but managed to escape on the outgoing liner *Grantully Castle*, and the police feeling certain of his arrest at Southampton telegraphed full particulars to England. Thomas would appear to be well served by confederates for, when the *Grantully Castle* arrived at Madeira, a telegram awaited him and he suddenly left the ship, alleging urgent business at Funchal, and stating his intention of coming on by the next boat.

When the next liner duly arrived at Southampton it brought an inspector of the Diamond Fields Police armed with the warrant for Thomas's arrest, but no one on whom to execute it. As usual, Thomas was a day ahead of his pursuers, and for a time no trace of him could be found. At length, through the *Castle* agent at Funchal, it was discovered that Thomas had remained but a day or two there, having taken passage for London in the *Bittern*, a cargo steamer trading to the Gold Coast.

The scene now changes to the Downs, where the inspector, in company with a London detective, awaited the *Bittern*. A slow sailer, she was believed to have encountered bad weather in the Bay of Biscay, and it was not until yesterday morning that she made her number off Deal, and was promptly boarded by the police in a pilot boat; but once again they were just too late.

Off the South Foreland a "hoveller" had tried to sell the *Bittern* some vegetables but instead secured a passenger in the person of Thomas, who struck a bargain with him, and was rowed ashore near Kingsdown. From there he appears to have walked to Walmer taking the train to Dover, where for the present he has been lost.

Thomas is stated to be a native of Colchester, for many years in Africa, and is described as a strongly built man of about forty, wearing a dark beard and moustache, and with a scar over the right brow caused by a dynamite explosion which blinded the eye.

Here was matter for reflection with a vengeance. As Pringle refilled his lamp and kindled the charred wick, his one thought was the possible identity of the cyclist with the man Thomas. The descriptions given in the *Chronicle* were inconclusive, but the cyclist had a very effective mask of dust and mud. True, he was beardless, but would not a shave be the first act of Thomas on arriving at Dover?

To Pringle it seemed such an obvious precaution that he dismissed the fact as irrelevant. The time, too, was sufficient for even an inexperienced rider to have cycled the distance. It was certainly a clever idea, and very characteristic of the man, to come by road rather than by the train with its scheduled times and its frequent stoppages, to say nothing of the telegraph wires running alongside.

As Pringle had almost conclusively proved, he had travelled up from the south by way of Tonbridge, yet he had shown an extreme desire to conceal the fact. Then, again, he talked of coming by the

Colchester road, and Thomas was said to be a native of Colchester. It was a small matter, no doubt; but the fugitive, anxious to hide his tracks, would be sure to speak of a neighbourhood he knew— or, rather, which he thought he knew, for it was clear that Thomas, if it were he, had forgotten the main features of the route.

But supposing Thomas to have been the cyclist, where were the diamonds? Surely, thought Pringle, he must have some with him. And at the thought of the treasure to which he had been so near his pulse quickened. Could Thomas have concealed it about his person? Hardly, in view of his possible capture. But what of the cycle? He had shown considerable solicitude for the machine— in fact, he had scarcely loosened his hold on it. And had not he, Romney Pringle, tested the possibilities of a cycle for concealing jewelry? Smiling at the recollection he sat down to his breakfast.

About nine o'clock Pringle started in search of his new acquaintance, but at the hotel he was met by a fresh difficulty—he knew no name by which to describe the stranger, and could only ask for "a gentleman with a bicycle."

"You may well say the gentleman with the bicycle," exclaimed the waiter as he took Pringle's judicious tip. "That's what we all call him. Why, he wouldn't let us put it in the yard last night, but he stuck to it like cobbler's wax, and stood it in the passage, where he could see it all the time he was eating. An' would you believe it, sir?"—sinking his voice to a confidential whisper— "he actually took the machine up to his bedroom with him at night!"

Pringle having expressed his horror at this violation of decency, the waiter continued—

"Ah! and when the guv'nor heard of it and went up to speak to him about it, he'd locked the door and pretended not to hear. He said it was a valuable machine, but I've got a brother in the trade and I know something about machines myself, and I don't see it's anything out of the way."

"What name did he give?"

"Think it was Snaky, or something foreign like that." The waiter consulted a slate. "Ah! here it is, sir— 'Snaburgh, No. 24; call 7:30.'"

"Has he gone, then?" inquired Pringle anxiously.

"Took his machine out with him soon after eight. The guv'nor objected to his going out before he'd paid his bill, seeing as he'd got no luggage, so he paid up, and then took a look at the time-table, and asked when lunch was on."

"What time-table was it?"

"'A B C' I saw him with."

"Do you expect him back?"

"Can't say for— Why, dash my wig, here he is, cycle an' all!"

The cyclist, holding a small black bag and wheeling the machine, wormed his way into the lobby resolutely declining the waiter's assistance. On seeing Pringle he started, then paused, and half turned back, but encumbered as he was his movements were necessarily slow, and Pringle, ignoring the action, advanced with his most engaging smile.

"I'm so pleased to find you're none the worse for your accident. Allow me!" He steadied the machine against the wall. "Have you been for a morning ride?"

"Only to do some shopping," was the ungracious reply.

Mr. Snaburgh, as he called himself, looked all the better for his morning toilet, and Pringle watched him closely in the endeavour to compare him with the rather vague newspaper description. He was certainly thick-set, and might have been any age from thirty to five-and-forty. His moustache was coal-black and drooped in cavalry fashion over his mouth; the chin had already grown a short stubble, and two fresh cuts upon his chops were eloquent of the hasty removal of a recent beard. There was a constant nervous twitching about the eyelids, but although shaded by the peak of the cap, a dirty-coloured corrugation over the right brow was quite apparent.

Pringle took special note of the right pupil. As Snaburgh stood he was in a full light, but yet it was unduly dilated, thus showing its insensibility to the light and the blindness of the eye.

"I must apologise for intruding on you so early in the day," said Pringle with all his wonted suaveness; "but a sprain is often at its worst a few hours after the accident."

"It's all right, thanks," gruffly.

"If I can be of any service to you while you're in town—"

"I'm not going to stay in town! Er—good morning!" And he resumed his elephantine struggle through the hall.

In face of this snub Pringle could do nothing, and fearful of rousing suspicions which might scare the fugitive into another sudden disappearance, he accepted the dismissal. As he passed out he overheard, "Shall I take the machine, sir?" and the reply, "No, I want a private sitting-room where I can take it."

Pringle meditated upon two facts as he turned homeward. He had ascertained beyond any reasonable doubt that the cyclist was Thomas, and that the machine was as much as ever the object of his idolatry. The extraordinary pains to keep it in sight, his refusal to part with it even in his bedroom, the saddling himself with it when, as he said, he only went shopping, all pointed to the fact that a machine intrinsically worth some three or four pounds had a very special value in his eyes.

One thing was a little puzzling to Pringle: the man had no luggage—not even a cycle-valise—the night before, yet at an early hour, almost before the shops were open, in fact, he had gone out and purchased a bag. Did he suspect how much comment his care of the cycle was arousing? Was he about to transfer its freight to the bag? Here again he displayed his usual shrewdness, for the "A B C" gave no hint as to the line he favoured.

Pringle wondered how much longer Thomas would remain at the hotel. He had certainly made inquiries about lunch, and the unloading of the cycle would take a little time. But then there was that story in the *Chronicle* to be reckoned with. Were Thomas to see that, he would be sure to connect it with Pringle's visit, and would promptly vanish. But was it in any other paper? Pringle made a large investment in the journalism of the morning and, mounting an omnibus, industriously skimmed the whole. The *Chronicle* alone printed it, and he decided to take the risk of Thomas reading it there.

Hard by Furnival's Inn is an emporium where the appliances of every known sport (and even of a few unknown ones) are obtainable. Pringle was no stranger to the establishment, and making his way to the athletic department, purchased a cheap cycling suit and sweater, with a cap which he ornamented with an aggressive badge. Downstairs among the cycling accessories he bought a "ram's-horn" handle-bar, and hurried back laden to his chambers.

His first step was to remove the characteristic port-wine mark on his right cheek with spirit, and then having blackened his fair hair and brows, he created the incipience of a moustache with the shreds from a camel-hair brush.

Although it would have been difficult for Pringle to look other than a gentleman, with his slim athletic figure clothed in the sweater, the cycling suit, and the cap and badge (especially the badge), he presented a fair likeness of the average Sunday scorcher. The manners of the tribe he fortunately saw no necessity to assume. To perfect the resemblance, the scorcher being comparable to a man who shall select a racehorse for a day's ride over country roads, it was necessary to "strip" his machine, so removing the mud-guards and brake, and robbing the chain of its decent gear-case, he substituted the "ram's-horn" for his handle-bar.

Towards noon Pringle rode down Arundel Street and alighting at a tavern commanding a view of the Embankment Hotel, sat down to wait in the company of a beer-tankard: but as he slowly sipped the beer, his vigil unrewarded and the barman beginning to stare inquisitively, the thought arose again and again that Thomas had given him the slip.

He almost decided on the desperate step of visiting the hotel and once more pumping the friendly waiter, when, shortly after one, he caught a momentary glimpse of a familiar face as its owner examined the street over the coffee-room blinds.

Pringle drew a long breath. He was on the right scent, after all: and ordering a cut from the joint he made a hearty lunch preserving an unabated watch upon the hotel door. This was a somewhat irritating task. It was the autumn season, and with a full complement of country and American cousins in the house, there was a constant movement to and fro.

Nevertheless, his persistence was rewarded after an hour by a slight but portentous occurrence: a waiter emerged with a cycle, which he propped against the curb. It was the hired crock. By this time Pringle could have identified it among some thousands at a cycle show. But the owner? Where was he? What, Pringle asked himself, could have soured his affection for the machine? What else but the removal of the treasure?

Pringle was saved further speculation by the appearance of Thomas himself. He was carrying the hand-bag, and entered on an earnest conversation with the waiter, the subject of discussion appearing to be the cycle itself. Presently the waiter opened the tool-bag, and taking a wrench from it, commenced to adjust the handlebar, which Pringle for the first time noticed was all askew. This took some little time, and when the man finished he pointed to the saddle as if that too required attention, an office which he straightway performed. And all the while Thomas, with the bag fast held, contented himself with supervising the task.

The sight was an instructive one for Pringle. The disarrangement of the cycle was an assurance that the contents had been transferred, and Thomas clearly regarded the machine but as a means of locomotion.

Resisting the waiter's attempt to hold the bag while he mounted, Thomas scrambled to the saddle and steered a serpentine course up the slope, the bag bouncing and trembling in his grasp. Even had he been capable of the feat of turning round, he would have felt no apprehension of the youth who followed at a pace regulated by his own.

In the case of every pastime some special Providence would seem to direct the novice: either he has an impregnable run of luck, or he performs feats which he can never after attain. So it was with Thomas.

An indifferent rider, he boldly plunged into the torrent which roared along Fleet Street: unscathed he shot the rapids of Ludgate Circus, and kept a straight and fearless course onwards up the hill. But in Queen Victoria Street the steering became too complicated and, forced to dismount, he pushed the cycle for the remainder of the way.

Pringle had followed in some alarm that they might be hopelessly separated in the traffic, and more than once had even entertained ideas of seizing the bag in the midst of a purposed collision and trusting to luck to dodge into safety between the omnibuses. But he dismissed them all as crude and dangerous; besides, his artistic ideals revolted at the clumsiness of leaving any details to mere luck.

The pursuit led on through the City till presently Pringle found himself descending the approach to the Great Eastern terminus. Inside all was bustle and confusion, and they had to elbow an arduous track through the crowd. Seeing wisdom in a less intimate attendance, Pringle withdrew to the shelter of a flight of steps, and while Thomas perspired he rested. But he never relaxed his watch, and the moment the other emerged from the booking-office and panted toward the labelling rack, Pringle followed on. As Thomas moved off with his machine Pringle palmed a shilling on the porter with the demand, "Same, please," and a few seconds later drew aside to read the label pasted on his spokes. It was *Witham*.

Handing the cycle to a porter he rushed to the booking-office and then on to the platform as the crock, in the indifferent absence of Thomas, was trundled into the van with customary official brutality; his own followed with a shade more consideration, and under the pretence of adjusting it he presently got into the van, and as he passed Thomas's machine buried a knife-blade in each of its tyres. He had just time to take his seat before the whistle sounded, and the train glided out of the station.

Witham was a good forty minutes off, and at every halt Pringle's shoulders blocked the carriage window. He feared lest Thomas should repeat his favourite strategy of alighting before his destination. But so long as they were in motion Pringle whiled the time by imagining fresh reasons for this mysterious journey.

He was staring at the map of the Great Eastern system which oppositely hung in the compartment, when his eye fell on a miniature steamboat voyaging a mathematically straight line drawn across from Harwich to the Hook of Holland. The figure suggested a new idea. Supposing the present trip had been arranged with an accomplice—could it in brief be a clever scheme to dispose of the diamonds in the best market? When more likely to disarm suspicion than for Thomas to cycle from Witham to Harwich?

"Witham!

Pringle, with every sense alert, looked out. No one alighting? Yes, here he was. The guard had already evicted the two cycles when Thomas, with the precious valise, hurried down the platform and seized his own. The supreme moment had arrived.

Pringle waited until the other had disappeared, and stepped on to the platform as the train began to move. There was no need for him to hurry; the damage he had inflicted on the crock would ensure its leisurely running. And true enough, when he reached the station door Thomas had got but a little way along the road in a bumpy fashion, which even to his inexperience might have told the rapid deflation of the tyres. His progress was further complicated by the presence of the bag, which he had no means of fastening to the cycle; and, slowly as Pringle followed, the distance between them rapidly shortened, until when Thomas turned into the main road he was nearly up to him.

Pringle halted a few seconds to allow a diplomatic gap to intervene, and then followed round the corner as Thomas shaped a painful course along the Colchester road. On and on, growing ever slower, the way led between high hedges, until with a pair of absolutely flat tyres there dawned upon Thomas's intelligence a suspicion that all was not well with the machine, and, dismounting, he leant it against the hedge.

"Can I lend you a repair? You seem badly punctured," piped Pringle in a high falsetto. He had shot by, and now, wheeling round, passed a little to the rear and propped his machine against a gate.

"I thought that was it. I haven't got a repair," was the least bearish reply that Pringle had yet heard from Thomas.

"You must get both tyres off—like this!" Pringle inverted the crock, and with the dexterity of long practice, ran his fingers round the rims and unnecessarily dragged out both the inner tubes for their entire length. "Catch hold for a second, will you, while I look for a patch."

Thomas innocently laid the bag at his feet and steadied the machine, when a violent thrust sent him diving headlong through the frame. With a spasm of his powerful back muscles he saved a sprawl into the hedge, and was on his feet in another second.

Pringle, the bag in hand, was already a dozen yards away. He had noted a fault in the hedge, and for this he made with all imaginable speed. The road sank just here, but scrambling cat-like up the bank, with a rending and tearing of his clothes, his bleeding hands forced a passage through the gap. Once clear of it he doubled back inside the hedge; beyond the gate there stood his cycle, and even as he neared it there was a scream of curses as the thorns waylaid Thomas in the gap.

In a bound Pringle was over the gate. The bag was hooked fast upon a staple; desperately he tugged, but the iron held until at a more violent wrench the leather ripped open. He seized the canvas packet within; it crisped in his fingers.

Behind there was a furious panting; he could almost feel the hot breaths, but as Thomas clutched the empty bag and collapsed across the gate, Pringle disappeared toward Colchester in a whirlwind of dust.

THE SILKWORMS OF FLORENCE

"And this is all that is left of Brede now." The old beadle withdrew his hand, and the skull, with a rattle as of an empty wooden box, fell in its iron cage again.

"How old do you say it is?" asked Mr. Pringle.

"Let me see," reflected the beadle, stroking his long grey beard. "He killed Mr. Grebble in 1742, I think it was—the date's on the tombstone over yonder in the church—and he hung in these irons a matter of sixty or seventy year. I don't rightly know the spot where the gibbet stood, but it was in a field they used to call in my young days 'Gibbet Marsh.' You'll find it round by the Tillingham, back of the windmill."

"And is this the gibbet? How dreadful!" chorused the two daughters of a clergyman, very summery, very gushing, and very inquisitive, who with their father completed the party.

"Lor, no, miss! Why, that's the Rye pillory. It's stood up here nigh a hundred year! And now I'll show you the town charters." And the beadle, with some senile hesitation of gait, led the way into a small attic.

Mr. Pringle's mythical literary agency being able to take care of itself, his chambers in Furnival's Inn had not seen him for a month past. To a man of his cultured and fastidious bent the Bank Holiday resort was especially odious; he affected regions unknown to the tripper, and his presence at Rye had been determined by Jeakes' quaint "Perambulation of the Cinque Ports," which he had lately picked up in Booksellers' Row.

Wandering with his camera from one decayed city to another, he had left Rye only to hasten back when disgusted with the modernity of the other ports, and for the last fortnight his tall slim figure had haunted the town, his fair complexion swarthy and his port-wine mark almost lost in the tanning begotten of the marsh winds and the sun.

"The town's had a rare lot of charters and privileges granted to it," boasted the beadle, turning to a chest on which for all its cobwebs and mildew the lines of elaborate carving showed distinctly. Opening it, he began to dredge up parchments from the huddled mass inside, giving very free translations of the old Norman-French or Latin the while.

"Musty, dirty old things!" was the comment of the two ladies.

Pringle turned to a smaller chest standing neglected in a dark corner, whose lid, when he tried it, he found also unlocked, and which was nearly as full of papers as the larger one.

"Are these town records also?" inquired Pringle, as the beadle gathered up his robes preparatory to moving on.

"Not they," was the contemptuous reply. "That there chest was found in the attic of an old house that's just been pulled down to build the noo bank, and it's offered to the Corporation; but I don't think they'll spend money on rubbish like that!"

"Here's something with a big seal!" exclaimed the clergyman, pouncing on a discoloured parchment with the avid interest of an antiquary. The folds were glued with damp, and endeavouring to smooth them out the parchment slipped through his fingers; it dropped plumb by the weight of its heavy seal, and as he sprang to save it his glasses fell off and buried themselves among the papers. While he hunted for them Pringle picked up the document, and began to read.

"Not much account I should say," commented the beadle, with a supercilious snort. "Ah! You should have seen our Jubilee Address, with the town seal to it, all in blue and red and gold—cost every penny of fifty pound! That's the noo bank what you're looking at from this window. How the town is improving, to be sure!" He indicated a nightmare in red brick and stucco which had displaced a Jacobean mansion.

And while the beadle prosed Pringle read:

CINQUE   TO ALL and every the Barons Bailiffs Jurat and Commonalty
PORTS   of the Cinque Port of Rye and to Anthony Shipperbolt Mayor
TO WIT   thereof:

WHEREAS it hath been adjudged by the Commission appointed under His Majesty's sign-manual of date March the twenty-third one thousand eight hundred and five that Anthony Shipperbolt Mayor of Rye hath been guilty of conduct unbefitting his office as a magistrate of the Cinque Ports and hath acted traitorously enviously and contrary to the love and affection his duty towards His Most Sacred Majesty and the good order of this Realm TO WIT that the said Anthony Shipperbolt hath accepted bribes from the enemies of His Majesty hath consorted with the same and did plot compass and go about to assist a certain prisoner of war the same being his proper ward and charge to escape from lawful custody NOW I William Pitt Lord Warden of the Cinque Ports do order and command you the said Anthony Shipperbolt and you are hereby required to forfeit and pay the sum of ten thousand pounds sterling into His Majesty's Treasury AND as immediate officer of His Majesty and by virtue and authority of each and every the ancient charters of the Cinque Ports I order and command you the said Anthony Shipperbolt to forthwith determine and refrain and you are hereby inhibited from exercising the office and dignity of Mayor of the said Cinque Port of Rye Speaker of the Cinque Ports Summoner of Brotherhood and Guestling and all and singular the liberties freedoms licenses exemptions and jurisdictions of Stallage Pontage Panage Keyage Murage Piccage Passage Groundage Scutage and all other powers franchises and authorities appertaining thereunto AND I further order and command you the said Anthony Shipperbolt to render to me within seven days of the date hereof a full and true account of all monies fines amercements redemptions issues forfeitures tallies seats records lands messuages and beréditaments whatsoever and wheresoever that you hold have present custody of or have at any time received in trust for the said Cinque Port of Rye wherein fail not at your peril. AND I further order and command you the said Barons Bailiffs Jurats and Commonalty of the said Cinque Port of Rye that you straightway meet and choose some true and loyal subject of His Majesty the same being of your number as fitting to hold the said office of Mayor of the said Cinque Port whose name you shall submit to my pleasure as soon as may be FOR ALL which this shall be your sufficient authority. Given at Downing Street this sixteenth day of May in the year of our Lord one thousand eight hundred and five.

GOD SAVE THE KING.

The last two or three inches of the parchment were folded down, and seemed to have firmly adhered to the back—probably through the accidental running of the seal in hot weather. But the fall had broken the wax, and Pringle was now able to open the sheet to the full, disclosing some lines of script, faded and tremulously scrawled, it is true, but yet easy to be read:

"To my son,—Seek for the silk-worms of Florence in
   Gibbet Marsh
   Church Spire SE x S, Winchelsea Mill SW ½ W.
   A.S."

Pringle read this curious endorsement more than once, but could make no sense of it. Concluding it was of the nature of a cypher, he made a note of it in his pocketbook with the idea of attempting a solution in the evening—a time which he found it difficult to get through, Rye chiefly depending for its attractions on its natural advantages.

By this time the clergyman had recovered his glasses, and, handing the document back to him, Pringle joined the party by the window. The banalities of the bank and other municipal improvements being exhausted, and the ladies openly yawning, the beadle proposed to show them what he evidently regarded as the chief glory of the Town Hall of Rye. The inquisitive clergyman was left studying the parchment, while the rest of the party adjourned to the council chamber. Here the guide proudly indicated the list of mayors, whose names were emblazoned on the chocolate-coloured walls to a length rivalling that of the dynasties of Egypt.

"What does this mean?" inquired Pringle. He pointed to the year 1805, where the name "Anthony Shipperbolt" appeared bracketed with another.

"That means he died during his year of office," promptly asserted the old man. He seemed never at a loss for an answer, although Pringle began to suspect that the prompter the reply the more inaccurate was it likely to be.

"Oh, what a smell of burning!" interrupted one of the ladies.

"And where's papa?" screamed the other. "He'll be burnt to death."

There was certainly a smell of burning, which, being of a strong and pungent nature, perhaps suggested to the excited imagination of the ladies the idea of a clergyman on fire.

Pringle gallantly raced up the stairs. The fumes issued from a smouldering mass upon the floor, and beside it lay something which burnt with pyrotechnic sputtering; but neither bore any relation to the divine. He, though well representing what Gibbon has styled "the fat slumbers of the Church," was hopping about the miniature bonfire, now sucking his fingers and anon shaking them in the air as one in great agony.

Intuitively Pringle understood what had happened, and with a bound he stamped the smouldering parchment into unrecognisable tinder, and smothering the more viciously burning seal with his handkerchief he pocketed it as the beadle wheezed into the room behind the ladies, who were too concerned for their father's safety to notice the action.

"What's all this?" demanded the beadle, and glared through his spectacles.

"I've dr-r-r-r-opped some wa-wa-wa-wax—oh!—upon my hand!"

"Waxo?" echoed the beadle, sniffing suspiciously.

"He means a wax match, I think," Pringle interposed chivalrously. The parchment was completely done for, and he saw no wisdom in advertising the fact.

"I'll trouble you for your name and address," insisted the beadle in all the pride of office.

"What for?" the incendiary objected.

"To report the matter to the Fire Committee."

"Very well, then—Cornelius Hardgiblet, rector of Logdown," was the impressive reply; and tenderly escorted by his daughters the rector departed with such dignity as an occasional hop, when his fingers smarted a little more acutely, would allow him to assume.

It still wanted an hour or two to dinnertime as Pringle unlocked the little studio he rented on the Winchelsea road. Originally an office, he had made it convertible into a very fair dark-room, and here he was accustomed to spend his afternoons in developing the morning's photographs. But photography had little interest for him today. Ever since Mr. Hardgiblet's destruction of the document—which, he felt certain, was no accident—Pringle had cast about for some motive for the act. What could it be but that the parchment contained a secret, which the rector, guessing, had wanted to keep to himself? He must look up the incident of the mayor's degradation. So sensational an event, even for such stirring days as those, would scarcely go unrecorded by local historians.

Pringle had several guide-books at hand in the studio, but a careful search only disclosed that they were unanimously silent as to Mr. Shipperbolt and his affairs. Later on, when returning, he had reason to bless his choice of an hotel. The books in the smoking room were not limited, as usual, to a few time-tables and an ancient copy of Ruff's "Guide." On the contrary, Murray and Black were prominent and above all Hillpath's monumental "History of Rye," and in this last he found the information he sought. Said Hillpath:

In 1805 Anthony Shipperbolt, then Mayor of Rye, was degraded from office, his property confiscated, and himself condemned to stand in the pillory with his face to the French coast, for having assisted Jules Florentin, a French prisoner of war, to escape from the Ypres Tower Prison.

He was suspected of having connived at the escape of several other prisoners of distinction, presumably for reward. He had been a ship-owner trading with France, and his legitimate trade suffering as a result of the war he had undoubtedly resorted to smuggling, a form of trading which, to the principals engaged in it at least carried little disgrace with it, being winked at by even the most law-abiding persons.

Shipperbolt did not long survive his degradation, and, his only son being killed soon after while resisting a revenue cutter when in charge of his father's vessel, the family became extinct.

Here, thought Pringle, was sufficient corroboration of the parchment. The details of the story were clear, and the only mysterious thing about it was the endorsement. His original idea of its being a cypher hardly squared with the simple address, "To my son," and the "A. S." with which it concluded could only stand for the initials of the deposed mayor.

There was no mystery either about "Gibbet Marsh," which, according to the beadle's testimony, must have been a well-known spot a century ago, while the string of capitals he easily recognised as compass-bearings. There only remained the curious expression, "The Silkworms of Florence," and that was certainly a puzzle. Silkworms are a product of Florence, he knew; but they were unlikely to be exported in such troublous times. And why were they deposited in such a place as Gibbet Marsh?

He turned for enlightenment to Hillpath, and poured over the passage again and again before he saw a glimmer of sense. Then suddenly he laughed, as the cypher resolved itself into a pun, and a feeble one at that.

While Hillpath named the prisoner as Florentine and more than hinted at payment for services rendered, the cypher indicated where Florentine products were to be found. . . . Shipperbolt ruined, his property confiscated, what more likely than that he should conceal the price of his treason in Gibbet Marsh—a spot almost as shunned in daylight as in darkness? Curious as the choice of the parchment for such a purpose might be, the endorsement was practically a will. He had nothing else to leave.

Pringle was early afoot the next day. Gibbet Marsh has long been drained and its very name forgotten, but the useful Murray indicated its site clearly enough for him to identify it; and it was in the middle of a wide and lonely field, embanked against the winter inundations, that Pringle commenced to work out the bearings approximately with a pocket-compass.

He soon fixed his starting-point, the church tower dominating Rye from every point of view; but of Winchelsea there was nothing to be seen for the trees. Suddenly, just where the green mass thinned away to the northward, something rose and caught the sunbeams for a moment, again and still again, and with a steady gaze he made out the revolving sails of a windmill.

This was as far as he cared to go for the moment; without a good compass and a sounding-spud it would be a dire waste of time to attempt to fix the spot. He walked across the field, and was in the very act of mounting the stile when he noticed a dark object, which seemed to skim in jerky progression along the top of the embankment. While he looked the thing enlarged, and as the path behind the bank rose uplifted itself into the head, shoulders, and finally the entire person of the rector of Logdown. He had managed to locate Gibbet Marsh, it appeared; but, as he stepped into the field and wandered aimlessly about, Pringle judged that he was still a long way from penetrating the retreat of the silkworms.

Among the passengers by the last train down from London that night was Pringle. He carried a cricketing-bag, and when safely inside the studio he unpacked first a sailor's jersey, peaked cap and trousers, then a small but powerful spade, a very neat portable pick, a few fathoms of manilla rope, several short lengths of steel rod (each having a screw-head, by which they united into a single long one), and finally a three-inch prismatic compass.

Before sunrise the next morning Pringle started out to commence operations in deadly earnest, carrying his jointed rods as a walking-stick, while his coat bulged with the prismatic compass. The town, a victim to the enervating influence of the visitors, still slumbered, and he had to unbar the door of the hotel himself. He did not propose to do more than locate the exact spot of the treasure; indeed he felt that to do even that would be a good morning's work.

On the way down in the train he had taken a few experimental bearings from the carriage window, and felt satisfied with his own dexterity. Nevertheless, he had a constant dread lest the points given should prove inaccurate. He felt dissatisfied with the Winchelsea bearing. For aught he knew, not a single tree that now obscured the view might have been planted; the present mill, perhaps, had not existed; or even another might have been visible from the marsh. What might not happen in the course of nearly a century?

He had already made a little calculation, for a prismatic compass being graduated in degrees (unlike the mariner's, which has but thirty-two points), it was necessary to reduce the bearings to degrees, and this had been the result:

Rye Church spire SE x S = 146° 15′.
Winchelsea Mill SW ½ W = 230° 37′.

When he reached the field not a soul was anywhere to be seen; a few sheep browsed here and there, and high overhead a lark was singing. At once he took a bearing from the church spire. He was a little time in getting the right pointing; he had to move step by step to the right, continuing to take observations, until at last the church weather-cock bore truly 146 ¼° through the sightvane of the compass.

Turning half round, he took an observation of the distant mill. He was a long way out this time; so carefully preserving his relative position to the church, he backed away, taking alternate observations of either object until both spire and mill bore in the right directions.

The point where the two bearings intersected was some fifty yards from the brink of the Tillingham, and, marking the spot with his compass, Pringle began to probe the earth in a widening circle, first with one section of his rod, then, with another joint screwed to it, and finally with a length of three, so that the combination reached to a depth of eight feet. He had probed every square inch of a circle described perhaps twenty feet from the compass, when he suddenly stumbled upon a loose sod, nearly impaling himself upon the sounding-rod; and before he could rise his feet, sliding and slipping, had scraped up quite a large surface of turf, as did his hand, in each case disclosing the fat, brown alluvium beneath.

A curious fact was that the turf had not been cut in regular strips, as if for removal to some garden; neatly as it was relaid, it had been lifted in shapeless patches, some large, some small, while the soil underneath was all soft and crumbling, as if that too had been recently disturbed. Someone had been before him!

Cramped and crippled by his prolonged stooping, Pringle stretched himself at length upon the turf. As he lay and listened to the song that trilled from the tiny speck just visible against a woolly cloud, he felt that it was useless to search further. That a treasure had once been hidden thereabouts he felt convinced, for anything but specie would have been useless at such an unsettled time for commercial credit, and would doubtless have been declined by Shipperbolt; but whatever form the treasure had taken, clearly it was no longer present.

The sounds of toil increased around. Already a barge was on its way up the muddy stream; at any moment he might be the subject of gaping curiosity. He carefully replaced the turfs, wondering the while who could have anticipated him, and what find, if any, had rewarded the searcher.

Thinking it best not to return by the nearest path, he crossed the river some distance up, and taking a wide sweep halted on Cadborough Hill to enjoy for the hundredth time the sight of the glowing roofs, huddled tier after tier upon the rock, itself rising sheer from the plain; and far and beyond, and snowed all over with grazing flocks, the boundless green of the seaward marsh.

Inland, the view was only less extensive, and with some ill-humour he was eyeing the scene of his fruitless labour when he observed a figure moving about Gibbet Marsh. At such a distance it was hard to see exactly what was taking place, but the action of the figure was so eccentric that, with a quick suspicion as to its identity, Pringle laid his traps upon the ground and examined it through his pocket telescope.

It was indeed Mr. Hardgiblet. But the new feature in the case was that the rector appeared to be taking a bearing with a compass, and although he returned over and over again to a particular spot (which Pringle recognised as the same over which he himself had spent the early morning hours), Mr. Hardgiblet repeatedly shifted his ground to the right, to the left, and round about, as if dissatisfied with his observations.

There was only one possible explanation of all this. Cleverer than Pringle had thought him, the rector must have hit upon the place indicated in the parchment, his hand must have removed the turf, and he it was who had examined the soil beneath.

Not for the first time in his life, Pringle was disagreeably reminded of the folly of despising an antagonist, however contemptible he may appear. But at least he had one consolation; the rector's return and his continued observations showed that he had been no more successful in his quest than was Pringle himself. The silkworms were still unearthed.

The road down from Cadborough is long and dusty, and, what with the stiffness of his limbs and the thought of his wasted morning, Pringle, when he reached his studio and took the compass from his pocket, almost felt inclined to fling it through the open window into the "cut." But the spasm of irritability passed. He began to accuse himself of making some initial error in the calculations, and carefully went over them again—with an identical result.

Now that Mr. Hardgiblet was clearly innocent of its removal, he even began to doubt the existence of the treasure. Was it not incredible, he asked himself, that for nearly a century it should have remained hidden? As to its secret (a punning endorsement on an old parchment), was it not just as open to any other investigator in all the long years that had elapsed? Besides, Shipperbolt might have removed the treasure himself in alarm for its safety.

The thought of Shipperbolt suggested a new idea. Instruments of precision were unknown in those days—supposing Shipperbolt's compass had been inaccurate? He took down Norie's *Navigation*, and ran through the chapter on the compass. There was a section headed "Variation and how to apply it," which he skimmed through, considering that the question did not arise, when, carelessly reading on, his attention was suddenly arrested by a table of "Changes in variation from year to year."

Running his eye down this he made the startling discovery that, whereas the variation at that moment was about 16° 31' west, in 1805 it was no less than 24°. Here was indeed a wide margin for error. All the time he was searching for the treasure it was probably lying right at the other side of the field!

At once he started to make a rough calculation, determined that it should be a correct one this time. As the variation of 1805 and that of the moment showed a difference of 7° 29′, to obtain the true bearing it was necessary for him to subtract this difference from Shipperbolt's points, thus:

> Rye Church spire SE x S = 146° 15′, deduct 7° 29′
> = 138° 46′.
> Winchelsea Mill SW ½ W = 230° 37′, deduct 7° 29′
> = 223° 8′.

The question of the moment concerned his next step. Up to the present Mr. Hardgiblet appeared unaware of the error. But how long, thought Pringle, would he remain so? Any work on navigation would set him right, and as he seemed keenly on the scent of the treasure he was unlikely to submit to a check of this nature. Like Pringle, too, he seemed to prefer the early morning hours for his researches. Clearly there was no time to lose.

On his way up to lunch Pringle remarked that the whole town was agog. Crowds were pouring in from the railway station; at every corner strangers were inquiring their road; the shops were either closed or closing; a stream roundabout hooted in the cricket-field. The holiday aspect of things was marked by the display on all sides of uncomfortably best clothing worn with a reckless and determined air of Pleasure Seeking. Even the artists, the backbone of the place, had shared the excitement, or else, resenting the invasion of their pitches by the unaccustomed crowd, were sulking indoors. Anyhow, they had disappeared. Not until he reached the hotel and read on a poster the programme of the annual regatta to be held that day, did Pringle realise the meaning of it all.

In the course of lunch—which, owing to the general disorganisation of things, was a somewhat scrambled meal—it occurred to him that here was his opportunity. The regatta was evidently the great event of the year; every idler would be drawn to it, and no worker who could be spared would be absent. The treasure-field would be even lonelier than in the days of Brede's gibbet. He would be able to locate the treasure that afternoon once for all; then, having marked the spot, he could return at night with his tools and remove it.

When Pringle started out the streets were vacant and quiet as on a Sunday, and he arrived at the studio to find the quay an idle waste and the shipping in the "cut" deserted. As to the meadow, when he got there, it was forsaken even by the sheep. He was soon at work with his prismatic compass, and after half an hour's steady labour he struck a spot about an eighth of a mile distant from the scene of his morning's failure.

Placing his compass as before at the point of intersection, he began a systematic puncturing of the earth around it. It was a wearisome task, and, warned by his paralysis of the morning, he rose every now and then to stretch and watch for possible intruders.

Hours seemed to have passed, when the rod encountered something hard. Leaving it in position, he probed all around with another joint, but there was no resistance even when he doubled its length, and his sense of touch assured him this hardness was merely a casual stone.

Doggedly he resumed his task until the steel jammed again with a contact less harsh and unyielding. Once more he left the rod touching the buried mass, and probed about, still meeting an obstruction. And then with widening aim he stabbed and stabbed, striking this new thing until he had roughly mapped a space some twelve by eight inches.

No stone was this, he felt assured; the margins were too abrupt, the corners too sharp, for aught but a chest. He rose exultingly. Here beneath his feet were the silkworms of Florence. The secret was his alone. But it was growing late; the afternoon had almost merged into evening, and far away across the field stretched his shadow.

Leaving the sounding-rod buried with the cord attached, he walked toward a hurdle on the river bank, paying out the cord as he went, and hunted for a large stone. This found, he tied a knot in the cord to mark where the hurdle stood, and following it back along the grass pulled up the rod and pressed the stone upon the loosened earth in its place. Last of all, he wound the cord upon the rod. His task would be an easy one again. All he need do was to find the knot, tie the cord at that point to the hurdle, start off with the rod in hand, and when all the cord had run off search for the stone to right or left of the spot he would find himself standing on it.

As he re-entered the town groups of people were returning from the regatta—the sea-faring to end the day in the abounding taverns, the staider on their way to the open-air concert, the cinematograph, and the fireworks, which were to brim the cup of their dissipation.

Pringle dined early, and then made his way to the concert-field, and spent a couple of hours in studying the natured history of the Ryer. The fireworks were announced for nine, and as the hour approached the excitement grew and the audience swelled. When a fairly accurate census of Rye might have been taken in the field, Pringle edged through the crowd and hurried along the deserted streets to the studio.

To change his golf-suit for the sea-clothing he had brought from town was the work of a very few minutes, and the port-wine mark never resisted the smart application of a little spirit. Then, packing the sounding-rod and cord in the cricketing hag, along with the spade, pick, and rope, he locked the door, and stepped briskly out along the solitary road.

From the little taverns clinging to the rock opposite came roars of discordant song, for while the losers in the regatta sought consolation, the winners paid the score, and all grew steadily drunk together.

He lingered a moment on the sluice to watch the tide as it poured impetuously up from the lower river. A rocket whizzed, and as it burst high over the town a roar of delight was faintly borne across the marsh.

Although the night was cloudy and the moon was only revealed at long intervals, Pringle, with body bent, crept cautiously from bush to bush along the bank; his progress was slow, and the hurdle had been long in sight before he made out a black mass in the water below. At first he took it for the shadow of a bush that stood by, but as he came nearer it took the unwelcome shape of a boat with its painter fast to the hurdle; and throwing himself flat in the grass he writhed into the opportune shade of the bush.

It was several minutes before he ventured to raise his head and peer around, but the night was far too dark for him to see many yards in any direction—least of all towards the treasure. As he watched and waited he strove to imagine some reasonable explanation for the boat's appearance on the scene. At another part of the river he would have taken slight notice of it; but it was hard to see what anyone could want in the field at that hour, and the spot chosen for landing was suggestive.

What folly to have located the treasure so carefully! He must have been watched that afternoon; round the field were scores of places where a spy might conceal himself. Then, too, who could have taken such deep interest in his movements? Who but Mr. Hardgiblet, indeed? This set him wondering how many had landed from the boat; but a glance showed that it carried only a single pair of sculls, and when he wriggled nearer he saw but three footprints upon the mud, as of one who had taken just so many steps across it.

The suspense was becoming intolerable. A crawl of fifty yards or so over damp grass was not to be lightly undertaken; but he was just on the point of coming out from the shadow of the bush, when a faint rhythmic sound arose, to be followed by a thud. He held his breath, but could hear nothing more. He counted up to a hundred— still silence. He rose to his knees, when the sound began again, and now it was louder. It ceased; again there was the thud, and then another interval of silence. Once more; it seemed quite close, grew louder, louder still, and resolved itself into the laboured breathing of a man who now came into view.

He was bending under a burden which he suddenly dropped, as if exhausted, and then, after resting awhile, slowly raised it to his shoulders and panted onwards, until, staggering beneath his load, he lurched against the hurdle, his foot slipped, and he rolled with a crash down the muddy bank. In that moment, Pringle recognised the more than usually unctuous figure of Mr.

Hardgiblet, who embraced a small oblong chest. Spluttering and fuming, the rector scrambled to his feet, and after an unsuccessful hoist or two, dragged the chest into the boat. Then, taking a pause for breath, he climbed the bank again and tramped across the field.

Mr. Hardgiblet was scarcely beyond earshot when Pringle, seizing his bag, jumped down to the water-side. He untied the painter, and shoving off with his foot, scrambled into the boat as it slid out on the river.

With a paddle of his hand alongside, he turned the head up stream, and then dropped his bag with all its contents overboard and crouched along the bottom.

A sharp cry rang out behind, and, gently he peeped over the gunwale. There by the hurdle stood Mr. Hardgiblet, staring thunderstruck at the vacancy. The next moment he caught sight of the strayed boat, and started to run after it; and as he ran with many a trip and stumble of wearied limbs, he gasped expressions which were not those of resignation to his mishap.

Meantime, Pringle, his face within a few inches of the little chest, sought for some means of escape. He had calculated on the current bearing him out of sight long before the rector could return, but such activity as this discounted all his plans. All at once he lost the sounds of pursuit, and raising his head, he saw that Mr. Hardgiblet had been forced to make a detour around a little plantation which grew to the water's edge.

At the next sound, Pringle seized the sculls, and with a couple of long rapid strokes grounded the boat beneath a bush on the opposite bank. There he tumbled the chest on to the mud, and jumping after it shoved the boat off again. As it floated free and resumed its course up stream, Pringle shouldered the chest, climbed up the bank, and keeping in the shade of a hedge, plodded heavily across the field.

Day was dawning as Pringle extinguished the lamp in his studio, and setting the shutters ajar allowed the light to fall upon the splinters, bristling like a cactus-hedge, of what had been an oaken chest. The wood had proved hard as the iron which clamped and bound it, but scarcely darker or more begrimed than the heap of metal discs it had just disgorged. A few of these, fresh from a bath of weak acid, glowed golden as the sunlight, displaying indifferently a bust with "Bonaparte Premier Consul" surrounding it, or on the reverse "Republique Française, anno XI, 20 francs."

Such were the silkworms of Florence.

THE BOX OF SPECIE

"Now then, sir, if you're coming!"

Mr. Pringle, carrying a brown gladstone, was the last to cross the gangway before it was hauled back on to the landing-stage. The steam ceased to roar from the escape pipes, impatiently tingled the bells in the engine-room; then, pulsating to the rhythmic thud of her screws, the liner swung from the quay and silently picked her way down the crowded Pool. As reach succeeded reach the broadening stream opened a clearer course, and the *Mary Bland* moved to the full sweep of the ebbing tide; a whitened path began to lengthen in her wake, for nearing Tilbury the Thames becomes a clean and wholesome stream, and its foam is not as that of porter.

The day had been wet and gusty, and although, when he stepped aboard, the declining sun shown brightly, there was a touch of autumn rawness in the air which induced Pringle to seek a sheltered corner. Such he found by the break of the poop, and here he sat and watched the stowing of the cargo, the last arrival of which encumbered the after-deck.

By the time Tilbury was in sight all had been sent down the after-hatch but three small cases which the mate and purser, who stood superintending operations, appeared to view with a jealous eye. They were clamped with iron, of small size (about fourteen inches long by seven wide and four deep), and Pringle, even from where he sat, could read the direction in bold, black letters on the nearest:

157

THE MANAGER

Ivory and Produce Company
Cameroons

These were obviously for transshipment, since the *Mary Bland's* route was but London to Rotterdam. It was to Rotterdam that Pringle was bound. The journey was not undertaken for pleasure; he was *en route* for Amsterdam on business of peculiar interest, and not unconnected with precious stones, Amsterdam, as everybody knows, being the headquarters of the diamond-cutting industry. But this by the way.

The men were about attaching the chain-tackle to the nearest of the three boxes when the captain came half-way down from the bridge.

"Haven't you got that specie stowed, Mr. Trimble? It'll be dark presently." He addressed the mate with just a little anxiety in the tone.

"All right, sir," interposed the purser. "We just wanted to get the deck clear before I opened the strong-room."

"Go ahead, then," and the captain returned to the bridge.

The purser disappeared below, and presently came his voice from the after-hatch: "Lower away, there!"

With much clanking and rattling of the chain, a case swung for a moment over the gulf, and then disappeared. A second followed, and a third was about to join them, when a voice from somewhere forward called:

"Steamer on the starboard bow!"

As the sun went down a grey mist, rising from the Cliffe marshes, had first blotted out the banks and then steamed across the fairway, which but a few minutes before had shown a clear course through the reach. It was quite local, and a big ocean tramp, coming slowly up stream, was just emerging from the obscurity as the *Mary Bland* encountered it.

"Hard a-starboard!" roared the captain, as he gave a sharp tug at the whistle lanyard. The man at the wheel spun it till the brasswork on the spokes seemed an endless golden ring. "Bang, clank!

bang, clank!" went the steam steering-gear with a jarring tremor on deck, answered by the furious din of the engine-room telegraph as the captain jammed the indicator at "full speed astern." And on came the tramp, showing bulkier through the mist.

"All hands forward with fenders!" and the men by the after-hatch scurried forward, the mate at their head. Slowly the vessels approached amid a whirr of bells and frantically shouted orders, their whistles hooting the regulation blasts. Suddenly, as but a few yards intervened, they obeyed their helms and slowly paid off, almost scraping one another's sides as they slid by, while at half-speed the *Mary Bland* plunged into the fog, her syren continuing the concert begun by the now silent tramp.

All at once there was a loud shout from the water, and a chocolate-coloured topsail, with a little dogvane above it, rose on the port-bow. Once more the captain's hand wrenched the telegraph to "full speed astern," but it was too late. There was a concussion, plainly felt allover the steamer, a grinding and a splintering noise, and the topsail with its little weathercock dogvane had disappeared. The after-coming crowd rushed back again to find the *Mary Bland* drifting with the tide through an archipelago of hay-trusses.

"Where in thunder are yer comin' to?" sounded in plaintive protest from the nearest truss. "Ain't there room enough roun' Coal-'ouse point for the likes of you?"

"What have we run down, Mr. Trimble?" demanded the captain, his hands quivering on the bridge rail in a spasm of suppressed excitement.

"I think it's a hay-barge, sir. It looks like a man floating on a truss over there on the port-beam," said the mate, pointing in the direction of the voice.

"Get a boat out then, lively, and pick him up! And send that look-out man to me—I want to speak to him."

The men were already handling the falls, and, as the hapless look-out man slouched aft, the first officer, jumping into the boat with four sailors, was lowered to the water, and rowed towards the survivor of the barge.

All this time Pringle had remained near the after-hatch. When the collision seemed imminent he was about to follow the general movement to the centre of interest, when a light suddenly flashed on the port side, and, even as he gazed in wonder, ceased as abruptly as it rose. He stopped and looked about him; the gathering gloom of the evening seemed deeper after the momentary light, everyone was forward, the deck quite deserted, and the box of specie for the time ignored. Not altogether, though. A sailor was coming aft, detailed, no doubt, to watch the treasure where it lay.

Noting how stealthily he approached, Pringle drew back into his corner and watched him. The man walked on tiptoe, with every now and then a backward glance; and, for all the dimness of the fog and the oncoming night, he stalked along, taking advantage of every slightest shadow. Clearly he imagined that everyone was forward; he never gave a glance in Pringle's direction, but moved "the beard on the shoulder." On he stole till he reached the deserted box, and there he stopped and crouched down. Faint echoes were heard from forward, but not a soul came anywhere near the after-hatch. The captain was, of course, on the bridge; but, having relieved his feelings at the expense of the look-out man, was now absorbed in trying to follow the progress of the mate among the hay trusses.

Presently the light shot up again, and now a little closer. As it flickered and oscillated, Pringle saw that it came from a slender cylindrical lamp, supported by a sort of conical iron cage topping a large, black coloured buoy, which floated some twenty feet off from the *Mary Bland*. The sight appeared to nerve the sailor to action; it seemed, indeed, as if he had waited for the buoy to reveal itself.

Dragging the box aside as gently as its weight allowed, he seized the chain placed ready for the tackle-hook, and tried to raise it. Again and again he made the attempt, but the weight seemed beyond his single strength. In the midst the light flared out once more; it was just opposite the ship, and as the buoy slowly dipped and turned, with a curtsey to this side and to that, the word "OVENS," in large white capitals, showed upon it before the light went out and all was dark again.

With a wrench and a groan, the man tilted the box on end; then, bracing himself, he raised it first to a bollard, and with a final and desperate heave to the gunwale. And then a curious thing happened. When presently the light shone the chest had disappeared, but, as if tracing its descent, the man hung over the side, his feet slipping and squirming to get a purchase, and as the light passed the sound of his struggling continued in the darkness.

At the next flash he was gone—all but a hand, which still gripped the gunwale, while his feet could be heard drumming furiously against the vessel's side; and now, as his fingers slipped from their agonising hold, he gave a shriek for help, and then another and another.

Pringle darted across the deck, but the unfortunate wretch was beyond help; his hand wedged fast in the chain, he had been dragged overboard by the momentum of nearly a hundred weight of specie. And as he plunged headlong into the river the beacon shimmered upon a fountain of spray, a few jets even breaking in cascade against the sides of the buoy.

The cries of the drowning man had passed unnoticed. The boat had reached the barge just as the truss began to break up in the swirl; the passengers were cheering lustily, and Pringle walked quietly forward and mingled unperceived with the crowd. While rescued and rescuers climbed on board, the captain telegraphed "full speed ahead," and the *Mary Bland* resumed her voyage, so prolific of incident.

A group of passengers were discussing the proper course to have pursued had the collision with the tramp steamer actually occurred. A burly man with a catarrhal Teutonic accent maintained that the only sensible thing to do would have been to scramble on board the colliding ship. "At the worst," said he, "she would only have had two or three of her fore compartments stove in, whilst we stood to have a hole punched in our side big enough for an omnibus to drive through. We should have sunk inside of ten minutes, whilst they would have floated—well, long enough to have got us comfortably ashore."

In this discussion Pringle innocently joined, with an eye on the captain, who paced the bridge in ignorance of the new anxiety in store for him. Meanwhile, the purser had remained at his post in the strong-room. He awaited the further storage of the specie; but, although he could hear the men returning to the hatchway, not a shadow of the box appeared. At length he cried impatiently:

"Lower away, there—oh, lower away!"

"There ain't no more up 'ere, sir," said one of the men, as he put his head over the coaming.

"*No more!*" repeated the purser in hollow tones from the depths. "Send down that third box of specie—the money, I mean. Ah, you jackass! Don't stand grinning there! Where's the box you were going to send down when that cursed hooker nearly ran into us? Where's Mr. Trimble?"

"'E's with the captain, sir. Ain't the box down there? Didn't we send it down atop of the other two 'fore we went forward?"

Bang! went the strong-room door as the purser, without further discussion, rushed up on deck.

"Where's that third box of specie, Mr. Trimble?"

The captain and the mate stared down at him from the bridge without answering.

"These idiots think they sent it down; but I've only received two, and it's nowhere about the deck."

The captain gasped and turned pale. "When did you last see it?" he asked the mate.

"Just before we got into the fog."

The captain suppressed an oath.

"Go down with the purser, Mr. Trimble, and see if it's fallen down the hatch."

Twenty minutes saw the mate return, hot and perspiring.

"Can't see a bit of it, sir," he reported; "and, what's more, Cogle seems to have disappeared as well!"

"Cogle?"

"Yes, sir. He was working the crane, but no one has seen him since. He can't have jumped overboard with the specie."

"Rot! Why, that box held five thousand sovereigns according to the manifest, and couldn't weigh an ounce less than three-quarters of a hundredweight altogether! You can't put a thing like that in your pocket, can you?"

The mate glanced doubtfully at the passengers on the saloon-deck, but none showed such a bulging of the person as might be expected from a concealed box of specie.

"How would it be to put back to Gravesend and inform the police?" he suggested. "Cogle must have tumbled overboard in the ruction."

"It's no good putting back," the captain decided gloomily. "That specie was delivered right enough, and I'm responsible for it. It can't have fallen overboard, so it's on the ship somewhere—that I'll swear. Can't you suggest anything?" he added testily, as the mate continued to cast a suspicious eye on all around.

"Why not search the passengers' luggage?"

"Search your grandmother!" returned the captain contemptuously. "How can I do that? Hold on, though—I'll send you ashore as soon as we get to Rotterdam, and we'll ask the police to stand by while the Customs fellows search the luggage. Not a mother's son leaves this ship except the passengers; and as to the cargo, our agent'll see after that." And he went below to "log down" the events of the day whilst they were fresh in his memory.

The one person who could have thrown any light on the mystery remained silent. Pringle had resolved to be the dead man's legatee. It would be a large order, no doubt, to fish the chest up again, but the light marked a shoal thereabouts, and the depth was unlikely to be great; and, thinking the affair over, Pringle had little doubt that it was the sight of the buoy, a fixed watermark, which had determined the man to jettison the specie where he did.

As soon as he got back to London again, Pringle devoted some time to a careful study of Pearson's *Nautical Almanac*. From this useful publication he learnt that at the time the *Mary Bland* was on her exciting course down the river it was the first of the ebb-tide—that is to say, about three-quarters of an hour after high-water. Now, inasmuch as a buoy is moored by a considerable length of chain, it is able to drift about within a circle of many feet; hence Pringle, to ensure success in his search, must choose a state of the tide identical with that prevailing when the box disappeared. At the same time, he proposed, for obvious reasons, to work at night, and preferably a moonless one.

At length he found that all these conditions were present about seven in the evening of the tenth day after his return.

Pringle, among his varied accomplishments, could handle a boat with most yachtsmen; and, leaving his chambers in Furnival's Inn for a season, he took up his residence at Erith. Here, attired in yachting costume, he spent depressing hours among the forlorn and aged craft at disposal, until, lighting on a boat suited to his purpose, he promptly hired it.

It was some eighteen feet long, half-decked, and carried standing lug and mizzen sails; but its chief attraction to Pringle was the presence of a small cabin in the fore-peak, and to the door, as soon as he had taken possession, he fitted a hasp and staple, and secured it with a Yale padlock. His next thought was of the dredging tackle, and this he collected in the course of several trips to London. In the end, when the day of his enterprise dawned, two fathoms of chain, with half a dozen grapnels made fast to it, together with a twelve-fathom rope and a spare block, were all stowed safely in the fore-peak.

"Nice day for a sail, sir," remarked the boat-keeper, as Pringle walked along the landing-stage soon after two o'clock in the afternoon.

"Yes; I want to take advantage of this north-west wind." And, getting into the boat, he was rowed towards the wooden railway-pier, off which his boat lay.

"Well, I didn't think you were a gent to take advantage of any-one," chuckled the man. He had a green memory of certain judicious tips on Pringle's part, and he spoke with an eye to other lay-outs of a like kind. Pringle smiled obligingly at the witticism, and made a further exhibition of palm-oil as they reached the yacht. Scrambling aboard he cast loose, and, hoisting the mizzen, paddled out into the stream and set the mainsail.

The tide was running strong against him, but the wind blew fairly fresh from the north-west and helped him on a steady course down the river. The sail bellied and drew, while the intermittent cheep-cheep from the sheet-block was answered by the continuous musical tinkle under the forefoot.

By six o'clock Pringle had got out of the narrower reaches, and it was nearly dark as he passed Tilbury. A slight mist began to steal across from the marshes, but, with a natural desire to avoid observation, he showed no light. His course was now easier, for the tide began to turn; but although he kept an intent watch for the buoy it perversely hid itself. He was just about to tack and run up stream again, concluding that he must have passed the spot, when suddenly the occulting light glimmered through the mist on his port-beam. Shooting up into the wind, he headed straight for the buoy, and as his bow almost touched it the light blazed clearly.

On the way down he had rigged up the spare block on the bumpkin about a foot beyond the stern, and through it rove his twelve-fathom rope, securing it by a turn round a cleat, the two-fathom chain with the grapnels fast on the other end. And now his real work began. He heaved the chain and grapnels overboard and began to tack to and fro and up and down upon the course he judged the *Mary Bland* had taken as she passed the buoy.

The night was chilly, and Pringle was proportionately ravenous of the cold-meat sandwiches he had stuffed into his pockets on starting—he knew better than to reduce his temperature by the illusory glow of alcohol.

It was very monotonous, this drifting with the stream and then tacking up against it, his cruising centred by the winking light: and every now and then he would shift his ground a few feet to port of starboard as the grapnel fruitlessly swept the muddy bottom.

Presently, while drifting down stream, the boat lost way, and looking over the stern he saw the rope taut as steel-wire. The grapnel had caught, and in some excitement he hauled on the rope. As the hooks came in sight he saw by the intermittent flare that they were indeed fast to a chain—not the crossed chain round the specie-box, but a sequence of ten-inch stud-links, green, encrusted with acorn barnacles, and with a significant crack or two—in short, a derelict cable.

Taking a turn of rope round the cleat, he hauled the links close up to the stern, and freeing them at the cost of a couple of grapnel-teeth, the cable with a sullen chunk dropped back to its long repose on the river-bed. But valuable time had been lost; he must avoid this spot in the future. Drifting some way off, once more he flung the grapnel overboard, and then resumed his weary cruise.

Time sped, and at least two hours had passed before the boat was brought up with a jerk—the grapnel had caught this time with a vengeance. At first he hauled deliberately, then with all his power, and as the grapnel held he tugged and strained until the sweat rained pit-a-pat from his brow. This, he thought, could be no cable—an anchor perhaps? He took breath, then threw all his weight upon the rope, but not an inch did he gain. He was almost tempted to cut the rope and leave the grappling-iron fixed, when all at once he felt it give a little, and slowly came the rope inboard—inch by inch, hand over hand.

Already was he peering for the first glimpse of the chain, when right out from the water grew a thing so startling, so unlooked for, that at the sight the rope slipped through his fingers, and it vanished. But the shock was only momentary. His was a philosophical mind, and before many feet had run overboard he was again hauling lustily.

Again the thing jerked up—to some no doubt a terrifying spectacle; it was a boot, still covering a human foot, and lower down a second showed dimly. Coarse and roughly made, they were the trade-marks of a worker, and Pringle asked no sight of the slimy canvas, shredded and rotten, which clung to the limbs below, to be assured that here was the victim of the tragedy whose sole witness he had been. His arms trembled with the immense strain he was putting on them, and, rousing himself, he hauled with might and main to end the task.

Presently, a shapeless, bloated thing floated alongside; and then a box, securely hooked by its crossed-chains, showed clear, the sodden mass floated out to its full length, and as the rope jerked of a sudden it broke loose and floated off upon the tide. Unprepared for so abrupt a lightening of the weight, Pringle slipped and fell in the boat, and the box sank with a noisy rattle of the chain across the gunwale.

In a moment he was on his feet, and, cheered by the prospect of victory, his fatigue vanished. Very soon was the chest at the surface again; then, by a mighty effort and nearly swamping the boat, he dragged it into the stern-sheets. It was a grisly relic he found within the cross-chains. Gripped hard, the arm had dislocated in the awful wrench of the accident; then later, half severed by an agency of which Pringle did not care to think, the work had finally been accomplished by the force which he had just used.

Looking away, he drew his knife, and, hacking the fingers from their death-grasp, sent the repulsive object to the depths from which he had raised it. Exhausted and breathless as he was, with characteristic caution, Pringle unshipped the block, and cutting the grapnel-chain from the rope dropped it over the side. He had just stowed the box at his feet, when a sudden concussion nearly flung him to the bottom of the boat.

"Hulloa, there, in the boat!" hailed a peremptory voice. "Why don't you show a light?"

Peeping round the lug-sail, Pringle beheld a sight the most unwelcome he could have imagined—a Board of Trade boat, with three men in it, had nearly run him down.

"I've been fishing, and lost my tackle. The night came up before I could beat up against the tide."

"Where have you come from?" inquired the steersman, an officer in charge of the boat.

"From Erith, this afternoon."

"Fishing for tobacco, likely," the other remarked grimly. "Throw us your painter. You must come with us to Gravesend, anyhow."

Pringle went forward and threw them the painter, and stepping back made as if to strike the lug-sail, when the officer interposed.

"Hold on there!" he exclaimed. "Keep your sail up—it'll help us against the tide."

Pringle, nothing loth, sat down behind the sail. The officer had not yet seen the box, and for the present the sail helped to conceal it. The address-letters and shipping marks were still legible on the case, and any way it was impossible for him to account for its possession legitimately. It was about nine; they would soon be at Gravesend, and once there discovery was inevitable. How on earth was he to escape from this unpleasant situation? Should he sink the box again? But the night was dark, and looking round he could see no friendly buoy or other mark by which to fix the spot in his memory.

Right ahead of them a steamer was coming down with the tide, and the officer edged away towards a large barge at anchor. Nearing her, Pringle noticed she had a dinghy streaming astern, and as they plunged into the deeper gloom she cast he had a sudden inspiration.

Catching the dinghy's painter with his boat-hook, he hauled her alongside, cut the painter, and gradually drawing it in secured it to the cleat in his stern. At once the rowers felt the extra load, and the officer hailed him to trim his sheet. Swiftly making his rope fast to the box-chain, he rove the other end through the ring in the dinghy's bow and knotted it tightly; then, with every muscle taut, scarce daring to breathe in fear of a betraying stertor, he dragged the box over the stern and let the rope run out. With the box depending from her bow, the dinghy sagged along with more than half her keel out of water, and the rowers were audibly cursing the dead weight they had to pull.

"Keep her up there, will you? I'd better come aboard and teach you how to sail!" growled the officer over his shoulder.

Pringle hauled the dinghy close up, cast off her painter, and deftly clambered over her bows, which for an agonising moment were nearly awash.

"Is that better?" he shouted. And the two boats so quickly shot away from him that he barely caught the cheery answer as, freed from the incubus of dinghy, man, and specie, the escort rowed on to Gravesend.

The tide fast lengthened the space between, and Pringle drifted back until the light of the patrol-boat was lost among those ashore; then, with his slight strength, he hauled upon the rope and tumbled the box into the dinghy.

Thud-thud! thud-thud! thud-thud!

A steamer was approaching, and looking round he saw the mast-head lights of a tug with a vessel in tow. Handling the dinghy's sculls, he paddled to one side and waited. On came the tug; at the end of a long warp there followed a three-masted schooner, with an empty boat towing astern of her. As soon as the ship came level with him he pulled diagonally across, and as the boat glided by, seized her with his hand, and for a while the craft ground and rubbed against each other in the swell as he held them side by side.

But the precaution was heedless; the crew of the homeward-bound were too busy looking ahead to notice anything astern.

Going forward and fishing up the painter from the dinghy's bows, he crept back with it, clawing along the boat's gunwale each way, and rove it through the boat's stern-ring. As he made fast, the dinghy swung round to her place in the rear of the procession; and, settling down aft beside the precious box, Pringle was towed upstream.

Gravesend was soon astern, and for the present he felt no fear of the patrol. Whether did they credit him with the feat of swimming off with some contraband object, or with merely falling overboard, they would never have suspected his presence in the dinghy that trailed behind the three-master's boat.

The voyage seemed endless, and as hour lengthened into hour he killed some time by scraping the address and stencil marks from the box. At first he thought they were bound for the Pool; but when the tug began to slow up, about two o'clock, he found they were off the Foreign Cattle Market at Deptford. The tide was now running slack, and, casting off from the boat, he rowed under the stern of a lighter at the end of a double column, all empty, judging by their height above the water; and, throwing his rope round one of the stays of her sternpost, he lay down in the dinghy to rest.

Soon, wearied with his long night's labour and soothed by the ripple of the tide, as turning and running more strongly it eddied round the lighter, he dropped into an uneasy doze. A puffing and slapping noise mingled with his slumbers, and then, as three o'clock struck loudly from the market, he awoke with a start.

At once he had a drowsy sense of movement; but, regarding it as a mere effect of the tide, he tried to settle some plan for the future. Any attempt to go ashore with the box at Deptford he knew would render him suspect of smuggling, and would land him once for all in the hands of the police. Safety, then, lay up the river, and the higher the better. He was thinking of sculling out into the stream and of running up with the tide, even at the risk of being challenged by another patrol, when it suddenly struck him that the shadowy buildings on either bank were receding. He stared harder, and took a bearing between a mast and a chimney-stack, and watched them close up and then part again. There was no doubt of it—he was moving! Presently they shot under a wide span, and dimly recognising the castellated mass of the Tower Bridge he knew that fortune was playing his game for him—or, as he might perhaps have read in manuscript, had his literary agency possessed any reality, "the stars in their courses were fighting for him."

The wind had died away and the night had grown warmer, but although he could have slept fairly in the boat—indeed, would have given worlds to do so—he dared not give way to the temptation. The lighters were bound he knew not whither; he must keep awake to cast off the moment they stopped. To fight his drowsiness he turned to the box again, and spent a little time in furbishing the surface, and finally, detaching the now useless chain, he dropped it overboard.

Gradually, as bridge succeeded bridge, the sky lightened, and as glow behind told the speedy dawn. Up came the sun, while the train of lighters dived beneath a grey stone bridge, and on the left a tall verandahed tower, springing from out a small forest, coruscated in warm red and gold. Pringle started up with a shiver, exclaiming, as the gorgeous sight pictured the idea:

Wake! for the sun, who scattered into flight
The stars before him from the field of night,
Drives night along with them from heaven, and
    strikes
The Sultan's Turret with a shaft of light!

Beside the tower a huge dome blazed like a gigantic arc-lamp, and shading his eyes from the glare Pringle made out the familiar lines of the palm house at Kew. This was high enough for his purpose; and while the flotilla, in the wake of a little fussy, bluff-bowed tug, sped onward, he cast off from the barge and sculled leisurely up stream.

The exercise warmed him after his long spell of frigid inaction; he turned towards the Surrey bank, and skirting the grounds of the Observatory, ran ashore just beyond the railway-bridge. A ragged object, asleep on the towing-path woke up as the boat grounded, and mechanically scratched itself.

"Mind the boat for yer, guv'nor?"

He looked like a tramp. From his obviously impecunious condition he was not likely to be overburdened with scruples.

"Yes; but find me a cab first, and bring it as near as you can."

As the man, scenting a tip, rose with alacrity, Pringle tumbled the box on to the shingle. It now showed little trace of its adventures, was already dry upon the surface, and, clear of the markings, bore an innocent resemblance to a box of ship's cocoa.

It was nearing seven when the emissary returned.

"Keb waitin' for yer up the road by the corner there," he reported.

"Give us a hand with this box, then," said Pringle. "It's quartz, and rather heavy."

"Why, but it's that!" ejaculated the man as he lifted one end with an unwonted expenditure of muscular force.

"Now, look here," said Pringle impressively, as they reached the cab. "I shall be back about noon, and I want you to look after the boat for me till then. That will be five hours—suppose we say at two shillings each?"

The tramp's eyes glistened, and he touched his cap-peak.

"Well, here's half a sovereign." Pringle shrewdly discounted the unlikelihood of the man's rendering any part of the service for which he was being paid in advance.

"Right yer are, guv'nor," agreed the tramp cheerfully, and slipped towards the river-bank.

The cab, with Pringle and the box inside, had scarcely disappeared round the corner when the tramp made off at a tangent toward Kew, and was seen no more. As to the boat, with a dip and a rock as the tide rose, it floated off into the stream, and resumed its travels in the opposite direction.

THE SILVER INGOTS

The morning was raw, the sun, when it deigned to shine, feeling chill and distant. There was no wind, and as they threaded the curves of the river the occasional funnels wrote persistent sooty lines upon the grey clouds. The park, with its avenues mere damp vistas of naked and grimy boughs, was deserted even by the sparrows, no longer finding a precarious meal at the hands of the children as yet only playing in their slums.

There is little pleasure in cycling towards the end of February, and, preferring walking to the perils of side-slip in the mud, Mr. Pringle had walked from Furnival's Inn by way of the Embankment and Grosvenor Road and now sat smoking on the terrace in front of Battersea Park.

There was a new moon, and the rubbish borne during the night on the spring tide from down stream was returning on the ebb to the lower reaches from which it had been ravished. As Mr. Pringle smoked and gazed absently at the river, now nearly at its lowest, a large "sou'-wester" caught his eye; it swam gravely with the stream, giving an occasional pirouette as it swirled every now and then into an eddy.

As it floated opposite him he caught a glimpse of some white thing below it—the whole mass seemed to quiver, as if struggling and fighting for life. Could it be a drowning man? Just there the river was solitary; not a soul was visible to help. Vaulting lightly over the low railings, Pringle sprang from the Embankment on to a bed of comparatively clean shingle, which here replaced the odorous

173

mud-level, and reached the water side just as the "sou'wester," in a more violent gyration, displayed in its grasp a woolen comforter.

Amused and a trifle vexed at his own credulity, Pringle turned, and, walking a yard or two along the beach, tripped and fell as his toe caught in something. Scrambling to his feet, he discovered a loop of half-inch manilla rope, the colour of which told of no long stay there. He gave it a gentle pull, without moving it in the slightest. A harder tug gave no better result; and, his curiosity now thoroughly aroused, he seized it with both hands, and, with his heels dug into the shingle, dragged out of the water just a plaited carpenter's tool-basket.

The rope, in length about six feet, was rove through the handles as if for carrying over the shoulder. Surprised at its weightiness, he peeped inside. They were odd-looking things he found—no mallets or chisels, planes or turnscrews, only half a dozen dirty-looking bricks.

Wondering more and more, he picked one up and examined it carefully. Towards the end was faint suggestion as it were of a scallop-shell, and, turning it over, he detected another and more perfect impression of the same with a crest and monogram, the whole enclosed within an oblong ornamental border, which a closer scrutiny revealed as the handle of a spoon. On another brick he identified a projection as the partially fused end of a candlestick; and, when he scraped off some of the dirt with his knife, the unmistakable lustre of silver met his gaze. All six ingots were of very irregular outline, as if cast in a clumsy or imperfect mold.

A cold sensation about the feet made him look down. Unnoticed by him, the tide had turned and he now stood to the ankles in water. For a moment longer he continued to crouch, while sending a cautious glance about him. In the quarter of an hour or less he had spent by the waterside only a single lighter had passed, and the man in charge had been too much occupied in making the most of the tide to spare any attention ashore. The terrace behind him was quite deserted, and he was sheltered from any observation from the bridge by a projection of the Embankment, which made of the patch of shingle a miniature bay. As to the little steamboat pier, to the naked eye his movements were as indistinguishable from that as from the opposite side of the river. His privacy was complete.

Straightening up, he turned his back on the water and directly faced the terrace. Right in front of him he could see a sycamore standing in the park, and, carefully noting its appearance, he scrambled up the ten feet or so of embankment wall, which at that point was much eroded and gave an easy foothold.

Once on the terrace, he walked briskly up and down to warm his frozen feet, and as he walked he tried to reason out the meaning of his discovery. Here was an innocent-looking carpenter's basket with half a dozen silver ingots of obviously illicit origin—for they had been clumsily made by the fusing together indiscriminately of various articles of plate.

Roughly estimating their weight at about eight pounds apiece, then their aggregate value was something over £100—not a large sum, perhaps, but no doubt representing the proceeds of more than one burglary. They must have been sunk below low-water mark, say, about a week ago, when they would have been covered at all states of the tide; now, with the onset of the spring tides, they would be exposed twice daily for an hour.

Could the owner have known of this fact? Probably not. Pringle hardly credited him with much skill or premeditation. Such a hiding-place rather pointed to a hasty concealment of compromising articles, and the chances were all against the spot having been noted.

On the whole, although it was a comparatively trifling find, Pringle decided it was worth annexing. Nothing could be done for the present, however. By this time the rising tide had concealed even the rope; besides, he could never walk out of the park with a carpenter's basket over his shoulder, even if he were to wait about until it had dried. No; he must return for it in clothing more suited to its possession.

As he walked back to Furnival's Inn, a clock striking half-past eleven suggested a new idea. By ten that night the basket would be again exposed, and it might be his last chance of securing it; the morning might see its discovery by someone else. The place was a public one, and although he had been singularly fortunate in its loneliness to-day, who could tell how many might be there to-morrow? This decided him.

About half-past ten that evening Pringle crossed the Albert Bridge to the south side, and turning short off to the left descended a flight of steps which led down to the water; the park gates had been long closed, and this was the only route available. His tall, lithe figure was clothed in a seedy, ill-fitting suit he reserved for such occasions; his tie was of a pattern unspeakable, his face and hands dirty; but although his boots were soiled and unpolished, they showed no further departure from their wonted, and even feminine, neatness. Since the morning his usually fair hair had turned black, and a small strip of whisker had grown upon his clean-shaven face, whilst the port-wine mark emblazoning his right cheek had disappeared altogether.

At the foot of the steps he waited until a nearing wagon had got well upon the bridge, and then, as its thunder drowned his footsteps, he tramped over the shelving beach, and rounding the projection of the embankment found himself in the little bay once more. With his back to the water, he sidled along until opposite the sycamore, and then, facing about, he went down on his hands and knees groping for the loop. Everything seemed as he had left it, and the basket, already loosened from its anchorage, came rattling up the pebbles as soon as he made a very moderate traction on the rope. What with the noise he made himself, slight though it was, and his absorption in the work, Pringle never heard a gentle step approaching by the path he had himself taken; but as he hastily arranged the ingots on the beach, and was about to hold the basket up to drain, his arm was gripped by a muscular hand.

"Fishing this time of night?" inquired a refined voice in singular contrast to the rough appearance of the speaker. Then, more sharply, "Come—get up! Let's have a look at you."

Pringle rose in obedience to the upward lift upon his arm, and as the two men faced each other the stranger started, exclaiming:

"So it's you, is it! I thought we should meet again some day."

"Meet again?" repeated Pringle stupidly, as for about the second or third time in his life his presence of mind deserted him.

"Don't say you've forgotten me at Wurzleford last summer! Let's see—what was your name? I ought to remember it, too—ah, yes, Courtley! Have you left the Church, Mr. Courtley? Seem rather down on your luck now. Why, Solomon in all his glory wasn't in it with you at Wurzleford? And you don't seem to need your glasses, either. Has your sight improved?"

Pringle remembered him before he had got half way through his string of sarcasms. He had not altered in the least, the shell might be rough, but the voice and manner of the gentleman-burglar were as Chesterfieldian as ever. Of all people in the world, he was the one whom Pringle would have least desired to see at that moment, and he prepared himself for a very bad quarter of an hour.

"It's lucky for you we haven't met before," continued the other. "If I could have got at you that night, it would have been your life or mine! Don't think I've forgiven you. I must say, though, you did it very neatly; it's something, I can tell you, to get the better of me. Why, I've never dared to breathe a word of it since; I should be a laughing-stock for the rest of my days. I, the 'Toff,' as they call me!

"But I can see a joke, even if it's against myself, and I've laughed several times since when I've thought of it. Fancy locking me in that room while you coolly walked off with the stuff that I'd been working for for months. And such stuff too! I think you'd have done better to act squarely with me. Those rubies don't seem to have done you much good. I never thought you'd do much with them at the time. It needs a man with capital to plant such stuff as that. But what's the game now? Who put you up to this?"

He had been taking short steps up and down the beach, half soliloquising as he walked, and now he broke off abruptly and fronted Pringle.

"No one." Pringle had now recovered his self-possession. They were alone; it was man to man, and anyhow, the "Toff" did not seem to be very vindictive.

"Then how did you know it was here? You're a smart fellow, I know; but I don't think you're quite smart enough to see to the bottom of the river."

"It was quite accidental," said Pringle frankly. "It was this way." And he sketched the doings of the morning.

"Upon my word," exclaimed the "Toff," "you and I seem fated to cross one another's paths. But I'll be kinder than you deserve. This stuff"—he kicked the ingots— "is the result of a 'wedge-hunt,' as we call it. Nervous chap, bringing it up the river, got an idea that he was being shadowed—dropped it from a steamer three days ago—wasn't certain of his bearings when he had done it. That comes of losing one's head. Now, if it hadn't been for you, I might never have found it, although it looks as if I was right in calculating the tides and so on. As you seem in rather hard case, I'll see you're not a loser over the night's work so long as you make yourself useful."

Pringle assented cheerfully; he was curious to see the end of it all. While the other was speaking he had decided to fall in with his humour. Indeed, unless he fled in cowardly retreat, there was nothing else to be done. The "Toff," as he knew, was wiry, but although in good form himself, Pringle's arm throbbed and tingled where it had been gripped. They were equally matched so far as strength went, unless the "Toff" still carried a revolver. Besides, the ingots were not worth disputing over. Had they been gold now—!

"Well, just lend a hand then." And, the "Toff" producing some cotton-waste, they commenced to pack the ingots back into the basket.

"Look here," the "Toff" continued as they worked; "why don't you join me? You want someone to advise you, I should say. Whatever your game was at Wurzleford, you don't seem to have made much at it, nor out of me, either—ah!"

The subject was evidently a sore one, and the "Toff's" face hardened and he clenched his hands at the memories it aroused.

"Yes," he went on, "you seem a man of some resource, and if only you'd join me, what with that and my experience—why, we'd make our pile and retire in a couple of years! And what a life it is! Talk of adventure and excitement and all that—what is there to equal it? Canting idiots talk of staking one's liberty. Liberty, indeed! Why, what higher stake can one play for?—except one's life, and I've done that before now. I've played for a whole week at Monte Carlo, and believe I broke the bank (I couldn't tell for certain—they don't let you know, and never close till eleven, in spite of all people think and talk to the contrary); I've played poker with some of the 'cutest American players; I've gambled on the Turf; I've gambled on the Stock Exchange; I've run Kanakas to Queensland; I've smuggled diamonds; I've hunted big game all over the world; I've helped to get a revolution in Ecuador, and nearly (ha! ha!) got myself made President; I've—hang it, what haven't I done?

"And I tell you there's nothing in all I've gone through to equal the excitement of the life I'm leading now. Then, too, we're educated men. I'm Rugby and John's, and that's where I score over most I have to work with; they sicken me with their dirty, boozy lives. They have a bit of luck, then they're drunk for a month, and have to start again without a penny, and the rats running all over them. Now, we two— Gentle! Don't take it by the handles. Wait a second. D'you hear anything?"

A cab trotted over the wooden-paved bridge, then silenced again. The "Toff" wound one end of the rope round and round his wrist, and motioned Pringle to do the same; then, with a sign to tread warily, he started to make the circuit of the promontory, the basket swaying between them as they kept step. Pringle, with an amused sense of the other's patronising airs, followed submissively behind him up the shelving beach. By the wooden steps the "Toff" paused.

"Under here," he directed; and they stuffed the basket under the bottom step.

"Now," he murmured in Pringle's ear, "you go up to the road, and if you see no one about walk a little way down, as if you'd come off the bridge, and stamp your feet like this." He stamped once or twice, as if to restore the circulation in his feet, but with a rhythmical cadence in the movement.

"Yes; what then?"

"There ought to be a trap waiting down the first turning on the opposite side of the road. If it doesn't come up, count twenty and stamp again."

"And then?"

"If nothing happens, come back and tell me."

When he stood at the top of the stairs Pringle felt much inclined, instead of turning to the left, to go the other way and cross the bridge, leaving the "Toff" to secure the ingots as best he could. Later on he had cause to regret that he had not done so; but for the moment love of adventure prevailed and, walking down the gradient from the bridge, he gave the signal. There was no one in sight, but the action was such a natural one on a damp and foggy night that had the street been ever so crowded it would have pass unnoticed.

Pringle counted twenty, and repeated the signal. By this time he had reached the corner, and looking down the side street, he distinctly saw the twin lights of a carriage advancing at a trot. He turned back and reached the stairs as a rubber-tyred miniature brougham pulled up beside him.

"Is it there?" whispered the "Toff" impatiently.

"There's a brougham stopping. I don't know—"

"Yes, yes; that's it. Lend a hand, now; we mustn't keep it waiting about."

Marvelling at the style in which the "Toff" appeared to work, Pringle helped to lug the basket up, and between them they bundled it into the carriage.

"Now," said the "Toff," fumbling in his waistcoat pocket, "what do you say about my proposal?"

"Well, really, I should like to think over it a little," replied Pringle evasively.

"Oh, I can't wait here all night while you're making up your mind. If you don't recognize a good thing when you see it, you're not the man for me. It's not everyone I should make the offer to."

"Then I think I had better say 'No.'"

"Please yourself, and sink a little lower than you are." The "Toff" appeared nettled at Pringle's refusal. He ceased to grope in his waistcoat, and drawing a leather purse from his trouser pocket, took something from it. "That's for your trouble," said he shortly; and the next minute was bowling swiftly over the bridge.

Pringle, who had mechanically extended his hand, found by the glimmer of a lamp that the "Toff" had appraised his services at the sum of seven shillings, and was moved to throw the coins into the river. As he hesitated over the fate of the florin and two half-crowns in his palm, a policeman approached and glanced suspiciously at him. His hand closed on the money, and he passed on to the bridge. He felt hot and grimy with his exertions; also his boots were damp, and the night wind began to grow chilly. Half way across he broke into a run, the elastic structure swaying perceptibly beneath his feet. Over on the other side the lights of a public-house pierced the mist, and he struck into the roadway towards it.

"Outside—on the right!" said a voice, as he opened the door of the saloon bar. For the time he had forgotten the shabbiness of his dress, enhanced as it was by the many things it had suffered in the course of the night's work, and with an unwonted diffidence he sought the public bar. There, with a steaming glass in hand, he stove to dry his boots at a gas-stove in one corner, but he still felt cold and miserable when, about half-past eleven, he rose to go.

"'Ere—what's this?" The barman had inserted the proffered coin in a *trier*, and giving it a deft jerk, now flung it, bent nearly double, across the counter.

"I beg your pardon," Pringle apologised, as he produced another. "I had no idea it was bad."

The barman threw the second coin upon the counter. It rang clearly, but doubled in the *trier* like so much putty.

"Bad!" chorused the onlookers.

"Fetch a constable, Ted!" was the solo of the landlord, who had come round from the other side of the bar.

For the second time that evening Pringle's nerve took flight. A horrible idea seized him—a crevasse seemed to open at his feet. Had the "Toff" played some treachery upon him? And as the door swung after the potman, he made a break for liberty. But the barman was quick as he, and with a cat-like spring over the counter, he held Pringle before he had got half across the threshold, several customers officiously aiding.

"I'm going to prosecute this man," announced the landlord; adding, for the benefit of the audience generally, "I've taken six bad half-crowns this week."

"Swine! Sarve 'im right! Oughter be shot!" were the virtuous comments on this statement.

As resistance was clearly useless Pringle submitted to his arrest, and was presently accompanied to the police-station by an escort of most of the loafers in the bar.

"What's your name?" asked the night inspector, as he took the charge.

Pringle hesitated. He realized that appearances were hopelessly against him. Attired as he was, to give his real name and address would only serve to increase suspicion, while a domiciliary visit to Furnival's Inn on the part of the police was to be avoided at all costs; the fiction of his literary agency as spurious as the coins which had landed him in his present plight, would be the very least discovery to reward them.

"Now, then, what is it?" demanded the inspector impatiently.

"Augustus Stammers," Pringle blurted, on the spur of the moment.

"Ah! I thought you were a stammerer," was the facetious remark of the publican.

The inspector frowned his disapproval. "Address?" he queried. Pringle again hesitated. "No fixed?" the inspector suggested.

"No fixed," agreed Pringle; and having replied to subsequent inquiries that his age was forty and his occupation a carpenter, he was ordered to turn out his pockets. Obediently he emptied his belongings on the desk, and as his money was displayed the landlord uttered a triumphant shout.

"There y'are!" he exclaimed, pouncing on a bright half-crown. "That makes three of 'em!"

This incriminatory evidence, together with a knife, being appropriated, Pringle was led away down some steps, through a courtyard, and then into a long white-washed passage flanked by doors on either side. Pushing one open, "In you go," said his conductor; and Pringle having walked in the door was shut and locked behind him.

Though lighted by a gas jet in the passage which shone through a small window above the door, the cell was rather dim, and it was some little while before his eyes, accustomed to the gloom, could properly take in his surroundings. It was a box of a place, about fourteen feet by six, with a kind of wooden bench fixed across the far end, and on this he sat down and somewhat despondently began to think.

It was impossible for Pringle to doubt that he was the victim of the "Toff's" machinations. He remembered how the latter's manner had changed when he positively refused the offer of partnership; how the "Toff" had ceased searching in his vest, and had drawn the purse from his trouser pocket. He supposed at the time that the "Toff," nettled at his refusal, had substituted silver for gold, and had thought it strange that he should keep his gold loose and his silver in a purse. It all stood out clear and lucid enough now. "Snide" money, as he knew, must always be treated with gentleness and care, and, lest it should lose the bloom of youth, some artists in the line are even accustomed to wrap each piece separately in tissue paper. The "Toff" evidently kept his "snide" in a purse, and, feeling piqued, had seized the opportunity of vindictively settling a score.

Pringle cursed his folly in not having foreseen such a possibility. What malicious fate was it that curbed his first impulse to sink the "Toff's" generosity in the river? With all his experience of the devious ways of his fellowmen, after all his fishing in troubled waters, to be tricked like this—to be caught like vermin in a trap! Well might the "Toff" sneer at him as an amateur! And most galling of all was the reflection that he was absolutely guiltless of any criminal intent. But it was useless to protest his innocence; a long term of imprisonment was the least he could expect. It was certainly the tightest place in which he had ever found himself.

Pringle was, fortunately, in no mood for sleep. He had soon received unmistakable evidence of the presence of the third of Pharaoh's plagues, and sought safety in constant motion. Besides, there were other obstacles to repose. From down the passage echoed the screams and occasional song of a drunken woman, as hysteria alternated with pleasurable ideas in her alcoholic brain; nearer, two men, who were apparently charged together, kept up an interchange of abuse from distant cells, each blaming the other for the miscarriage of their affairs; right opposite, the thunderous snoring of a drunken man filled the gaps when either the woman slumbered or the rhetoric of the disputants failed. Lastly, at regular intervals, a constable opened a trap in the cell doors to ascertain by personal observation and inquiry the continued existence of the inmates.

As time passed the cells overflowed, and every few minutes Pringle heard the tramp of feet and the renewed unlocking and sorting out as fresh guests were admitted to the hospitality of the State.

After a time the cell opposite was opened, and the voice of the snorer arose. He objected to a companion, as it seemed, and threatened unimaginable things were one forced upon him. He was too drunk to be reasoned with, so a moment after Pringle's door was flung open, and at the decision, "This un'll do," his solitude was at an end.

It was a dishevelled, dirty creature who entered; also his clothes were torn rawly as from a recent struggle. He slouched in with his hands in his pockets, and with a side glance at Pringle, flung himself down on the bench. Presently he expectorated as a preliminary to conversation, and with a jerk of the head towards the opposite cell, "I'd rawther doss wiv' im than wiv' a wet unbreller! What yer in for, guv'nor?"

"I'm charged with passing bad money," replied Pringle affably.

"Anyone wiv' yer?"

"No."

"'Ow many'd yer got on yer?"

"They found three."

A long whistle.

"That's all three stretch for yer! Why didn't yer work the pitch 'long o' someone else? Yer ought ter 'ave 'ad a pal outside to 'old the snide, while you goes in wiv' only one onyer, see?"

Pringle humbly acknowledged the error, and his companion, taking pity on his greenness in the lower walks of criminality, then proceeded to give him several hints, the following of which, he assured Pringle, would be "slap-up claws!"

Later on he grew confidential, told how his present "pinching" was due to "collerin' a red jerry from a ole reeler," and presently, pleading fatigue, he laid him down on the bench and was soon snoring enviably. But his slumbers were fitful, for, although but little inconvenienced by the smaller inhabitants of the cell, having acquired a habit of allowing for them without waking, he was periodically roused by the gaoler's inspection. On many of these occasions he would sit up and regale Pringle for a time with such further scraps of autobiography as he appeared to pride himself on—always excepting his present misfortune, which, after his preliminary burst of confidence, he seemed anxious to ignore as a discreditable incident, being "pinched over a reeler." In this entertaining manner they passed the night until eight o'clock, when Pringle authorized the expenditure of some of his capital on a breakfast of eggs and bacon and muddy coffee from "outside," his less affluent companion having to content himself with the bare official meal.

Soon after breakfast a voice from a near cell rose in earnest colloquy. "Hasn't my bail come yet, gaoler?"

"I tell yer 'e's wired 'e'll come soon's 'e's 'ad 'is breakfast."

"But I've got a most important engagement at nine! Can't you let me out before he comes?"

"Don't talk tommy-rot! You've got to go up to the court at ten. If yer bail comes, out yer'll go; if it doesn't, yer'll have to go on to Westminster."

"Must I go in the van? Can't I have a cab—I'm only charged with being excited!"

"Yer'll 'ave to go just like everybody else."

Bang! went the trap in the door, and as the footsteps died up the passage Pringle's companions chanted:

But the pore chap doesn't know, yer know—
'E 'asn't bin in London long!

About an hour later the cells were emptied, and the prisoners were marched down to the courtyard and packed away in the police-van to be driven the short intervening distance to Westminster Police Court. There was no lack of company here. On arrival the van-riders were turned into a basement room, already half full, and well lighted by an amply barred window which, frosted as were its panes, allowed the sun freely to penetrate as if to brighten the over-gloomy thoughts of those within.

Punctually at ten the name of the first prisoner was called. It was the hysterical lady of the police cells, who disappeared amid loudly expressed wishes of "Good-luck!" The wait was a tedious one, and as the crowd dwindled, Pringle's habitual stoicism enabled him to draw a farcical parallel between his fellows and a dungeonful of aristocrats awaiting the tumbril during the Reign of Terror. The noisy converse around him consisted chiefly of speculations as to the chances of each one being either remanded, "fullied," or summarily convicted.

Pringle had no inclination to join therein; besides his over-night companion had long ago decided, with judicial precision, that he would be either "fullied"—that is, fully committed for trial—or else remanded for inquiries, but that the chances were in favour of the latter.

The room was half empty when Pringle's summons came, but the call for "Stammers" at first brought no response. He had quite forgotten his alias (not at all an unusual thing, by the way, with those who acquire such a luxury), and it was not until the gaoler repeated the name and everyone looked questioningly at his neighbour that Pringle remembered his ownership and passed out, acknowledging with a wave of the hand the chorus of "Good-luck" prescribed by the etiquette of the place.

Up a flight of steps, and along a narrow passage to a door, where he was halted for a season. A subdued hum of voices could be heard within. Suddenly the door opened.

"Three months, blimey, the 'ole image! Jus' cos my 'usband 'it me!"

And as a red-faced matron, with a bandaged head, flounced past him on her way downstairs, Pringle stepped into the iron-railed pen she had just vacated. In front of him was a space of some yards occupied by three or four desked seats, and on the bench beyond sat a benevolent-looking old gentleman with a bald head, whom Pringle greeted with a respectful bow.

The barman was at once called; he had little to say, and said it promptly.

"Any questions?" Pringle declined the clerk's invitation, and the police evidence, officially concise, followed.

"Any questions?" No, again.

"Is anything known of him?" inquired the old gentleman.

An inspector rose from the well in front of the bench, and said:

"There have been a number of cases in the neighbourhood lately, sir, and I should be glad of a remand to see if he can be identified."

"Very well. Remanded for a week." And so, after a breathless hearing of about two and three-quarter minutes by the clock, Pringle found himself standing outside the court again.

"'Ow long 'ave yer got?" Instead of going along the passage, Pringle had been turned into a room which stood handy at the foot of the steps, where he was greeted by a number of (by this time) old acquaintances.

"I'm remanded for a week."

"Same 'ere," observed his cell-fellow of the night before. "I'll see yer, mos' likely, at the show."

"Any bloke for the 'Ville?" inquired a large, red-faced gentleman, with a pimple of a nose which he accentuated by shaving clean.

"Yus; I've got six months," said one.

"Garn!" contemptuously replied the face. "Yer'll go to the Scrubbs."

"Garn yerself!" retorted the other; and as the discussion at once became warm and general Pringle sat down in a far corner, where the disjointed shreds of talk fused into an odd patchwork.

"'E sayd you're charged with a vurry terrible thing, sayd 'e (hor! hor! hor!). I tell yer, ef yer wants the strite tip—don't you flurry yer fat, now—so, says I, then yer can swear to my character—they used to call it cocoa-castle, strite they did—"

"Answer your names, now!" The gaoler was holding the door open. Beside him stood a sergeant with a sheaf of blue papers, from which he called the names, and as each man answered he was arranged in order along the passage. It was a welcome relief. Pringle began to feel faint, having eaten nothing since the morning, and, what with the coarse hilarity and the stuffy atmosphere by which he had been environed so many hours, his head ached distractingly.

"Forward now—keep your places!" The procession tramped into an open yard, where a police van stood waiting. With much clattering of bars, jingling of keys, and banging of doors, the men, to the number of a dozen or so, were packed into the little sentry-boxes which ran round the inside of the van, its complement being furnished by four or five ladies, brought from another part of the establishment. This done, the sergeant, closing the door after him, gave the word to start, and the heavy van, lumbering out of the yard, rolled down the street like a ship in a gale.

"Gimme a light," said a voice close to the little trap in Pringle's cell door. Looking out, he found he was addressed by a youth in the opposite box, who extended a cigarette across the corridor.

"Sorry, I haven't got one," Pringle apologised.

"'Ere y'are," came from the box on Pringle's right, and a smouldering stump was handed to the youth, who proceeded to light another from it.

"'Ave a whiff, guv'nor?" courteously offered the invisible owner. An obscene paw, holding the returned fag, appeared at the aperture.

"No, thanks," declined Pringle hastily.

"Las' chance for a week," urged the man, with genuine altruism.

"I don't smoke," protested Pringle to spare his feelings, adding, as the van turned off the road and came to a stand, "Is this the House of Detention?"

"No; this is the 'Ville."

The van rumbled under an archway, and then, after more banging, jingling, and clattering, half a dozen men were extracted from the boxes and deposited in the yard.

"Goodbye, Bill! Keep up yer sperrits!" screamed a soprano from the inmost recesses of the van.

"Come and meet us at the fortnight," growled a deepest base from the courtyard.

A calling of names, the tramp of feet, then silence for a while, only broken by the champing of harness. Presently a brisk order, and, rumbling through the arch again, they were surrounded by the noise of traffic. But it was not for long; a few minutes, seconds even, and they halted once more, while heavy doors groaned apart. Then, clattering through a portico full of echoes, and describing a giddy curve, the van abruptly stopped as an iron gate crashed dismally in the rear.

"'Ere we are guv'nor!" remarked the altruist.

THE HOUSE OF DETENTION

Clang, clang! Clang-a-clang, clang!

As the bell continued to ring Mr. Pringle started from an unrestful slumber, and, sitting up in bed, stared all around. Everything was so painfully white that his eyes closed spasmodically.

White walls, white-vaulted ceiling, even the floor was whitish-coloured—all white, but for the black door-patch at one end, and on this he gazed for respite from the glare. Slowly he took it all in—the bare table-slab, the shelf with its little stack of black volumes, the door, handleless and iron-sheeted, above all the twenty-four little squares of ground-glass with their horizontal bars broadly shadowed in the light of the winter morning.

It was no dream, then, he told himself.

The thin mattress, only a degree less harsh than the plank bed beneath, was too insistent, obstinately as he might close his eyes to all beside. And, as he sat, the events of the last six and thirty hours came crowding through his memory. How clearly he saw it all! Not a detail was missing.

Again he stood by the riverside, the bare trees dripping in the mist; again he saw the ingots, and lent unwilling aid to save them, fingered the contemptuous vails, sole profit of their discovery. He was crossing the bridge; beyond shone the lights of the tavern, and there within he saw the frowsy crowd of loafers, and the barman proving the base coin he innocently tendered. And then came the arrest, the police cell, the filthy sights and sounds, the court with its sodden, sickening atmosphere, and, last of all, the prison. What a trap had he, open eyed, walked into! For a second he ground his teeth in impotent fury.

The bell ceased. Dejectedly he rose, wondering as to the toilet routine of the establishment. Shaving was not to be thought of, he supposed, but enforced cleanliness was a thing he had read of somewhere. How long would last night's bath stand good for? He looked at the single coarse brown towel and shuddered. Footsteps approached; he heard voices and the jingling of keys, then the lock shot noisily, and the door was flung open.

"Now, then, put out your slops and roll your bedding up."

Pringle obeyed, but his bed-making was so lavish of space that when the warder peeped in again, some ten minutes later, he regarded the heap with a condescending grin, and presently returned with a prisoner who deftly rolled the sheets and blankets into a bundle whose end-on view resembled a variegated archery target. Then the hinges creaked once more, the lock snapped, and Pringle was left to his meditations. They were not of a cheerful nature, and it was with an exceeding bitter smile that he set himself to seriously review his position. Already had he decided that to reveal himself as the proprietor of that visionary literary agency in Furnival's Inn would only serve to increase the suspicion that already surrounded him, while availing nothing to free him from the present charge—if even it did not result in fresh accusations! On the other hand, unless he did so he could see no way of obtaining any money from his bankers so to avail himself of the very small loophole of escape which a legal defence might afford.

He had one consolation—a very small one, it is true. Money is never without its uses, and it was with an eye to future contingencies that he had managed to secrete a single half-sovereign on first arriving at the gaol. Whilst waiting, half-undressed, to enter the searching room, he bethought him of a strip of old-fashioned court-plaster which he was accustomed to carry in his pocket-book. He took it out, and, waiting his opportunity, stuck half a sovereign upon it and then pressed the strip against his shin, where it held fast.

"What's that?" inquired a warder a few minutes later, as Pringle stood stripped beneath a measuring gauge.

"I grazed my skin a couple of days ago," said he glibly.

"Graze on right shin!" repeated the warder mechanically to a colleague who was booking Pringle's description; and that was how the coin escaped discovery such time as he was being measured, weighed, searched, examined, and made free of the House of Detention. As he paced up and down the cell, occasionally fingering the little disc in his pocket, its touch did something to leaven his first sensations of helplessness, but they returned with pitiless logic so soon as he thought of escape. Bribery with such a sum was absurd, and he saw only too plainly that the days of Trenck and Casanova were gone forever.

Chafing at the thought of his sorry fate, Pringle turned for distraction to the inscription which on all sides adorned the plaster walls. They were scarcely so ornate as those existing in the Tower, and their literary merit was of the scantiest; nevertheless they were not without a human interest, especially to a fellow sufferer like Pringle.

The first he lighted on appeared to be the record of a deserter: "Alf. Toppy out of Scrubbs 2nd May, now pulled for deserting from 2nd Batt. W. Norfolk."

"H. Allport" informed all whom it might concern that he was "pinched for felony." Another soldier—it is to be hoped not a criminal—was indicated by the simple record, "Johore, Chitral, Rawal Pindi."

One prisoner had summed up his self-compassion in the ejaculation, "Poor old Dick!"

"Cheer up, mate, you'll be out some day," was no doubt intended to be comforting, whilst there was a suggestion of tragedy in the statement, "I am an innocent man charged with felony by an intoxicated woman."

It seemed to be the felonious etiquette for prisoners to give their addresses as well as their names—thus, "Dave Conolly from Mint Street."

"Dick Callaghan, Lombard Street, Boro, anyone going that way tell Polly Regan I expect nine moon," set Pringle wondering why on earth Dick had not written to Polly and delivered his message for himself. An ingenuous youth was "Willie, from Dials, fullied for taking a kettle without asking for it," with his artless postscript, "only wanted to know the time," but perhaps he passed for a humorist among his acquaintances, while "Darky, from Sailor's kip the Highway, nicked for highway robbery with violence," had a matter-of-fact ruffianism about it which spoke for itself.

From these sordid archives Pringle turned to the printed rules hanging from a peg in the cell, but they were couched in such an aridly official style as to remind him but the more cruelly of his position, and in considerable depression he resumed his now familiar tour—four paces to the window, a turn, and four paces back again, which was the utmost measure of the floor space.

He had almost ceased to regard any plan of escape as feasible, when the idea of Free-masonry occurred as a last resort. Amongst his other studies of human nature Pringle had not neglected the mummeries of The Craft; he had even attained the eminence of a "Grand Zerubbahel." Now, he thought, was the time to test the efficacy of the doctrines he had absorbed and expounded; he would try the effect of masonic symbolism upon the warder.

Soon again the keys rattled and the doors banged; nearer came the sounds, the echoes louder, but now there was a clattering as of tinware. The door was flung open, the warder took a small cube loaf of brown bread from the tray carried by a prisoner, and slapped it, with a tin resembling a squat beer-can, down on the table board. The tin was full of hot cocoa, and, quickly raising it with a peculiar motion of the hand, Pringle inquired genially, "How old is your mother?"

The warder stopped in the act of shutting the door; he pulled it open again, and glared speechless at the audacious questioner. For quite a minute he stood; then, with an accent which his emotion only rendered the purer, he growled:

"None of yer larrks now, me man!"

As the door slammed Pringle mechanically tore the coarse brown bread into fragments, and soaking them in the cocoa, swallowed them unheedingly. His last scheme had gone the same road as its predecessors, and he no longer attempted to blind himself to the consequences. He scarcely noticed when the breakfast-ware was collected, silently handing out his tins in obedience to the summons.

He was still sitting on the stool, with eyes staring at the frosted windows which his thoughts saw far through and beyond, when the eternal unlocking began again. Listlessly he heard a voice repeating something at every door; he did not catch the words, but there was a tramp of many feet, and a bell was ringing. The voice grew louder; now it was at the next cell. He stood up.

"Chapel!

Pringle stared at the warder—a fresh one this time.

"Get yer prayer-book and 'ymm-book, and come to chapel! Put yer badge on," he added, looking back for a minute before continuing his monotonous chant.

Pringle picked up the black volumes and sent an inquiring glance around for the "badge." Prisoner after prisoner defiled past the open door as he waited; then all at once he saw the warder's meaning. Each man displayed a yellow badge upon his breast, and, looking round again, he saw, dangling upon his own gas-burner, a similar disc of felt, with the number of the cell stamped upon it. Hanging the tab upon his coat button, Pringle entered a gap in the procession duly labelled "B.3.6." for the occasion.

Right overhead an endless column marched; on the gallery below he saw another, and all around was a rhythmic tramp-tramp in one and the same direction. Down a slope of stairs they went, across a flying bridge, and then along a gallery whose occupants had preceded them. Tramp, tramp, tramp, tramp. Another bridge, and then a door opened into a huge barn of a hall.

Backless forms were ranged in long rows over the wooden floor, with here and there a little pew-like desk, from which the warders piloted their charges to their seats. The prisoner ahead of him was the end man of his bench, and Pringle, motioned to the next one, headed the file along it and sat down by the wall at the far end, with a warder in one of the little pews just in front.

"What yer in for, guv'nor?" asked someone in a husky growl.

Pringle looked round, but his immediate neighbour was glaring stolidly at the nearest warder, whose eye was upon them, and there was no one else within speaking distance but a decrepit old creature, obviously very deaf, on the row behind, and beyond him again a man of apparent education wearing a frock coat. From neither of these could such an inquiry have proceeded.

"Eyes front there! Don't let me catch you looking round again." It was the warder who spoke in peremptory tones, and Pringle started at the words like a corrected schoolboy.

"Hymn number three."

The chaplain had taken his stand by the altar, and the opening bars of Bishop Ken's grand old hymn sounded from the organ. There was a rustle and shuffling of many feet as the whole assembly rose, the organist started the singing, and the many-voiced followed on with a roar which could not wholly slaughter the melody. Half-way through the first verse Pringle felt a nudge in the ribs, and, barely inclining his head, caught the eye of his stolid neighbour as it closed in a grotesque wink. Keeping one eye on the little pew in front the man edged towards him, and repeated, in a sing-song which fairly imitated the air of the hymn:

"What yer in for, matey?"

Taking his cue, Pringle changed back: "Snide coin," and then a strange duet was sung to the old Genevan air.

"Fust time?"

"Yes."

"Do a bloke a turn?"

"What's that?"

"Change badges—I'll tell yer why at exercise presently. Won't 'urt you, an' do me a sight er good!"

The hymn ceased, and the chaplain began to intone the morning prayers. As they all sat down, Pringle's neighbour dropped his badge on the floor, and, pretending to reach for it, motioned to him to exchange.

The warder's attention was elsewhere, and Pringle obligingly re-labelled himself "C. 2.24."

A short and somewhat irrelevant address, another hymn, and
the twenty minutes' service was over. As bench after bench emptied, the monotonous tramp again echoed through the bare chamber, and a dusty haze rose and obscured the texts upon the altar. It
was a single long procession that snaked round and round the cor-
ridors, and, descending by a fresh series of stairways and bridges,
disappeared far below in the basement. The lower they got, the
atmosphere became sensibly purer and less redolent of humanity,
until at the very bottom Pringle felt a rush of air, welcome for all
its coldness, and there, beyond an open grille, was an expanse of
green bordered by shrubs, and, above all, the cheery sunlight.

"And earth laughed back at the day," he murmured.

The grass was cut up by concentric rings of flagstones, and
round these the prisoners marched at a brisk rate. Between every
two rings were stone pedestals, each adorned with a warder, who
from this elevation endeavoured to preserve a regulation space
between the prisoners—that is to say, when he was not engaged in
breathing almost equally futile threatenings against the conversation which hummed from every man who was not immediately in
front of him. And what a jumble of costumes! Tall hats mingled
with bowlers and seedy caps that surely no man would pick from
off a rubbish heap. Here the wearer of a frock-suit followed one
who was literally a walking rag-shop; and, conspicuous among all
with its ever-rakish air in the sober day-time, an opera hat spoke
of hilariously twined vine-leaves.

"Thankee, guv'nor," came a hoarse whisper from behind
Pringle; "yer done me a good turn, yer 'ave so!"

The speaker was slight and sinuously active, with a cat-like
gait—a typical burglar; also his hair was closely cropped in the style
of the New Cut, which is characterised by a brow-fringe analogous
to a Red Indian's scalp-lock, being chivalrously provided for your
opponent to clutch in single combat.

"What do you want my badge for?" inquired Pringle with less
artistic gruffness.

"Why, the splits 'll be 'ere in a minute ter look at us—bust 'em!
An' I'll be spotted—what ho! Well, they'll take my number from

this badge o' yourn, 'B.3.6,' an' they'll look up your name an' think it's a alias of mine—see? An' then they'll go an' enter all my convictions 'gainst you—haw, haw!"

"Against me! But, I say, you know—"

"Don't you fret—it'll do you no 'arm! Now when I goes up on remand termorrer there won't be nothing returned 'gainst me, so the beak'll let me off light 'stead o' bullyin' me—"

"Yes, yes; I see where you come in right enough," interrupted Pringle. "But what about me?"

"No fear, I tells yer strite. When yer goes up again, if the split ain't found out 'is mistake an goes ter say anythink 'gainst yer respectability, jest you sing out loud an' say it's all a bito' bogie—see? Then the split'll see it's not me, an' 'e'll ave ter own up, an' p'raps the beak'll be that concerned for yer character bein' took away that he'll—"

"Halt!"

Pringle, in amused wonderment at the cleverness of an idea founded, like all true efforts of genius, on very simple premises, walked into the man ahead of him, who had stopped at the word of command. Those in the inner circle were being moved into the outermost one, and there the whole gathering was packed close and faced inwards.

Measured footsteps were now audible; but when the leaders of this new contingent came in view it was clear that whatever else they might be they were certainly not a fresh batch of prisoners. For one thing, they wore no badges; moreover, they conversed freely as they drew near. Well set up, and with a carriage only to be acquired by drilling, they displayed a trademark in their boots of a uniform type of stoutness.

"'Tecs, the swabs!" was the quite superfluous remark of Pringle's neighbour. Along the line they passed, scanning each man's features, now exchanging a whispered comment, and anon making an entry in their pocket-books. Pringle himself was passed by indifferently, but it was quite otherwise with the wearer of badge "B.3.6." He, evidently a born actor, underwent the scrutiny with an air of profound indifference, which he managed to sustain even when one of the police returned for a second look at his familiar features.

"Forward!"

As the recognisers left the yard the prisoners were sorted out again, and resumed their march round the paved circles.

"That's a bit of all right, guv'ner!" And Pringle's new friend chuckled as he spoke. "Haw, haw! See that split come ter 'ave another look at me? Strite, I nearly busted myself tryin' not ter laugh right out! Shouldn't I like ter see the bloke's face when yer goes up—oh, daisies! Yer never bin copped afore?"

"No. Is there any chance of getting out?"

"What—doin' a bolt? Bless yer innercent young 'art, not from a stir like this! Yer might get up a mutiny, p'raps," he reflected, "so's yer could knock the screws (warders) out. But 'ow are yer ter do that when yer never gets a chance ter 'ave a jaw with more than one at a time? There's the farm now," indicating an adjacent building with a jerk of the head.

"The what?"

"'Orspital. If yer feel down on yer luck yer might try ter fetch it, p'raps. But it's no catch 'ere where yer've no work and grups yerself if yer like. Now, when yer've got a stretch the farms clahssy."

Again the bell rang, and the spaces grew wider as the prisoners were marched off by degrees. On the stairs, as they went in, Pringle and his new friend exchanged badges, and the old prisoner, with a muttered "Good luck," passed to his own side of the gaol and was seen no more.

Back in the solitude of his cell Pringle found plentiful matter for thought. The events of the morning had enlarged his mental horizon, and roused fresh hopes of escaping the fate that menaced him. As his long legs measured the cell—one, two, three, four, round again at the door—so lightened was his heart that he once caught himself in the act of whistling softly, while the hours flew by unnoticed.

He swallowed his dinner almost without tasting it, and the clatter of supper tins was all that reminded him that he had eaten nothing for five hours. He was not conscious of much appetite; after all, haricot beans are filling, and a meal more substantial than the pint of tea and brown loaf might have been thrown away upon him. With supper the gas had been kindled, and as he sat and munched his bread at the little table, the badge suspended on the bracket shown golden in the light.

Since morning he had endowed it with a special interest—indeed, it largely inspired the thoughts which now cheered him. True, it was not a talisman at whose approach the prison doors would open wide, but it had taught him the important fact that the prisoners were known less by their faces than by the numbers of their cells.

Escape seemed less and less remote, when a plan, bold and hazardous in its idea, crystallised from out the crude mass of projects with which his brain seethed. This was the plan—he would lag behind after service in chapel the next morning, conceal himself in a warder's pew, and lie in wait for the first official who might enter the chapel—such a one, in the graphic phrase of his disreputable friend, he would "knock out," and, seizing his keys and uniform, would explore the building. It would be too daring to attempt the passage of the gate, but it would be hard luck indeed if he discovered no ladder or other means of scaling the wall.

Such was his scheme in outline. He was keenly alive to its faultiness in detail; much, far too much, was left to chance—a slovenliness he had ever recoiled from. He felt that even the possession of the uniform would only give him the shortest time in which to work; and, while he risked the challenge of any casual warder who might detect his unfamiliar face, his ignorance of the way about would inevitably betray him before long. But his case could hardly be more desperate than at present; and, confident that if only he could hide himself in the chapel the first step to freedom would be gained, he lay down to rest in happier mood than had been his for two days past.

At the first stroke of the morning bell Pringle was on his feet, every nerve in tension, his brain thrilling with the one idea. In his morning freshness and vigour, and after a singularly dreamless sleep, all difficulties vanished as he recalled them, and even before the breakfast hour his impatient ear had already imagined the bell for chapel. When it did begin, and long before the warder was anywhere near his cell, Pringle was standing ready with his badge displayed and the little volumes in his hands.

The moment the door opened he was over the threshold; he had walked a yard or two on while the keys still rattled at the next cell; the man in front of him appeared to crawl, and the way seemed miles long. In his impatience he had taken a different place in the procession as compared with yesterday, and when at length he reached the haven and made for his old seat at the end of the bench against the wall he was promptly turned into the row in front of it. His first alarm that his plans were at the very outset frustrated gave way to delight as he found himself within a few inches only of the warder's pew without so much as a bench intervening, and, lest his thoughts might be palpable on his face, he feared to look up, but gazed intently on his open book.

The service dragged on and the chaplain's voice sounded drowsier than ever as he intoned the prayers, but the closing hymn was given out at last, and Pringle seized a welcome distraction by singing with a feverish energy which surprised himself. A pause, and then, while the organist resumed the air of the hymn, the prisoners rose, bench after bench, and filed out.

The warder had passed from the pew towards the central aisle; he was watching his men out with face averted from Pringle. Now was the supreme moment. As his neighbours rose and turned their backs upon him, Pringle, with a rapid glance around, sidled down into the warder's pew and crouched along the bottom.

Deftly as he had slid into the confined space, the manoeuvre was not without incident—his collar burst upon the swelling muscles of his neck, and the stud with fiendish agility bounced to the floor, while quaking he listened to the rattle which should betray him. Seconds as long as minutes, minutes which seemed hours passed, and still the feet tramped endlessly along the floor. But now the organ ceased. Hesitating shuffles told the passing of some decrepit prisoner, last of the band, there was a jingling of keys, some coarse-worded remarks, a laugh, the snapping of a lock, and then—silence.

Pringle listened; he could hear nothing but the beating of his own heart. Slowly he raised himself above the edge of the desk and met the gaze of a burly man in a frogged tunic, who watched him with an amused expression upon his large round face.

"Lost anything?" inquired the big man with an air of interest.

"Yes, my liberty," Pringle was about to say bitterly, but, checking himself in time, he only replied, "My collar stud."

"Found it?"

For answer Pringle displayed it in his fingers, and then restored the accuracy of his collar and tie.

"Come this way," said the befrogged one, unlocking the door, and Pringle accepted the invitation meekly. Resistance would have been folly, and even had he been able to take his captor unawares, the possible outcome of a struggle with so heavy a man was by no means encouraging.

As the key turned upon Pringle and he found himself once more in the cell which he had left so hopefully but a short half-hour ago, he dropped despondently upon the stool, heedless of the exercise he was losing, incurious when in the course of the morning a youngish man in mufti entered the cell with the inquiry:

"Is your name Stammers?"

"Yes," Pringle wearily replied.

"You came in the night before last, I think? Did you complain of anything then?"

"Oh, no! Neither do I now." Pringle began to feel a little more interested in his visitor, whom he recognised as the doctor who had examined him on his arrival at the prison. "May I ask why you have come to see me?"

"I understand you are reported for a breach of discipline, and I have come to examine and certify you for punishment," was the somewhat officially dry answer.

"Indeed! I am unaware of having done anything particularly outrageous, but I suppose I shall be told?"

"Oh, yes; you'll be brought before the governor presently. Let me look at your tongue. . . . Now just undo your waistcoat—and your shirt—a minute. . . . Thanks, that will do."

The doctor's footsteps had died away along the gallery before Pringle quite realized that he had gone. So this was the result of his failure. He wondered what form the punishment would take. Well, he had tried and failed, and since nothing succeeds like success, so nothing would fail like failure, he supposed.

"Put on yer badge an' come along o' me."

It was the Irish warder speaking a few minutes later, and Pringle followed to his doom. At the end of the gallery they did not go up, as to chapel, nor down to the basement, as for exercise, but down one flight only to a clear space formed by the junction of the various blocks of the prison, which starred in half a dozen radiations to as many points of the compass.

As his eye travelled down the series of vistas with tier above tier of galleries running throughout and here and there a flying crossbridge, Pringle noted with dismay the uniformed figures at every turn, and the force of his fellow-prisoner's remark as to the folly of a single-handed attempt to escape was brutally obvious.

He was roused by a touch on the shoulder. The Irish warder led him by the arm through an arched doorway along a dark passage, and thence into a large room with "Visiting Magistrates" painted on the door. Although certainly spacious, the greater part of the room was occupied by a species of cage, somewhat similar to that in which Pringle had been penned at the police court. Opening a gate therein the warder motioned him to enter and then drew himself up in stiff military pose at the side. Half-way down the table an elderly gentleman in morning dress, and wearing a closely cropped grey beard, sat reading a number of documents; beside him, the ponderous official who had shared Pringle's adventure in the chapel.

"Is this the man, chief warder?" inquired the gentleman. The chief warder testified to Pringle's identity, and "What is your name?" he continued.

"Give your name to the governor, now!" prompted the Irishman, as Pringle hesitated in renewed forgetfulness of his alias.

"Augustus Stammers, isn't it?" suggested the chief warder impatiently.

"Yes."

"You are remanded, I see," the governor observed, reading from a sheet of blue foolscap, "charged with unlawfully and knowingly uttering a piece of false and counterfeit coin resembling a florin." Pringle bowed, wondering what was coming next.

"You are reported to me, Stammers," continued the governor, "for having concealed yourself in the chapel after divine service, apparently with the intention of escaping. The chief warder states that he watched you from the gallery hide yourself in one of the officer's pews. What have you to say?"

"I can only say what I said to the chief warder. My collar stud burst while I was singing, and I lost it for ever so long. When I did find it in the warder's pew the chapel was empty."

"But were you looking for it when you hid yourself so carefully? And why did you wait for the warder to turn his back before you looked in the pew?"

"I only discovered it as we were about to leave the chapel. Even if I had tried to escape, I don't see the logic of reproving a man for obeying a natural instinct."

"I have no time to argue the point," the governor decided, "but I may tell you, if you are unaware of it, that it is an offence, punishable by statute, to escape from lawful custody. The magistrate has remanded you here, and here you must remain until he requires your presence at"—he picked up the foolscap sheet and glanced over it— "at the end of five more days. Your explanation is not altogether satisfactory, and I must caution you as to your future conduct. And let me advise you not to sing quite so loudly in chapel. Take him away."

"Outside!"

Stepping out of the cage Pringle was escorted back to the cell, congratulating himself on the light in which he had managed to

present the affair. Still, he felt that his future movements were
embarrassed; plausible as was the tale, the governor had made no
attempt to conceal his suspicions, and Pringle inclined to think he
was the object of a special surveillance when half a dozen times in
the course of the afternoon he detected an eye at the spy-hole in
the cell door. It was clear that he could do nothing further in his
present position. He recalled the advice given him yesterday, and
determined to "fetch the farm." There only could he break fresh
ground; over there he might think of some new plan—perhaps concert it with another prisoner. Anyhow, he could not be worse off.

But here another difficulty arose. He was in good, even robust,
health; and the doctor, having overhauled him twice recently, could
hardly be imposed upon by any train of symptoms, be they never
so harrowing in the recital.

Suddenly he recalled a statement from one of those true stories of prison life, always written by falsely-accused men—the number of innocent people who get sent to prison is really appalling!

It was on the extent to which soap-pills have been made to serve
the purpose of the malingerer. Now the minute slab upon his shelf
had always been repellent in external application, but for inward
consumption—he hurriedly averted his gaze! But this was no time
for fastidiousness; so, choosing the moment just after one of the
periodical inspections of the warder, he hurriedly picked a corner
from the stodgy cube, and, rolling it into a bolus, swallowed it with
the help of repeated gulps of water. As a natural consequence, his
appetite was not increased; and when supper arrived later on he
contented himself with just sipping the tea, ignoring the brown
loaf.

Sleep was long in coming to him that night; he knew that he
was entering upon an almost hopeless enterprise, and his natural
anxiety but enhanced the dyspeptic results of the strong alkali.
Toward morning he dropped off; but when the bell rang at six there
was little need for him to allege any symptoms of the malaise which
was obvious in his pallor and his languid disinclination to rise.

"Ye'd better let me putt yer name down for the docthor, Stammers," was the not unkindly observation of the Irish warder as he

collected. Pringle merely acquiesced with a nod, and when the chapel bell rang his cell door remained unopened.

"Worrying about anything?" suggested the doctor, as he entered the cell about an hour afterwards.

"Yes, I do feel rather depressed," the patient admitted.

A truthful narrative of the soap disease, amply corroborated by the medical examination, had the utmost effect which Pringle had dared to hope; and when, shortly after the doctor's visit, he was called out of the cell and bidden to leave his badge behind he was conscious of an exaltation of spirits giving an elasticity to his step which he was careful to conceal.

Along the passage, through a big oaken door, and then by a flight of steps they reached the paved courtyard. Right ahead of them the massive nail-studded gates were just visible through the inner ones which had clanged so dismally in Pringle's ears just three nights back.

"Fair truth, mate, 'ave I got the 'orrors? Tell us strite, d'yer see 'em?" In a whisper another and tremulous candidate for "the farm" pointed to the images of a pair of heraldic griffins which guarded the door; the sweat stood in great drops upon his face as he regarded the emblems of civic authority, and Pringle endeavoured to assure him of their reality until checked by a stern "Silence there!"

"Turn to the left," commanded the warder, who walked in the rear as with a flock of sheep.

From some distant part of the prison a jumbled score of men and women were trooping toward the gate. They were the friends of prisoners returning to the outside world after the brief daily visit allowed by the regulations, and as their paths converged towards the centre of the yard the free and the captive examined one another with equal interest.

"Ough!" . . . "Pore feller!" . . . "'Old 'im up!" . . . "Git some water, do!"

The tremulous man had fallen to the ground with bloated, frothing features, his limbs wrenching and jerking convulsively. For a moment the two groups were intermingled, and then a little knot of four detached itself and staggered across the yard. A visitor, rushing from his place, had compassionately lifted the sufferer from the ground, and, with the warder and two assisting prisoners, disappeared through the hospital entrance.

In surly haste the visitors were again marshalled, and a warder beckoned Pringle to a place among them. For a brief second he hesitated. Surely the mistake would be at once discovered. Should he risk the forlorn chance? Was there time? He looked over to the hospital, but the Samaritan had not re-appeared.

"Come on, will yer? Don't stand gaping there!" snarled the warder.

The head of the procession had already reached the inner gate; Pringle ran towards it, and was the last to enter the vestibule. Crash! He was on the right side of the iron gate when it closed this time.

"How many?" bawled the warder in the yard.

Deliberately the man counted them, and Pringle palpitated like a steam-hammer. Would he never finish? What a swathe of red-tape! At last! The wicket opened, another second— No, a woman squeezed in front of him; he must not seem too eager. Now! He gave a sob of relief.

In the approach a man holding a bundle of documents was discharging a cab. Pringle was inside it with a bound.

"Law Courts!" he gasped through the trap. "Half a sovereign if you do it quickly!"

A whistle blew shrilly as they passed the carriage gates. Swish— swish! went the whip. How the cab rocked! There was a shout behind. The policeman on point duty walked over from the opposite corner, but as the excited warders met him half-way across the road, the cab was already dwindling in the distance.

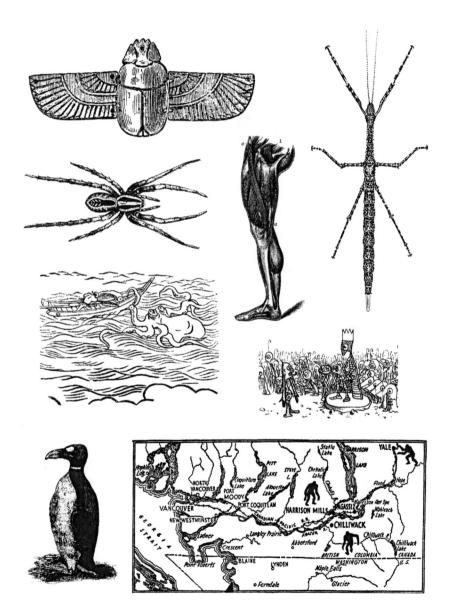

NOVEMBER JOE

DETECTIVE OF THE WOODS

H. HESKETH-PRICHARD

NOVEMBER JOE

ISBN 1-61646-013-X

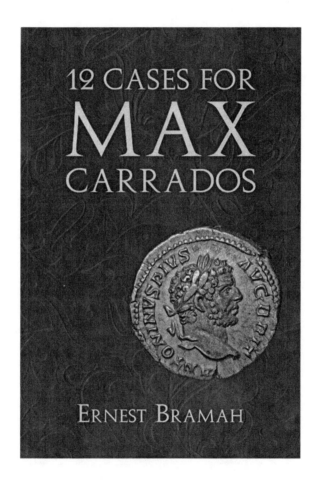

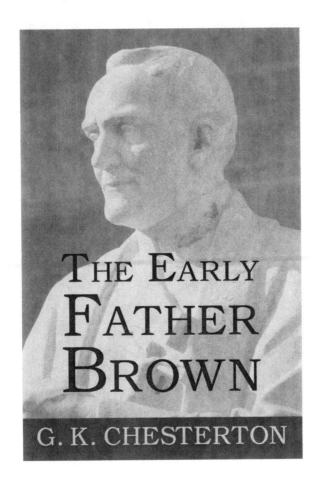

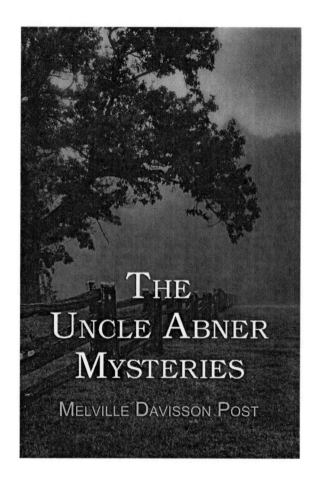

CPSIA information can be obtained at www.ICGtesting.com
Printed in the USA
BVOW05s0031060515

399156BV00002B/43/P

9 781616 460907